Gambling to Kill

GAMBLING TO KILL

First paperback edition printed in 2021 in the United Kingdom

A catalogue record for this book is available from the British Library

ISBN
Paperback 978-1-910236-62-8
Kindle 978-1-910236-82-6

Published by The Creative Peak(TCP)

Book Design: T M Goble
Cover Image: Copyright Shutterstock

T M Goble's Website

www.tmgoble.com

Action Thrillers
Detective Murder Mysteries
Standalone Murder Mysteries
Historical Fiction
Contemporary Fiction
History of Peak District Literature
Seasonal Recipes
I occasionally send newsletters with details on new releases, special offers and other bits of news relating to my books. www.tmgoble.com/joinemail.html

01

Relaxing under the bright sun from the extensive glass roof, my spirits soared as I drifted through Blackford Shopping Mall with Josh. The brightly lit shop windows displayed all the latest fashions and my eyes constantly searched the vast array of goods on offer. Like most women, I relished a few hours of shopping, always hoping to pick up a bargain. Unlike my brother, Josh, who wasn't in the least bit interested in fashion, which was one reason we were here today. Most of the clothes he possessed had seen better days, so he needed sorting out.

A casual approach was fine, but Josh was erring towards scruffy, which was not acceptable. By the time we'd finished our shopping trip, Josh would have new clothes and we wouldn't be leaving until I'd accomplished my mission. My mouth twitched with excitement as my mind whirled through the best shops to visit.

Josh had needed persuasion to join me for a jaunt around the shops, especially after I'd explained that he would buy some new outfits. Somehow, we don't seem to meet up that often these days, which is a pity as we both enjoy each other's company. Glancing across at him as we meandered along, he didn't appear to be taking much notice of the fashions on display. He was too busy eyeing up a striking blonde woman who had stopped near the escalators to chat excitedly on her mobile phone.

I nudged him playfully in the ribs and shook my head. The mischievous expression on his face made me giggle. Spending time with him today will be fun. My mind wandered as a young couple gazed into a jeweller's shop examining a display of engagement rings. A deep breath didn't suppress the flutter of excitement which rippled through me.

This evening will be dinner with Scott, who has booked an exclusive Italian restaurant. The only other time we'd been there, we had been celebrating our decision to live together. It was such a romantic setting, with its cosy alcoves, subdued lighting and candles everywhere. My heart pounded. Would we be celebrating again tonight? Is he building up to propose?

Josh and I strolled through the Mall after bumping into Maddie, who I knew from school. We'd been in the same year group although we had our own circle of friends and had associated little with each other. Suppressing the chuckle that rose in my throat, 'You took a particular interest in Lynette, Maddie's friend.'

Amusement twinkled in his eyes, 'I had a quick chat while you were busy exchanging the latest news with Maddie. She was a bit nervous but never stopped talking.' We meandered through the centre and peered into a few shop windows, but every time I pointed out an item of interest Josh shook his head.

Placing my hands on my hips, I surveyed him with a solemn expression, 'Now we have arrived at the crucial time. Blackford Police have promoted you to Detective

Sergeant, so you must smarten your appearance. We will buy new clothes for you, but first we will dispense with that despicable beanie.' I pointed towards his pocket where the offending item dangled out.

Josh screwed up his face in silent disapproval, but I ignored his discomfort. It was time for him to face reality and update his wardrobe. Appearances are important. That leather jacket is rubbed and the ridiculous beanie will be in the waste bin before the end of the day.

It's not only his appearance that needs an overhaul, but his timekeeping also requires a serious rethink. As usual, he arrived late to meet me. Why doesn't he ever arrive on time? Today, I will buy him a new watch with all the latest gadgets and alarms. It will appeal to his sense of humour. No doubt he will protest, but I can always win him around. After all, I'm his big sister and I always get my own way.

'Before we begin a serious bout of shopping,' he rolled his shoulders and gave a melodramatic groan, 'I shall pop to the loo.' With the hint of a nod and a resigned expression, he plonked himself down on a bench in the concourse outside the building society. Walking away from him, my determination to succeed was at an all-time high. In anticipation of his reluctance, I'd booked lunch at the only posh restaurant in the Mall. I wanted him to have an enjoyable day. Despite my positive approach, a doubt still lingered in the back of my mind. Could I make him buy new clothes and smarten his image?

02

A door burst open. A figure fully dressed in black and wearing a mask sprinted into the corridor. From the same door, a second black figure emerged. Relaxing, I smiled. It must be a prank. The first person ran along the corridor and dropped a small cylinder. 'Hey!' A third person in black crashed into me.

'What the...!' Bouncing off the wall, my high heels wobbled, I staggered, then crashed to the floor. The red cylinder lying in front of me belched smoke. I gasped, inhaled the billowing fumes and struggled for my next breath. I wanted to scream but didn't have enough air as a suffocating sensation tightened my throat. My eyes stung and a ball of fear formed in my stomach. What was happening? With my hand at my throat, 'Josh! Josh!' A shout, but only a whisper.

Shaking and disorientated, my feet slipped and my knees buckled as I tried to push myself from the floor. The smoke thickened. I must escape. Which way to go? Panic gripped me. I couldn't breathe. Clawing at the wall for support, I struggled to my feet. Shaking and wobbling, I leaned against it then kicked off my shoes. Disorientated by my collapse, I twisted and staggered.

With my hand across my mouth to stop the toxic fumes, I cried out, 'Josh!' A feeble sound emanated as my mouth burned. My heart thudded and my body weakened, overwhelmed by the lack of oxygen. I needed air, but as the smoke reached my lungs, I coughed and retched. The burning of my eyelids increased. My eyes stayed shut from the fear of opening them. Tears escaped and rolled down my cheeks. What can I do? Why is this happening? 'I can't see you, Josh!' I clutched at the burning sensation in my throat as I gasped for air, 'Where are you?'

My shout produced a wheeze, but no noise. Dropping to the floor, on my hands and knees, I slithered along the corridor. Had I chosen the right direction? My body shook and my throat rasped. Blood rushed through my head. Dizziness swarmed. In the distance, people screamed. A faint voice reached me. My name.

'Ellie! Ellie!' Josh's voice. I wanted to scream his name so he would find me. Opening my mouth, the sound disappeared as I fought for breath and consciousness. The stars increased. Overwhelmed with nausea, the world spun. My body slumped. Darkness enveloped me.

03

Constable Tom Collins sat with his patrol partner, Gemma Jones, in a police Range Rover. Would it be a quiet day? The radio from central control remained silent. With a contented sigh, he closed his eyes. His wife would be out this evening. With a timely finish to his shift, a bite to eat, he could enjoy an evening's fishing on the canal. The idea fetched a smile to his lips. Tonight, he'd head along the towpath to his favourite spot, near the lock. Forcing aside the pleasant images, he switched his attention back to the present, flicked his eyes open and gazed around with interest.

The bright sun of a surprisingly mild winter morning shone from a cloudless sky. The overnight rain glistened on the bushes and trees, giving them a jewelled appearance. With a silent groan, he shuffled to relieve his aching back.

On a standard patrol with no incidents, he'd parked at one of his favourite spots in Blackford, which allowed a panoramic view over the ravine, with its river and a railway. It was a popular area for dog walkers as a myriad of paths wound their way downwards through Blackford's industrial relics.

A chuckle from his police partner interrupted his

thoughts, 'You're a funny old sod.' Tom twisted his heavily jowled face towards the young lass, with her short auburn hair and slim figure. Giving an indulgent smirk of amusement, 'What have I done now?'

'You're older than my dad, but you're still a constable.' The corners of her mouth twitched as she gazed, waiting for his reply.

Tom grinned, 'I have been happy as a constable.'

'You're a good copper,' Gemma wound down her window to let in the cool breeze.

'Believe nothing you hear about me, it'll be wrong.' He closed his eyes and rested his head on the back of the driver's seat. As his body relaxed, he drifted back to thinking about his evening's fishing and which bait to use.

The police radio blared into life. 'All units, major incident at the shopping mall. Every available unit to respond.' In an instant, Tom transformed from his laggardly morning. He shot up straight in his seat. With a flowing movement, the car jolted into life. The tyres screeched and spun on the cobbles, but finally gripped. Gemma was thrown back in her seat before she could respond on the radio. He flicked on the blue flashing lights. The siren screamed into life.

Tom shouted, 'Control. Tango X-ray Two responding at speed. ETA three minutes.' The traffic stopped for the Range Rover with its blue flashing lights and siren blaring as it squealed into the middle of the road. The cars split apart like an axe cleaving a log. He accelerated hard; Gemma gripped her seat.

Tom barked at the radio, 'Control, where's the incident?'

'Blackford Building Society.'

'One minute,' bellowed Tom. 'We'll go in the exit. There are no barriers.' Tom swung the Range Rover between the posts into the gloomy concrete parking area. 'Car park is full of smoke coming from the building society end.' He accelerated hard. Two young lads sprinted across the car park and into the street.

'Do we chase them, Tom?'

'No, I recognised them. We'll deal with the incident first.' A roar of motorbikes gripped his attention. Three bikes hurtled out of the smoke towards him.

The police radio blared, 'Armed raid on the building society. All personnel warned to approach with caution. Firearm units deployed.'

Tom didn't flinch as the bikes drove down the middle of the car park, heading for the Range Rover. Slamming on the brakes of the vehicle to prevent a collision, the bikes skidded past. Gemma scrawled the numbers and radioed them to control. The last rider tossed a smoke canister at the police car. It landed on the bonnet with a loud thud and then bounced onto the floor. Smoke enveloped the car.

Tom edged the car forward through the thick grey cloud. Voices and screams echoed throughout the car park. A woman appeared in the swirling mist like a ghostly image. He needed to differentiate between perpetrator or innocent victim. She screamed and pointed. The echo reverberated through the concrete shell. Victim shot through his mind.

He followed the woman's line of sight. A figure, clad in black with a mask, held a woman tight to him with a knife at her throat. The man dragged her towards the motorbike stand. A bike lay abandoned on the floor. 'His bike didn't start.' Stopping the car, he opened the driver's door.

Gemma grabbed his arm, 'We're supposed to wait for the armed unit.'

Tom ignored her, 'Get into the driver's seat, block off the end of the car park.'

'What will you do?' Gemma climbed over the central console into the driver's seat.

'Release that poor terrified woman.' The smoke swirled as the robber stared at the motor bike on the floor.

The lithe figure in black could move quickly. Tom could not catch him. Even in his younger days, sprinting had not been his forte. Tugging a handkerchief from his pocket, he forced it over his mouth. The smoke burned his throat. How could he free the woman?

The victim's terrified eyes streamed from the smoke. Taking slow and steady steps, Tom silently willed the captor to release her and leave on the bike. Gemma in the Range Rover had followed his instructions and disappeared. Tom focused on the terrified woman and her abductor.

Distant sirens approached, but they would not distract him. Had Gemma told control to close the car park? If a member of the public arrived, the result could be catastrophic. Tom took steady paces towards the pair. It was essential to make no hurried movements, as the man might panic and injure the woman. Progress was slow as he paused between each step. 'Keep back or I'll kill her,' came a muffled threat from the man's black mask.

'Calm down. Take the bike, I won't stop you.' Tom with cautious yet deliberate steps continued to move in their direction.

'Stop!' yelled the muffled voice again.

'I'm not armed.' Tom moved his hands away from his

side with palms facing upwards.

'The belt! The belt!' roared the hood.

The lout wouldn't understand the equipment on his belt. Despite the large number of years in the police, he'd never been trained for firearms or tasers. The paraphernalia he carried was harmless. Tom unbuckled it with deliberate movements and let the belt drop to the floor. 'Stay calm, we don't want anyone hurt.' Tom kept inching forward. 'Let her go!' Tears streamed down her desperate face as she gasped for breath. The knife shook in a nervous hand a few inches from her throat. Tom controlled a smoke induced cough but struggled to squint through his watering eyes. He stopped. The man scanned the car park, searching for an escape. He dragged the woman with him, the knife still at her throat. She shook violently, drawing in desperate breaths.

Tom willed him to try the bike. 'The bike; take the bike and escape! I only want the woman unharmed.' The handkerchief did not prevent the smoke from burning his throat. A movement at the edge of the car park caught his attention. Gemma's voice penetrated the smoke, but her words were indecipherable. Someone had come through the cordon. This could be a disaster. He didn't want the raider to panic and hurt the woman. Focusing on the masked man, he used his peripheral vision to assess the incomer. A scruffy man in a brown jacket and beanie inched across the car park.

Tom focused on the captive. He recognised the scruffy man, the new Detective Sergeant for Blackford. Tom raised his palm towards the Sergeant, urging him to stop. Which he did. No one moved. The raider seemed frozen with indecision. His eyes searched the area.

'Stay back, or I'll use the knife on her.' He grabbed the woman tighter and lifted her on to tiptoe. The woman opened her mouth as though to scream, but no sound emerged. Only three metres away from the raider and his captive, 'Let her go. Take the bike. Go!'

The silence was broken as tyres screeched and reverberated through the concrete structure. A twisting and turning motorbike accelerated in through the exit. One bike that had shot past him as they arrived, had returned. Would the rider have a gun? It skidded near him and close to the man in black.

He shoved the woman towards Tom and leapt on the back of the bike. The woman lay sprawled across the concrete, sobbing. With a wheelie take off, the bike sped towards the exit, narrowly missing a fire engine coming the other way.

04

Oh my God, I can't stop shivering. The knife against my throat. I thought I would die. What a nightmare. The scenario haunts me and I can't shake it from my mind as I've never been so terrified. What would have happened if one accomplice hadn't returned to pick him up? What would he have done to me?

Whimpering fear clenched like a tight fist around my chest. The policeman's jacket, although thick and warm, didn't ease my trembling. The rasping smoke still lingered in my throat. My eyes still sting, but the paramedics' drops have helped the itching. Blue lights fill the space between the concrete walls. The pulsating beams shot through the gloomy grey vault. Fluorescent jackets shone under the strobing flashes. Despite shivering, my heart continued to thud as though it wanted to burst from my rib cage. Gulping air didn't improve the sandpaper of my throat.

Josh placed his hand on my arm, 'Let the paramedics take you to hospital, Eleanor.'

'No, not yet. The police officer who saved me has requested a statement.' I couldn't disappoint such a brave man. The attempt to shake my head was a disaster as the world spun.

Josh gave me a strange glance, 'Yes, I understand, we encourage witnesses to make early statements, but I'm concerned about you, sis. If witnesses need medical attention, that must take priority and we wait until later.'

'Josh, it's okay, the worst is over.' I attempted to force my lips into a smile, but even that became difficult. They wouldn't cooperate. Talking hurt my throat. I didn't want Josh to know that fear enveloped me. 'Although I'm still shaking, a doctor will calm me down. Then I need to rid my mind of the terrible fright. I'm safe, that's most important. He didn't harm me. Here's the constable who rescued me. His bravery and courage were outstanding.' Josh sat close to me, 'Do you know him?'

'I've only met him once, when he manned reception at the police station on the day of my interview. Tom is a long service officer but has remained a constable.'

'With no thought for his own safety, he saved me.' The image of Tom moving towards me while the knife pricked my throat filled my mind. My heart hammered as I relived the sensation of the cold steel against my skin. He appeared so calm. In control. Focused.

Tom's eyes narrowed, his brow creased as he approached. He stopped, flexed his back and rolled his shoulders, then plodded in my direction. Josh had been called away. How many times in his long career had Tom experienced these situations? A female paramedic moved to sit next to me on the concrete steps in the car park, 'Can you cope with the police?'

'Yes, that's my brother, Josh.' I pointed towards the police car parked nearby. 'He's a Police Sergeant.' Josh strode back towards us. Although he had suffered the effects of the smoke, he made less fuss than me. His policeman's mind and actions must have conquered his smoke induced problems. Like Josh, I must be brave. Automatically, I stood as Tom approached.

A quick smile crossed the rugged face, but the creases returned. 'Please sit down, ma'am, I'm sure you feel weak.'

'I can't thank you enough, Constable, you were unbelievably brave.'

Giving another fleeting smile, 'I wanted him to make a run for it. If he escaped on the motorbike, he couldn't take you with him.'

Josh arrived, 'Tom, this is my sister, Eleanor.'

Rubbing his chin and with the glimmer of a smile, 'I didn't realise.' His voice held a hint of surprise. 'After the release, I helped my patrol partner, Gemma. The paramedics took over with you.' Josh dropped his arm from my shoulder and shook Tom's hand. 'You are a brave man.'

Tom nodded, 'Can I ask some questions?'

'Yes, but I saw little.'

'Don't worry about that, Ellie. Explain the best you can when Tom asks you questions. 'I'll leave you in his care as I shouldn't hear your account as it might cloud future investigations.'

Josh and Tom were dedicated police officers and even under stress never forgot the expectations required of them. Making myself as comfortable as I could, I pulled the thick fluorescent jacket tight around me. My hand shook as sickness rolled in my stomach.

Tom dropped his large body with a groan onto the steps next to me. Again, he stretched his back, 'There is no need to tell me all that happened as we have several witnesses including your brother's version.' Rubbing my fingers across my forehead, I revisited the terrifying experience, 'What do you want to know?'

'Can you tell me what happened before and after your brother found you in the corridor?'

As I mentally ran through the chaos of the smoke, I became convinced my stomach wouldn't hold out. The shaking had moved from my hands to my arms, so I pulled the jacket tighter. Tom waited. 'I called to Josh in the smoke of the corridor but became disoriented. When I regained my senses, Josh appeared sliding along the floor and found me. He wrapped me in his arms, but my legs were too weak to move.' My stomach churned violently as a cold sweat spread through my body as the memories flooded back.

I gulped, 'Josh lifted me as two men in black emerged from the smoke.' Tom concentrated on me. 'You said two men. Can you think back? Are you certain they were men? Any ideas of height or size?'

Trying to recall my senses during the chaos, 'I assumed they were men. My eyes streamed so I can't recall their size or shape.' The initial encounter came to me, 'As I passed the baby changing room in the corridor, they barged into me, they were about my height.'

Tom caught my hand, 'You're doing well. What build? Were they as large as me?'

'No, definitely not. They were about my height and slim.'

'So, could they have been female?'

'The robber had strength in his arms. When he spoke, his voice sounded deep and gruff.' Tom took a few minutes, concentrating on his notebook and recording the information with slow and ponderous handwriting. 'They shoved Josh away and one grabbed my clothes.'

'Can you remember exactly how?'

'Around my neck and waist. He could lift me without a problem and dragged me into the car park where you found me.'

'Perfect.' Tom gave a friendly smile as he left me to wait for Josh's return. I shivered, but the scare and frights had begun to subside.

05

Staying seated, I waved away the paramedic while waiting for Josh. Would his return to Blackford be successful? I wanted him to prosper, but why be a policeman? There would have been many opportunities in whatever field he had chosen.

Even when we were young, he had a stubborn and independent streak. Once he fixed on an idea, no amount of pleading would change his view. I understand him but choosing a job where your life is on the line daily is unbelievable. After being a troubled teenager, always in bother at school, why choose the police? He approached and sat next to me. Josh had never answered my question about his career choice. He either changed the subject or refused to reply. Why won't he justify his choice? Has an event happened in his life that he has wanted to keep secret? Something must have driven him to make such a choice. But what?

Popping his arm around me, 'Who did we meet when we arrived in the shopping centre?'

Bringing my thoughts back to the current situation, 'Why?'

'The police will wish to contact them to discover

whether they noticed suspicious activities.' Opening his notebook, he waited for my reply.

He must be dedicated to his job as he is carrying his police notebook with him, even though not working today. Despite my shaking state, I smiled as the encounter came back to me. 'We met Maddie and her friend. Your eyes lit up when you spoke to Lynette.'

'I've her number, I might give her a ring.'

'On police business?' I grinned.

'Personal, I'll let one of the team interview her.' Josh made notes.

My mind drifted. Why rob a building society? They must be desperate people. What prompts them to become criminals? They are vicious individuals who should be locked up. Police officers like Josh and Tom must deal with them every day. I wrung my hands together. Now I've seen Josh's job from firsthand experience, I will fear for him every day. 'I spoke to Maddie. We were in the same year group at school. For a short period, she joined the airline where I work.' The conversation became more relaxed as the blue lights disappeared from the car park. A few constables remained and continued to string police tape across the entrance.

'Were you friends?'

'No, she was always in trouble and had no interest in learning.'

'What was Maddie's job on the airline?'

'Cabin crew, but she only stayed about a year.'

'When we met, she appeared nervous and kept glancing over her shoulder and checking the clock near the jeweller's shop.'

'Maddie is not a nervous person, but I never asked

why she appeared agitated. Perhaps she had an important appointment. Or she was meeting up with a friend.'

06

Waiting patiently in the hospital corridor for the result of my blood test, I took rapid sighs, which became my attempt to calm from the trauma.

'Eleanor, what has happened to you?' Scott rushed along the fluorescent lit hospital corridor and dropped into a seat next to me. Kissing me briefly on the cheek, he stared intently and his solemn face was anxious, as his eyes scanned my face. 'You are pale.'

'Calm down, darling.' Reaching across, I patted him reassuringly on the arm and concentrated on forcing my lips into something resembling a grin. 'I'm not hurt but became caught in a raid at the shopping centre.'

Stripping off his denim jacket, he folded it and draped it across his lap. After rubbing his face, he ran his fingers through his short blonde hair. His expression remained drawn and tense.

'The robbers used smoke canisters, so the medical staff have examined me and I am waiting for the result of a blood test.' Shuffling on his seat, he leaned over and with extreme gentleness rubbed the back of my hand. The wide-eyed expression indicated his alarm after receiving the call from the police. His face was pale and pinched and for a long moment he just stared as his gaze travelled over my face and searched my eyes. Blinking hard to dispel the vivid images which scurried through my brain, my breath caught in my throat. With an effort I struggled to keep my expression positive, 'No harm done, it's only a check-up.'

'Will you still be able to fly?'

'Yes, I fainted from the terror, I don't need a check.'

'That's a relief.'

The silence stretched as his focus dropped to the floor. What was he thinking? Had he recalled an important event?

Attempting to regain his attention I wriggled around on the uncomfortable plastic chair, 'Don't worry, darling, I can fly to Bangalore when I return to work from holiday so it won't mess up your staff schedules.' Moistening my dry lips, I forced out a small laugh to show to him I hadn't been hurt and that he shouldn't be concerned.

Scott took a deep breath and settled, which helped me to relax and his presence would ease the distress of the attack. 'I came from the office, it's a nightmare setting up a new airline office in India. Procedures are different there. Every process takes three times longer than expected, I shall never complete the set-up on time at this rate.'

The stresses and strains of his job had been taking their toll. During the past few months, he'd become agitated and short tempered. A holiday, somewhere warm and relaxing, would suit both of us. I gave him a kiss on the cheek. 'There. I'm calm, so don't worry.'

'Why did you come to Blackford? When I left the flat this morning you had decided on a shopping trip to Manchester.'

'Josh rang as he has a few days off before he starts his

new job so I agreed to meet him. By coming to Blackford, I could pop in to see mum and dad. Just before you arrived, she rang and is coming to pick me up which leaves you free to return to work.' Leaning across, I kissed him once again on the cheek, 'Thanks for coming to check, I am okay.'

For some reason he ignored the kiss and my words of appreciation and huffed out a long breath as his eyes scanned the corridor. 'Why didn't you text to tell me your change of plan?' Anxiousness percolated his voice although the concerned look had disappeared from his face.

'It was no big deal as I would have mentioned it this evening. As I have some free time, I've agreed to stay with mum and dad for a few days. It's also a chance to see Josh who has just been promoted to Detective Sergeant in Blackford.' The proudness in my voice was evident as I explained about his elevated role in the police force.

Scott wrung his hands together, so I leaned across and squeezed his arm in a reassuring gesture. Why won't he stop worrying about me? 'Will your brother be on the team investigating the robbery?'

The question took me by surprise as he didn't normally take any interest in Josh. 'I have no idea.'

Scott's eyes wandered around the hospital corridor turned into a waiting area, 'Do you know the details of what happened at the shopping centre today?'

I tensed but had decided that I wouldn't explain what had happened to me as I didn't want him to make a fuss. With the stress he was under, I didn't want him worrying about me as it would add to his burden. Only Tom, Josh and I had any knowledge about the raid, and they wouldn't tell. 'Josh and I had wandered around the shops. Mum asked me to help him buy some new clothes as he's so scruffy.' Scott concentrated on my face. 'The robbers came from the toilets and dropped smoke canisters. I became disoriented, but Josh and I escaped into the car park.'

'Did any of them hit or grab you?'

'No.'

A strained tense expression flooded his face.

07

At one point earlier today, I hadn't expected to see my family again. My hand flew to my throat. Would I ever forget the sensation of that long sharp blade resting against my skin? As we pulled into the drive the sight of the familiar red brick detached house brought tears to my eyes and a fresh sense of belonging overwhelmed me. It had been my childhood home. A place of safety and always full of love.

Although the hospital had treated me well, it was a relief to arrive here where I would be fussed over and comforted. After easing the soreness in my throat from the smoke inhalation, the accident and emergency department had released me. Stepping from the BMW, I paused in the familiar surroundings and allowed the sense of peace to envelop me. My skin tingled and I kept yawning, but my trepidation had improved as the hours passed.

'Do you want me to help you into the house, Ellie?'

'No, mum.' The weakness in my legs had gone. A blackbird flew with a screech from a nearby bush which momentarily startled me. Would I always be this jumpy after the terror of today? The familiar sound of the gravel crunching under my feet as we walked to the front door was strangely reassuring. Mum wearing smart blue trousers and a cream blouse walked alongside with worry written over her face. With a nervous gesture, she touched the back of her short blonde hair as her eyes searched my face.

'Come in and relax, your father and I will take care of you.' They were the same reassuring words I'd heard so often when growing up. Relief flooded through me; I was so lucky to have such a wonderful family.

'Hello, my darling.' Dad stood in the doorway with a large welcoming smile. His grey hair matched his chinos and was complemented by a short-sleeved blue shirt. A fresh wave of emotion surfaced as he wrapped his arms around me and gave me an enthusiastic squeeze. Releasing me he rested his hands on my shoulders and with a concerned expression studied my face. Retirement suited him. The healthy glow on his cheeks was evident from time spent pottering in the garden or on the golf course.

Aware that he needed the reassurance that I was unhurt, I gulped back the wave of tears that threatened. I stretched my lips into a smile and let out a long slow breath, 'It's great to be home, dad.'

'Come and sit in the lounge, you look pale and fragile.'

'I'm still jittery, but the shaking of my hands has stopped and breathing is much easier.' The familiar smell of fresh furniture polish and the strong fragrance from a vase of lilies greeted me. The softness of the green carpet under my feet had a soothing effect. It was all so familiar and reassuring. Relaxing my shoulders, I sank into an armchair.

Dad perched on the edge of the couch, 'Do you want to talk? It might help allay your fears.' Shaking my head, 'I can't free myself from the smoke despite the hospital saying my body is clear. The smell lingers, it's so vivid. I can't believe I was caught in the middle of an armed robbery.'

Dad examined my eyes, 'Did you tell them you still had the smell?'

'Yes, it's not uncommon and no cause for concern, my breathing and throat have returned to normal.'

Mum entered the room with an anxious expression. 'You are pale, Ellie.'

'Can we stroll in the garden? The fragrances will overpower the lingering smoke.'

Dad focused on me as though trying to read my mind. 'Are you sure?'

'Yes, come on dad, let's walk.' My legs trembled as I stood, but I wouldn't give in. Dad opened the French Doors and slipped on outside shoes.

The family had reverted to calling me by my childhood name. I had been fifteen, when I announced to the world as a naïve adolescence, I preferred Eleanor and not Ellie. When Josh tried to find me in the smoke, he'd called Ellie. Mum has used the same name. Today has shocked those who love me.

The freedom of the garden was such an antidote after being confined and threatened by that vicious man. As the winter's day was mild, I kicked off my shoes and left them on the patio as I meandered across the wet surface of the lawn. Whatever the season, I always enjoyed being barefoot on grass. The simple pleasure of the garden fragrance drew me towards the nearest Lonicera blossom. Dad strolled alongside me. He had always been a caring and patient man, so he wouldn't give his thoughts or opinions but would allow me to speak when I chose.

Not wishing to recall the attack, I chose a topic that had given me concern for years. 'Why did Josh become a policeman?' As I had no sensible answer, perhaps Dad would know. Josh and I, close to each other in age, grew up fighting and squabbling. As we moved into maturity and he forsook his wayward ways, we established a close bond.

I don't know Eleanor,' his face had a bewildered expression. 'During his years at secondary school we had nothing but trouble from him. Fights and not doing his work took us to his school many times. Almost overnight, he became a reformed character and then set his mind on joining the police.'

'You let me choose my career but did you try to persuade Josh to follow you and become a pilot?'

'I suggested it, but he showed no interest.' Dad chuckled, which helped me calm. It reminded me of my youth. He could never keep serious for long. 'When you were in your teens, you showed an interest in planes. I had talked less to you about them, but it was your chosen career. But Josh never entertained the idea.'

Lifting my face to the watery sun, I closed my eyes and sighed. 'Today conveyed to me how dangerous it is to be a policeman. As the whole incident unfolded the police officers and the other emergency services entered the shopping centre not knowing what to expect. Without doubt they were in danger, but none shirked their responsibilities.'

'No one can doubt their bravery and dedication to duty.'

'Although Josh suffered from the smoke, he switched into his police mode to talk to his colleagues.'

Tears came to my eyes and streamed down my face. 'One older policeman thought nothing for his own safety, as he tried to help me.' The vision of Tom advancing had been imprinted on my mind forever. He hadn't hesitated and wasn't armed. Such a brave man.

'Are you all right darling? Is it too much for you?'

I linked my arm into dad's as we sauntered past the fragrance of the Lonicera again. 'No, I'm fine dad, but I'll never stop worrying about Josh.'

'Mum and I have tried persuading him many times to change career. When he was a young boy, he could be stubborn and he hasn't changed. But he doesn't seem as enthusiastic about his job as previously. If he wants to change career then many of my old colleagues gave up flying early and started their own businesses. It wouldn't be difficult to find him a good job, but he dismisses the idea as soon as I mention it.'

08

'Eleanor, there's a policeman here to talk with you. If you're feeling unwell, I'll tell him to come back later.'

As mum emerged from the French Doors, I wrapped my arms around her shoulders, 'I'm okay. The police told me they would send someone so I could sign my statement.'

Mum adjusted her necklace and then tugged at her sleeve, 'I don't like the idea, he will upset you by forcing you to recall the events.'

'Criminals must be caught and I can't let Josh down.' I drifted past mum with a reassuring smile. 'Hello Tom, I didn't expect it to be you.'

A small grin flashed across his face. Standing in the middle of the green carpet with his helmet tucked under his arm, he towered over me, while his alert and twinkling eyes studied me carefully.

Mum twisted her hands together in anxiety, 'Can we stay?'

Tom screwed up his face, 'Yes, although I need to take Eleanor through her statement and you might find it distressing.'

Mum and dad mimicked each other as they squared

their shoulders. Mum perched on a small chair near the window, with her hands in her lap and her lips pressed tightly together as she scrutinised my face. Dad preferred standing when there was a serious matter to discuss, so he moved to his favourite place in front of the fireplace and stood with his hands behind his back and legs slightly apart. They wanted to protect me and would agonise if I suggested they leave.

'Can you read your statement and check for omissions or mistakes?' Tom eased himself onto the edge of a large cream armchair decorated with an assortment of cushions and placed his helmet on the floor.

An involuntary shudder reverberated through my whole body. Had I left out any relevant information? As I read, the images swirled through my mind. Smoke everywhere, not being able to breathe. The terror. The screams echoing through the mall. An icy shiver swept through me. Three pairs of eyes focused on me as I placed the paper in my lap.

'I'm afraid this isn't much help.' I tapped my statement, 'It's vague.'

Tom's weather-beaten face relaxed, 'Don't worry, you did well. Can I ask some questions?' Although he didn't intend menace, his deep and serious voice made my stomach turn. A tightness formed in my throat, forcing me to take several deep gulps. The harsh smell and taste of the smoke returned.

Dad took a step forward, 'You've gone pale.'

Forcing my reluctant lips upwards, I struggled to form an acceptable smile. 'Stop fussing dad. Tom has a job to do.' As I signed my name my hands trembled. Annoyed with myself for not being able to cope, I gritted my teeth and sat up straight, 'Ask away, Tom.'

'When you emerged from the smoke, your jumper had ridden up.'

'Oh, my God.' Mum raised a hand to her throat.

I didn't respond or even glance in her direction but remained focused on Tom. 'When the man grabbed you in the corridor, did he touch you sexually?'

'This has gone too far.' Dad's words had an authoritative edge. He hadn't raised his voice, but I could hear the agitation. 'Can't you see she's distressed by the ordeal without constant reminders.'

Tom ignored him.

'He did not grab me sexually, although he yanked at my clothes several times but not in a specific place. He dragged me along the ground by the waist and neck. The bruising is visible in both places, so my recollection is correct.' The silence lengthened as Tom wrote in his notebook, then his eyes focused on me, ignoring my parents as though they weren't there.

The thud of the front door closing reverberated through the silent room. Josh entered the lounge, 'Hello, Tom. This is a surprise as I didn't expect to meet you here. Are you following up the statement? I stayed with the on-site team until they had finished.'

Josh threw his jacket over the back of a nearby chair, 'I've come home to check on Eleanor.'

I smiled and closed my eyes at the same time. Josh would pick up the message that he shouldn't be concerned. Hesitating, he glanced at our parents and his face transformed into policeman mode. 'This isn't the place for you.'

'We're supporting Eleanor.' Dad glared at him.

'Tom is being diplomatic because I'm in the police

force. Parents of children over eighteen are not allowed in interviews. And Ellie hasn't been eighteen for some time,' he chuckled. 'Let's make it easy for everyone. Eleanor will fret about your reactions if you stay. Tom needs to ask questions. Calm down. Have a walk in the garden and leave him to finish.'

'Mum, dad, please do as Josh suggests. I'm willing to answer questions, even if it brings back the memories. Go into the garden. When Tom has finished, I'll come to find you.' Josh ushered mum and dad out of the room, closing the French Doors behind them.

Tom glanced at his notebook again, 'The cameras in the shopping centre showed you meeting two women before the robbery. You took group photos.'

'I'd forgotten about them. Maddie, I knew from school and she also worked at the airline for a short while. Lynette is her friend; I'd not met her before.' Flicking through my phone, I showed Tom the photos of Lynette and Maddie.

09

The early morning sun streamed into the bedroom as Josh dropped onto the edge of his bed. Yesterday had been traumatic for poor Ellie, but by the evening she had relaxed. His mind drifted. It hadn't been a good way to meet his new colleagues. He had planned a relaxing week before starting his new job, but he would report for duty early and begin his new role.

The previous Saturday had been a disastrous day. Looking forward to an enjoyable evening out, he had been dumped by his girlfriend. Josh rubbed his hand over the stubble on his chin. Why did his job make it so difficult to keep a girl? He hadn't been surprised when Julie announced their relationship had ended as he'd let her down so many times. To be fair to her, she'd given him many last chances. Saturday couldn't be helped, he needed to work. He arrived an hour late, but she had been good about ending it. No histrionics and no recriminations.

He pictured her sitting on the bar stool with one elbow resting on the bar next to her drink. In the other hand she held her mobile phone, which occupied her attention. Her pretty face, gorgeous black hair and slim figure were imprinted on his memory. As he had strode across the bar, she raised her head and her blue eyes studied him. Perching on the bar stool next to her, he had leaned forward and kissed her on the cheek. She had given him no greeting and had faced him with a sorrowful expression before announcing that their relationship was over. It made it worse because she had been so calm.

While he had tried his best to persuade her to change the decision, he could understand her reason. She'd heard the excuses before. So, she finished her drink, scooped up her bag and left without a backward glance.

He had ordered a Budweiser and sat watching the people in the bar. Many were couples, some deep in conversation, others holding hands while many laughed together. Did his involvement with work doom a relationship before it started? It had lasted two months with Julie. Longer than most but frustratingly he'd returned to square one.

Flicking the blue duvet back into place, he padded across the thick cream carpet to the wardrobe. On his way, he picked up a towel from the ensuite to dry his hair. Living at home had always been easy. Mum and dad dealt with everything and his room had been completely renovated last week. They had organised the decorators, resulting in no effort for him. His mum had chosen blue, not that he had a strong preference. Bending down, he picked up a large box of chocolates and a bottle of his Dad's favourite single malt from a plastic bag. Scribbling a note of thanks, he placed them on the chest of drawers for his mum to find later.

After taking his first job in nearby Manchester he had become determined to buy his own flat but it had never happened. The constant jibes about living at home sometimes niggled him. Most men, in their thirties were living with their partner. The blue alarm clock digits on the bedside table flashed as it changed to eight o'clock. He would be late again, assuming his duty started at nine.

It would be good to greet his new colleagues, especially those he'd met at the shopping centre raid, so he pulled on dark jeans and picked a blue polo shirt from the wardrobe. Eleanor will still want to buy clothes for him, so she'd insist on another shopping trip. He'd be happy to spend time with her as it didn't happen often. She'd made a success of her life and had decided on her career before leaving school. Pride in her always rose to the fore whenever he spoke about Eleanor to his friends or colleagues.

Staring at the mirror, he gave his hair a quick brush. But it wouldn't behave this morning and stuck out at strange angles. Never mind, he would cover it with a beanie. He moved his head and rubbed his chin; a shave could wait until later. As to the stubble, celebrities made it trendy, so he could live with it. Which jacket to wear from the multitude in the wardrobe? Many were destined for the charity shop. He chose the usual chocolate brown leather jacket as it was the most comfortable. His black beanie had already been stuffed into a pocket.

Phone, cash and car keys. He stopped and checked the small black leather holder on the chest of drawers. The cause of his problems. Would this shiny holder give him alternative ways of changing his life? He shook his head and opened it. The new plastic inside glinted in the light. He read the words on the warrant card, Detective Sergeant Josh Anderson.

Had he imagined reaching this role when he'd joined the police force? An image of himself in his first police uniform flickered into his mind. He had been pleased and proud as he'd imagined himself strolling through the streets, greeting people, being respected and solving crimes. Reality never reached the heady, rose-tinted view. Why had he chosen the police? It had started at school. A poacher cum gamekeeper would be an accurate analogy. His eyes flashed with amusement. He read the words on the warrant card again, a Detective Sergeant.

The promotion should never have gone through. He'd struggled to be a Detective Constable as he could not fathom out the solution to crimes but couldn't face going back to the uniform division, so he'd stuck with it. A few lucky breaks had come his way on investigations. Then, before he knew it, he had been pressed into applying for promotion.

The Inspector had told him in no uncertain terms that ambition held the key to becoming a successful police officer. He had no alternative but to apply and he couldn't believe they didn't reject his application. The promotion panel hadn't progressed well as he hadn't known the answers to many questions so in his usual style he had prevaricated. The worse questioning had been the imagined scenarios. He'd given some ridiculous answers, which in retrospect would never be workable. He shook his head in dismay. But they gave him promotion. Why?

Then the vacancy here in his home town had appeared. Chief Inspector Haskins had been ruthless when he interviewed him. Probing questions and hypothetical situations to which he had no sensible answers. They confused him and it showed in his lacklustre performance.

Then the phone message came through. It hadn't been dramatic. A young lass from personnel told him he'd been accepted and she would make the arrangements for the transfer. That was it. No fanfare of celebratory trumpets, just a brief letter a few days later confirming his appointment. A new job in the town where he'd been brought up. It hadn't sunk in for several days and he had told no one. Why give it to him? His ambition had waned dramatically and had almost disappeared.

He remained apprehensive about the promotion. Was he destined to be a complete failure? It would be a fresh start, but could he succeed? But the return to Blackford meant the past had the potential to rise again. The idea made him shudder. Surely the past was long forgotten.

The blue digits on the bedside clock flicked, so he inspected his new card once more. Yes, it said Detective Sergeant Josh Anderson. He closed it and tucked it away in the inside pocket of his jacket.

10

'Don't leave your plate and mug there, Tom. Wash them up. It only takes two minutes and they will be ready when you arrive home from your shift.' Sandra pulled her bright red coat around her ample frame and checked her make-up and hair in a small compact mirror which she'd taken from her handbag.

Tom picked up the white functional mug and plate from the Formica table. The lights in the kitchen gave a fluorescent harshness to the room highlighting the tired worn cupboards of the kitchen units. Sandra had been nagging him about a new kitchen for ages. The small window over the stainless steel sink faced north so didn't catch the morning light which came in the front of the terraced Victorian house. In some ways Sandra was right; it needed brightening up with a more modern approach. A soft sigh escaped his lips. Another job to add to the list. If he retired, he'd be far busier than remaining in the police force. Not a pleasant thought early in the morning.

'Will you be in when I finish?'

'What time?'

'The shift ends at five today.'

'No, you know I won't be here.' Tutting at him, she

raised her eyebrows, 'You never remember, no matter how many times I tell you, it's my Pilates class this afternoon, but I'll pop back to change before the book club.'

Tom had already donned his police jacket, so he removed it and hung it on the back of the chair as his Sergeant always moaned about the mess down the front of his uniform. Soapy splashes from washing dishes would be noticeable. The sink, too low for him, made his back ache. 'So, what time will you be back?'

He grimaced as the water scalded his fingers. Sandra concentrated on her make-up so he swapped to the other tap and washed his mug and the plate in cold water.

'I'm lunching with the girls and then onto Pilates so I won't be having supper this evening. I'll be out late as we've a long discussion at the book club.'

Tom didn't turn to look at his wife and gazed out of the kitchen window into the small back garden as he dried his mug and plate. Another lonely evening beckoned, a too familiar pattern these days as they rarely went out together. The weekly trip to the local pub had dwindled away under the pressure of her classes and clubs. 'I'll buy my tea in the police canteen.'

'If I'm late, don't wait up, the book club session will not finish until ten.'

Tom nodded and put on his black windcheater style jacket for the second time. Although he preferred the traditional tunic, he would be on patrol today so needed to wear his personal protection equipment.

Sandra finished depositing various items into her bag. Tom kissed her on the forehead, 'See you later, luv.' The wood in the door had swelled with the damp as he struggled to open it. 'That's another job that needs sorting.'

'Yes, I know.' His shoulders tensed, but he made no additional comment but anticipated her next remark.

'When you retire, you'll have time to do the jobs around the house. There's a backlog, but they won't take you long. Have you handed in your application yet?'

He couldn't leave until he'd replied, so he pushed the door closed, 'I'm still thinking about it.'

'But you've a full pension, I can't see the point in staying on.'

'I'll have a chat with the Inspector, but I'm still thinking.'

A frown crossed Sandra's face, but Tom opened the door and stepped out into the mild winter's morning. 'Keep safe, Tom.'

He ambled the short path to the back gate, which had nearly fallen off its hinges from lack of maintenance. With a grimace he lifted it open, just enough for him to squeeze through and closed it following the same procedure. The old Vauxhall parked outside the shabby prefabricated garage constructed by a previous owner was covered in dew. It was in a poor condition. Dents and scratches were all too prevalent. Once upon a time it had been a glossy racing green but it now was more akin to matt sludge. Should he buy a new car? These days he hardly drove it as they didn't go out often. Why would he need a new car?

Letting the warmth of the morning's winter sun seep into him, the prospect of retirement filled him with dread as Sandra would find an endless list of jobs for him to achieve. She wanted him to help at the charity shop where she worked three days a week. It didn't appeal. The thought of sorting through other people's discarded items made him shudder.

He couldn't fish all the time, so what else? It was obvious that his bosses struggled to understand him. Tom smiled to himself. He never worried about their views. Traditional policing had gone, his colleagues of the same ilk had retired, so he'd become a lone bastion of the old ways. Tolerated, by the senior staff they waited for the day he would hang up his helmet. As he climbed into his old car, and settled himself into the worn driver's seat, he smiled again. They would have a long wait.

11

Josh rubbed his face as he sat in his dark blue Audi outside the police station. What would today be like? It would be his first official day as a Sergeant after volunteering to sacrifice his holiday and start his new role immediately. Scary moments in the police happened, but yesterday the fright reached a higher level because Eleanor had been involved.

His body ached as he hadn't slept well last night as the scary memories of the smoke kept forcing themselves back into his mind. His stomach churned and he couldn't stop shivering. The weak state had been hidden from his parents and Eleanor as they would nag at him to leave the job. Helping Eleanor through the trauma was a priority. How would she react in the coming weeks? Would she be able to overcome the constant flashbacks to the terrorising ordeal? Too many questions but no answers.

His face tightened and he pressed his lips together in a thin hard line. This new role as a Sergeant had been scheduled to start next week, but his new colleagues would expect him to come early after the events of yesterday. It was the strange ethos of the police. Today all eyes will be on him, watching his every move to gauge how he responded to the pressure.

Life as a Detective Sergeant in Blackford awaited. Would he enjoy it? He wrung his hands together, pursed his lips and tried to relax his shoulders, but the empty feeling wouldn't go away. This morning he would meet his new boss. He'd only met him once before at the disastrous interview.

Standing beside his car his eyes scanned the building, his new place of employment. The thirty-year-old shell was weathered and worn. The concrete had lost its initial shine and was now covered with grime. The bright sunshine did nothing to lift his spirits and did little to enhance the bleak grey structure of the police station. Checking his watch as he reached the entrance of the monstrosity, a sigh escaped his lips. Only a few minutes late. Would anyone notice? Pausing on the steps next to the concrete planter bowls, which had seen better days and had degenerated into rubbish bins and ashtrays, he braced himself for the day ahead.

With a smile fixed firmly he strode into the building. Some officers, on duty in the reception area, gave a small wave. Josh appreciated the welcoming gesture. Moving down the corridor with a stiff straight back and the smile still firmly planted across his lips, second thoughts poked and jabbed at him like a sharp stick. Would he manage to be a success as a Sergeant?

On reaching the door, with a sign that read, Detective Chief Inspector Jeremy Haskins, he gave a sharp knock, took a deep breath and waited. 'Come.'

Slipping inside the office, the man who had interviewed him sat at a large shiny mahogany desk. His stern watchful face showed a flicker of surprise. The meticulously organised desk did little to raise Josh's faltering spirits. It wasn't his style. The arranged files in a neat pile, a picture of his family angled towards him and a precisely placed fountain pen beside his large day book. The keyboard and computer screen to the side were clean and shining. Was his desk ever covered with a haphazard scattering of papers as he worked? Did he ever make a mess? 'Josh! I hadn't expected you.' The corners of his lips quirked into a light smile and he flapped his hand towards the vacant chair, 'Come in and sit down. How's your sister?'

'Bearing up remarkably well under the circumstances, sir.'

'Good, we're short of staff so I'm glad you've arrived.'

Jeremy Haskins in his light blue suit, white shirt and dark blue tie leaned back in his chair and stared across at him, his gaze alarmingly direct. Would they develop a good working relationship? Time would tell. Josh had checked him out. In his mid-forties, he had been in the police force all his working life. Known by his colleagues as a serious and meticulous man, he didn't tolerate slack methods or informality. 'As you are a witness to the raid at the shopping centre, I cannot allow you to work directly on the case.'

'Perhaps I can help in the background.'

He inclined his head the smallest fraction, 'I'm the Chief Investigating Officer and have set up an incident room. Blackford does not need a daylight robbery that terrifies the public. One aspect you could work on is whether it is related to a robbery at a post office a few months ago.'

'Are there similarities?'

'Motorbikes for the getaway.'

'I'll check it out.'

'Assign yourself to the Incident Room,' he raised

his chin and studied Josh intently, 'I want a quick result.' Josh hated being confined in an Incident Room. The duty would make it a terrible start to his new role.

The Chief flicked through a file on his desk while Josh sat and waited. 'I'll be honest with you Josh, your interview was poor, but you were the only applicant. Your reference from Manchester was good, so I appointed you.' A blow to his confidence on his first morning.

It was important to remain positive, so he asked, 'Why didn't I come across well, sir.'

'You lack the dynamism I require from my teams. Police work is action and detail, I won't have guesswork that occurs in other stations. We catch criminals by meticulous hard work.'

His heart sank at his Chief's opinion as he favoured finding information from people and not the tedium of detailed paperwork. Josh admitted to himself he lacked dynamism and had become too laid back. Also, he cut corners with paperwork, which he found boring. His new boss wouldn't approve as he appeared well organised. Perhaps his new colleagues would compensate and be more tolerant, Josh flashed a lopsided grin.

The Chief Inspector surveyed him with a critical eye, 'I appreciate that in the force we need to dress casually and not stand out, but can I ask you to be smarter.' Josh didn't think it worth answering, so dipped his head in a quick nod. 'An experienced uniformed Sergeant runs the Incident Room. Introduce yourself and he'll allocate tasks for you.'

Not the best of welcomes from his new boss. With such a meticulous man as his senior officer the future did not look promising. It would be a bumpy ride.

His deep serious voice cut through Josh's thoughts, 'As you appreciate, I'm busy. We'll leave a welcoming drink for you on hold until we clear up this raid.'

Josh would not be dismissed as he had an important issue on his mind. 'Yesterday I witnessed Tom Collins's fearless approach in freeing my sister from the man holding her at knife point. What's the procedure to recommend someone for an award or commendation.'

The Chief Inspector held up his hand, 'Ahh! Tom Collins. The man is an enigma. The senior officer at the scene recorded witness statements. A recommendation for his bravery in rescuing your sister has already been made.' With deliberate care he picked up his fountain pen and rearranged its position next to his diary. Shaking his head slowly from side to side he refocused his attention on Josh. 'Tom Collins has been in Blackford police longer than the life of this building. I try to give him the benefit of the doubt, but his approach is from another era. I've told him frequently we cannot look back and must look forward, but it's water off a duck's back.'

'He must be near retirement age.'

The Chief Inspector laughed.

'I came here five years ago when everyone expected Tom to retire. We sometimes wonder what we will do with him, but he is a serving officer…'

Josh interrupted, '… a very brave one.'

The Chief Inspector's eyes narrowed. He didn't like being interrupted, 'Yes, a brave officer.'

'I thanked him yesterday but as I've officially started, I would like to formally thank him again. Do you know if he's in today?'

'You'll find he is on duty most days as he rarely takes

his days off and personnel complain that he doesn't take his full entitlement of holidays. One attribute I can say about him, he is an observant officer. Yesterday as he swung into the car park, he recognised two young lads. They come from the Mercer family who own the demolition firm near the bypass. The head of the family is the lads' grandfather, Arthur Mercer. When they were both young men, Arthur was one of Tom's first arrests, so he is interviewing him about his grandsons.'

'Is it likely that the family could have been involved?'

'Yes, would be my guess. Arthur and his sons have convictions for armed robbery.' A crisp knock came on the office door. The Chief Inspector frowned. 'Come! Perfect timing, Claire. Meet Josh.'

She gave the briefest of smiles to the Chief Inspector and shook hands with Josh. Her piercing brown eyes travelled up and down his whole body in a quick scan. No welcoming smile appeared, and her expression was serious. 'Claire Harris. Welcome to Blackford.'

Josh had never like cropped hair on a woman, but she had a splendid figure, although a little overweight. She wore a cream blouse and straight blue trousers with elegance.

'As the two Sergeants on my team you will work closely together.' She smiled at the Chief and handed him a file, but her stony expression returned as her gaze slid back to him.

Josh studied her. Young, he guessed under thirty so about five years his junior. To become a Detective Sergeant before thirty meant she would have been identified as a high-flyer. He'd have preferred an experienced officer for a close colleague as she would make as many mistakes as him, but how would they handle them? He had a sense of foreboding that he would often shoulder the blame.

'Claire is the new breed of police officer I want for my team, she's been with us for six months and has had a major impact, I hope you can do the same, Josh.'

The words cut through Josh as he doubted his capability to fulfill such high expectations. With an inward sigh, he gave the expected reply, 'I'll do my best.'

The Chief Inspector eyed them, 'Right, Let's get on with it!'

As they moved down the corridor, she paused and surveyed him with a serious expression, 'Sorry about your sister but it's good you've arrived as it's hell here. The boss,' she nodded her head toward his office, 'is all right but uptight and he's slow compared to what I'm used to.'

'Where did you come from?'

'The Met, they perform faster.'

'What made you choose Blackford?'

Her scowl implied too much of a personal question. 'To broaden my experience. Must go!' With a suddenness that surprised him she twisted away and strode down the corridor. Why hadn't she been more welcoming and offered to show him around? It was obvious he would be on his own. So far there weren't many plus points about starting his job in Blackford.

12

'Welcome, I assume you're Josh, the boss informed me you were arriving this week.' The large room, bright from the vast windows, had been filled with a mismatch of desks, tables and computer equipment. Some blinds had been half pulled to control the glare from the low winter sunshine which cut across the space while others hung broken and twisted. Peeling faded paintwork and brown old fashioned carpet tiles added to the air of neglect. The uniformed Sergeant had a firm handshake and a pleasant smile. 'It's chaos, but I'm sure that's nothing new to you. Will you do incoming analysis?'

Groups of four desks were crammed throughout the room with only enough space to squeeze between them. Each desk had a computer with a screen balanced on top. Old technology which had become grimy from years of use. A mixture of police officers and civilians manned the desks, which were cluttered with paperwork, folders and an assortment of mugs and paper cups. Their animated chatter and the occasional bout of laughter filled the air, along with the whirr of the printers and the photocopy machine.

The offered role of analysing the incoming data did

nothing to boost his mood. He gave a quick forced smile to cover his unwillingness. It was a job he hated.

'It's a crap job, but it will help the team having someone experienced checking through the info as it filters through. Sorry to desert you but I need to go to a meeting. Why bosses assume a meeting will solve a crime, I'll never know.' Josh liked his fellow Sergeant. His down to earth comment appealed to him. 'Gemma, can you show Josh around?'

The officer sitting behind a bank of computers stood up. Petite, she wore her auburn hair in a bun. She'd been Tom's patrol partner when they'd arrived at the raid. Giving him a friendly grin. 'Hi, Sarge, how's your sister?'

Drifting towards her, 'Bearing up. What about you? Did the smoke irritate your throat?'

She laughed, 'A good idea according to my colleagues as it stops me talking so much. Come on, I'll take you on a tour of the station unless you've had one already.'

'No, a tour will be great. Aren't you with Tom today?'

As they left the room, 'He's on a one-man Tom Collins' mission,' her eyes shone with amusement. 'He wants no one with him.'

'I worked with a few old stagers in Manchester and they always preferred lone working.'

'He's a good copper. Make sure he's assigned to your team. And his driving is wicked, though a little scary.' She chuckled, 'He's like a man possessed once he turns on the blue flashing lights and the siren. He's missed his vocation, as he should have been a rally driver.'

Gemma kept glancing at him as they meandered along the corridor. She smiled every time he caught her eye. 'Here's the most important part of the station, the canteen. Shall we have a cup of tea while we're here? Then you can tell me about your move to Blackford.' Bright and bubbly with a friendly smile. Josh would enjoy her company. What a contrast to straight laced Claire.

He took a step towards the counter to buy the teas. 'No, my treat, you are working for paperwork Haskins and have Miss Perfection as your Sergeant colleague, best of luck with both. You will need more than a cup of tea dealing with them.'

Her petite figure moved to the counter. She joked with the staff. In the past he had resisted a relationship with a fellow officer apart from one occasion. Would it be too complicated? Shaking his head, he would be casual as she could be in a long term relationship although she didn't wear a ring. It would be difficult, but he would be constrained in his approach. It was his first day in Blackford so chatting up a pretty colleague would have to wait.

13

The steel frames of the fences and gates had seen better days, but the razor wire that topped them was shiny suggesting it had been a recent addition. The pungent smell of diesel and oil greeted Tom as he ambled across the muddy car park, doing his best to avoid the large puddles. This morning he had driven to a less salubrious part of town, often described in the newspapers as a brown site. It had previously held nineteenth-century industries that had long since vanished. On arrival he had parked his patrol car across the road in front of the disused rectangular mill building which had survived from the eighteenth century.

A gap in the showers brought out the sunshine, but it didn't improve the vista. His eyes swept towards his intended destination and he marched through the gate of Mercer's Demolition, the principal groundworks company in Blackford. The dull thud of heavy machinery caused the ground to tremble so he would keep his wits about him. The source of the thudding came closer. Tom stopped and waited as a huge caterpillar machine, painted bright orange, rumbled in front of him with the dinosaur jaws swinging with the motion. The driver stared down at Tom but showed no reaction and carried on trundling his huge beast across the site.

Kicking the mud from his boots, he stamped his feet on the wooden slope as he strode into the Portakabin office of Mercer's Demolition.

'What the bloody hell do you want? The authorities should have pensioned you off years ago, you useless lump.'

Arthur Mercer's outbursts had always been ignored by Tom. Standing in the entrance, he surveyed the scene as it was best not to hurry this interview. Taking his time, he allowed the silence to lengthen before he answered, 'Good morning, Mr Mercer. How are you today?'

'A damn sight worse now that you've turned up.' Arthur glared at him with burning reproachful eyes and snorted with derision. 'The quicker you tell me what you want, the quicker you'll leave. Get on with it, I don't like you creeping around my premises.'

Tom lips almost curved into a smile, but he concentrated on keeping his deadpan expression, 'No law-abiding citizen or business needs to fear a policeman.' He took a moment to survey the office. Untidy papers were everywhere and it was in desperate need of a coat of paint. 'What have you been up to?' Tom stared hard waiting for a reaction and his eyebrows rose, 'I'm suspicious otherwise you wouldn't want me to leave so quickly. And you haven't even offered me a cup of tea.'

'So, you've turned up on one of those visits have you,' snarled the short wiry man with grey hair. He folded his arms across his grubby brown overalls and scowled. The desk in front of him was stacked high with an assortment of papers and the tatty office chair squeaked alarmingly as he leaned back. 'I have nothing to say. The last time you lot became involved with me it cost you a few grand for false arrest.' A self-satisfied grin crossed his unshaven face.

Tom drifted to the far side of the office, scanning the desk files and diagrams on the wall. 'I want to help.'

Arthur groaned, crossed to the filing cabinet and opened the top drawer. 'I've no time to sit around talking to you. I've a business to run.' He flapped through the files, interspersed with the occasional loud huff.

'How are your grandsons these days, Arthur?'

He paused, twisted round and focused on Tom. His eyes narrowed, 'They're good kids. No trouble. You leave them alone.' His voice was low and held the hint of a threat.

'I only make enquiries when it's related to a crime.'

Arthur banged the metal filing cabinet drawer, which rattled closed with a metallic grind. Squaring his shoulders, his hands clenched. 'You're trying to stitch them up, aren't you?'

That accusation amused Tom, even though he'd heard it so often.

'You might not like me Arthur, for good reasons, as you spent eight years in prison because of me. However, we've known each other for longer than either of us care to remember and you know I have never fitted anyone up for a job they didn't do.' The two men stared at each other.

Arthur switched his gaze to a woman sat at a nearby desk, who had stopped working and listened to the conversation. Young and blonde, she stared with arms folded across her ample bosom. He frowned, 'Margaret, can you go to the house and fetch those files we spoke about earlier?'

Without a word she stood, sneered at Tom and left the office. 'The kettle has boiled. Don't think this will happen again.' Within a minute, Tom had a mug of strong brown tea in front of him. He had made progress. The mention of his grandsons had given Arthur enough uncertainty. 'So, what do you think my grandsons have done?'

Tom ignored the question, 'Before I go, I want to check your motorbikes.'

Arthur's eyes bored into him and his shoulders tensed. 'How can I have been so daft! The robbery at the shopping centre. They used motorbikes for their getaway. So, you think with my record and my love of bikes it might be me.'

'Or your family.'

'You leave them alone, especially the grandkids, I've told them to keep their noses clean, work hard and they can take over this business.'

Tom sipped his tea, 'They were in the shopping centre car park when the raid took place.'

'If you think I'm falling for that line you've another think coming, I suppose there's some dodgy witness who wants to stitch me up and says my grandkids were there. Why don't you check out the reliability of the witness before coming to see my family and making false accusations about them?'

Tom pulled himself up to his full height and glared down on Arthur Mercer, 'I arrived first in the car park in response to the raid. Your grandsons ran across the car park. One had a blue jacket and the other a brown hoodie. Does that seem familiar to you?'

Arthur had been carrying on with his work but slammed the filing cabinet door which had inched open while they had been talking. The metal structure bounced.

Tom sipped his tea and waited.

'If you were racing to a crime scene, you didn't have time to identify them, all youngsters wear the same clothes.'

Tom's lips curled; his expression hardened as he stared at Arthur Mercer. 'If you persist with your current attitude, I shall return with a warrant for their arrest.'

'I'm not falling for that, you've no grounds for a warrant.'

'They are present at the scene of a major crime, witnessed by a police officer. Your family, including yourself, has a history of robberies. Everyone in town knows you like fast bikes, so it won't take much to convince the magistrate to issue a warrant.'

Arthur Mercer slumped into a chair, 'Will you go easy on them? Honestly, they have done nothing wrong. Being in the mall doesn't implicate them.'

With slow precision, Tom flicked to the page in his notebook. 'I have questioned them twice about shoplifting and one has been charged with riding a motorbike without a licence.'

'That's daft bringing that up. So, the bike was more powerful than his licence, hardly puts him in line as a bank robber.'

'I need not explain to you that lookouts are a key part of a successful raid.'

'Bloody hell!' Arthur's fist hammered down onto his paper-strewn desk and his expression hardened. 'You think they kept watch?'

'A theory, but I want a word.' Arthur Mercer fiddled with a broken and leaking biro. His confidence had gone. 'I can do this in two ways. Either a warrant for their arrest or you summon them here now.'

'As they are under eighteen, I want to stay with them.'

Tom nodded.

Arthur picked up the phone and thumped the number pad with his finger. 'I want you over in the office now and bring your brother.' He waited, then shouted, 'Don't give me any of your lip, get yourself over here straightaway or I'll give you a bloody good clip around the ear.' He then slammed down the phone, crossed his arms and scowled. They waited in silence.

14

Despite Josh's best efforts, he would arrive late. He trotted across Market Square in the twilight drizzle with his beanie pulled tight on his head. Would she still be there? Would she wait? It had been deadly quiet in the Incident Room but he needed to show willing and had stayed on for an extra hour. Nothing changed with the boring job of checking the incoming information.

As he intended leaving, a query came from a patrol. By the time he'd found the relevant information, he had been late leaving the police station. Approaching the front door of The Grapes, he glanced at his watch. Ten minutes late at the pub for a first date. Josh wouldn't blame her if she hadn't waited.

The Grapes had a good reputation, but it didn't impress. The sound of loud chatter and hearty laughter greeted him as he entered the bar that was half full of office workers who had popped in for a drink on the way home. The red carpet, scratched tables and chairs had seen better days. The people, in groups of three or four, sat drinking and joking. The lively atmosphere reflected friends meeting regularly. He weaved his way through to the far end of the bar, but he couldn't see her. Another failure before it had even started.

Josh bought a pint of IPA and sat on a bar stool with a dogeared copy of the local free newspaper. He glanced at his watch. Fifteen minutes late. His time keeping needed to improve. As the door opened a smile crossed his face. 'Hi, Lynette.'

'Josh, so sorry to be late, I'm hopeless at timekeeping and although I made a special effort for our first date, I failed miserably. Thanks for waiting.'

'Calm down, it's no hassle for me. Relax. Drink?' A grin crossed his face, they shared a common trait.

'I've had a terrible day, large G & T please.' She slipped off a stylish long red coat, folded it and placed it on a nearby chair, then nipped on to the bar stool next to him. Her tight thin red cotton top showed off her figure. The white skirt revealed plenty of leg as she made herself comfortable. A stunning figure, with a beautiful face. This evening she was full of smiles unlike their first meeting in the shopping mall when she had been rather serious. At first sight he'd taken a liking to her and as she sat on the bar stool, he was glad about asking her for a date.

'Why was work bad today?'

'Cheers,' they touched glasses and she savoured a long sip of her drink.

'Work's boring, there are better topics.'

Josh nodded, jobs wouldn't be a topic for tonight and he hoped when he eventually told her that he was a policeman she wouldn't dump him.

Giving him a devastating smile, 'What music do you like?'

Rubbing his chin, he laughed.

She nudged him, 'What's so funny, it's a simple question?'

He raised his eyebrows and gave a broad grin, 'Classical.'

'Doesn't fit with disco dance music.' She caught his eye and they laughed together.

Josh relaxed, he would enjoy the evening.

'I'm excited as I'm riding tomorrow.'

'A horse?' Josh signalled for the drinks to be replenished.

'Fool! Yes, only because I haven't found camels in Blackford.'

The laughter ceased as he paid for the drinks. He faced her, 'This isn't a good pub.'

She shrugged, 'It the best in the town centre. Where do you suggest?'

'Let's visit the new Tapas bar and then go to the Ibiza Club.'

'Brill!' she wriggled on her stool, revealing more leg. Her eyes sparkled.

15

Josh wanted an excuse to leave the Incident Room. Scanning the room, he searched for inspiration. Amateurish notes and drawings relating to the shopping centre raid had been stuck on the wall and half used lukewarm coffee cups lined the desks. The room had the familiar feel of an investigation progressing nowhere. To stretch his legs and relieve the boredom he wandered across the room to study the wall charts. Nothing there to help his excuse to leave. Acknowledging others in the room, he returned to his seat and clicked on the mouse. Could he find a reason to leave in the next batch of incoming information?

'Any fresh developments, Josh?' The Chief Inspector's voice behind him made him jump. Dressed in shirtsleeves, he was in a busy mood, as he checked with the other officers before returning. 'Why isn't Tom here?'

'He recognised a name and is following it through.'

'What's the name?'

'Jack Monroe.'

'The name means nothing to me. What about you?'

'No, sir.' Josh logged on to the police computer and typed in the name, Jack Monroe. He pointed towards the screen, 'Convictions for assault, affray and grievous bodily harm.'

The Chief Inspector frowned and rubbed a hand across his brow. 'There's no mention of robbery in his record. Old dogs don't learn new tricks. What's your opinion?'

Josh scrolled down the screen, 'I agree. No evidence of robbery according to these statements. He becomes tanked up and then lashes out. Nasty bit of work, but I can't see him planning a robbery. The only hope would be that he helped a fellow villain.'

The Inspector's face tightened and he narrowed his eyes, 'Tom is spending too much time on his own wild goose chases.' His tone was challenging, bordering on argumentative, 'When he comes back instruct him to return to the checking of the cameras. Monroe's a loner.'

Tom wouldn't be pleased as he'd been moaning about camera checks. The noise of a police radio on full volume disrupted the quiet. Tom entered with the radio strapped to his fluorescent jacket near his lapel. He concentrated on the cackling noise of the call. 'I'm back in the station, where's the nearest car?' The reply was unintelligible to Josh, 'I can be there in seven.' Again, the crackle, 'I'm on my way.'

'What is it?' the Chief Inspector frowned at the disruption that Tom had caused.

'A dog walker has reported finding a body at the top end of Blackdam reservoir.'

'You're supposed to be in here, not on call.'

'The nearest free car is twenty minutes away. There's an accident on the motorway.'

'Very well,' a tight smile appeared, 'you'd better go.' Josh opened his hand to indicate whether he should follow

Tom. The Chief wiped his hand over his face, 'Go with Collins. If it's suspicious, I don't want a heavy-footed copper treading on the evidence.'

In less than a minute Josh jumped into the passenger seat of the Range Rover. Tom laboured to the driver's side and hauled himself in. Then his movements changed to become fast and multi-tasked. The siren screeched and blue lights flashed. The full power of the Range Rover came through as Tom's foot hit the accelerator.

16

A car driver panicked and pulled out in front of them. Josh closed his eyes and braced himself for the impact, but it didn't happen. The siren changed tone and when he opened his eyes again, the Range Rover weaved around the terrified motorist stuck in the middle of the road.

Tom aimed for a space between two closing articulated lorries. Josh closed his eyes again only daring to peep when they sped away without a crash. Eyes closed seemed the best idea.

Swinging the patrol car onto a dusty track, 'You're local, so will know where we're headed.'

After a few hundred metres, the tranquil blue reservoir appeared on the left. The trees, bare of leaves, increased in density as the track became rougher while the houses lining the track became larger and more isolated. An open gate led to a field lined by trees and the reservoir. They bounced forward along an uneven mixture of gravel and mud.

The radio blared the identity of the dog walker, a Mr Humphries, who had indicated that he would wait until the police arrived. 'There he is,' shouted Josh. The old man had a brown and white spaniel sat at his feet. Josh nipped out as soon as the car came to a halt. 'Mr Humphries?' He showed his warrant card. The obedient dog sat at his master's feet but wagged his tail. Josh couldn't resist fussing the dog as he surveyed the scene. Behind Mr Humphries, a rocky outcrop formed the edge of the water. A gravel beach joined the rocks to the woods.

The old man pointed past the outcrop. 'She's on the far side of the rocks.' Josh examined the potential routes to reach her as he moved from foot to foot.

'No need to rush. She's dead. My dog wouldn't come back. He always comes when he's called, so I went to investigate. I'm too old to reach the lass.'

Josh opened his hand, indicating he wanted the man to show him. Tom had parked the patrol car and joined them. The gravel petered out and the mud became thick within a few steps. Josh's shoes leaked, so he glanced at Tom's feet. After parking, he'd pulled on a pair of wellies. The old man also wore wellington boots. With a silent sigh, Josh plodded on with soggy socks and wet feet. The rock outcrop stretched inland from the reservoir. The straightforward route up was via natural steps, a continuation of the reservoir track. Impassable for vehicles, but walkers would have no problem. The man struggled to reach the uppermost point of the rocks. 'You can see from here but can't reach her.'

The woman's lifeless body lay at the bottom of the rocks directly below the highest part of the outcrop and underneath the only cliff edge. The cliff about five metres high could make a fall fatal. Her leggings and tracksuit top, with thick trainers, indicated a runner. Her face was submerged in the water, but her body lay twisted on the rocks. One leg stretched out at an unnatural angle. Tom peered over the edge and grunted, 'I'll call from the car.'

A fellow runner? A meeting? Josh shook his head. Not likely in this remote spot. He had little doubt she'd fallen or been pushed from the top of the rocks. This might be a simple case as it would be difficult to sneak up on someone. Turning to Mr Humphries, 'Has it upset you?'

A smile crossed his grim face. 'Sergeant, I'm fine. I spent twenty years as a paramedic, so it hasn't distressed me apart from the sadness for the young woman with her life ahead of her.'

Josh took the man's address and let him hobble away with his dog.

'I've called the whole circus.' Tom pulled himself to the top of the rocks. 'We'd better cordon off the muddy area otherwise the Chief will think we've missed a trick, although I wouldn't expect any of the footprints to be useful.'

They conducted a preliminary search of the immediate area, but it gave no clues as to the young woman's death. Sitting on a rock they waited for investigation colleagues to take the case to the next stage. The tranquil scenery of the large reservoir with its treelined shores was in sharp contrast to the grim discovery of a body. A noisy swarm of Canada geese flew overhead and landed on the smooth surface of the reservoir. The water gently lapped against the rocky shoreline and the breeze sighed as it passed through the bare branches of the trees. Such a beautiful place. What a shame to sully such a bright vibrant setting with the grim morbidity of death.

Would he be transferred to the case? Josh mulled the evidence. He couldn't work out a scenario that would make it an accidental death. At least with a murder enquiry, he would have a fresh case to start his career in Blackford. His contemplations were interrupted as a black Mitsubishi Shogun four wheel drive crunched its way along the track. Tom picked up a roll of blue police tape and methodically tied it around a tree to cordon off a nearby ditch.

'Who's that?' Josh peered across at Tom.

'He's not normally this fast. It's Professor Sutherland, the pathologist.'

Josh rubbed his hands together and moved across to join Tom, 'We can make progress.'

'He's good if handled the right way, otherwise he's a bloody nuisance and won't give early details. He makes a strict demarcation between his job and ours.'

Josh studied the tall slim man, with thin greying hair and an oblong clean-shaven face. He gave the officers no acknowledgement as he climbed down from his car and donned his white overalls over his suit trousers. After placing his feet in white wellingtons, he placed an elastic cap on his head and strode towards them.

'Constable Collins.' He greeted Tom with a nod.

'Detective Sergeant Josh Anderson, sir.' But Josh received no recognition or smile.

'Where is she?' he frowned at the cordoned areas.

Josh led him along the same route as the old man had taken them. The Professor peered down from the rock outcrop. Josh went to speak, but Tom shook his head. 'I'll complete an initial investigation.'

'Will you call if you need us, sir?'

'Yes, Constable.'

The noise of two vehicles made Josh turn.

A forensics van, part of the professor's team, edged

its way along the bumpy track, followed by the Chief Inspector's shiny maroon BMW. Tom muttered, 'There will be fur flying.'

Josh had warmed to Tom. His bravery was beyond question. Although he appeared a disinterested bystander, he understood people.

The Chief Inspector, wound down his window and raised his eyebrows, waiting for a report from Josh.

'Young woman on the rocky edge of the water.' He climbed from his car opened the boot and extracted a pair of pristine wellington boots. 'She fell from the top of the outcrop. The Professor is making a preliminary examination.'

'You'll be on this case Josh unless it's accidental. I'll find out the initial conclusion from the Professor.'

Josh had already picked up the hint from Tom and didn't move. Tom smiled as the Professor's sharp voice cut through the air, 'Chief Inspector, I have not given you permission to advance that close to the deceased as I'm still conducting my examination.'

'Professor! This could be a murder case. An investigation team needs to be organised.'

'Chief Inspector...'

Tom and Josh moved away from the top of the outcrop. Both had wry smiles. 'It's the same every time they meet.' Tom kept his voice low, 'The Professor becomes annoyed and then doesn't give us any early information.'

Tom and Josh waited as the forensics team set about their task. The Professor strutted back towards them, 'I will write up my report.'

'When?' The Professor ignored the question from the

Chief Inspector and marched away.

The Chief muttered, 'Always hampering us in doing our job. Josh, when you've finished here, set up a murder Incident Room at the station. Even without his help,' he raised his arm and pointed at the Professor, 'it's a suspicious death.' He stomped across to his car, threw his boots into the back, slid into his smart BMW now splattered in mud and drove away.

The case could start without information from the Professor. 'Thank you for attending quickly, Professor.'

He scrutinised Josh as he changed his boots, 'I appreciate your patience in allowing me to conduct the initial examination without interference.' He glared at the Chief Inspector's car bouncing along the track in the distance. 'There is no sexual assault, but it's a suspicious death.'

'Can you explain how you came to that conclusion, sir?'

'Two head wounds, one caused by the fall. The second is a smooth indented fracture of the skull. My estimate would be a metal bar. There is no identification or personal possessions on the body.'

'The metal bar used for jacks in cars?'

The Professor nodded. His team loaded the black sealed bag, 'Show the officers the face.' One attendant unzipped the bag. 'White female about your age, Sergeant.'

Josh stared down at the bloated, bruised face covered with blotches. The black bag was closed. What were her last memories? Had she known fear? Did she know she would die?

'She has been dead for many hours. Immersion causes the puffiness. I'll have more details when I examine her on the table.'

17

Deep in thought, I nibbled at the biscuits mum had brought to the garden for me. A chilly wind had blown throughout the afternoon. Spits and spots of rain came and went from the heavy grey sky. That's the last of Dad's onion sets planted and it's good to be performing normal tasks again. Although not a suitable day for gardening, the desire to be outside had become urgent as the frightening images appeared less frequently.

'Are you mad? The weather is terrible.' Josh's voice made me smile. I'd stepped into the shed away from the biting wind, pulled my anorak tighter and drank my tea down in one. The taste of the smoke had gone, although my legs were shaky. 'I'm helping dad.'

'In this weather?'

'If I sit with mum in the lounge, my mind runs ragged, so I'm happy concentrating on onion sets.' Josh laughed. I didn't need to explain, we had an understanding. He squeezed into the small shed as it rained even harder. 'Any progress?'

'None with the young lads. It will be a long haul of trawling through the video footage.'

I rubbed my brow, 'Why would youngsters be involved. I don't understand police methods.'

'The youngsters could have been the lookouts. But we've dropped interest in them.'

'Why?'

'The family won a harassment case against the police so the seniors aren't interested in taking out a warrant unless there is a definite link with the shopping centre crime.'

'Any additional information on the cameras?'

'I don't know, as I've been moved to another case. A dog walker found the body of a woman at Blackdam reservoir.'

'That's appalling. How sad. Suicide?'

He stared at me, 'No, murder.'

I clutched my jacket about me as his words, so matter of fact, scared me. Josh has a frightening job; I wish he would change to another career. A shadow of concern swept across his face.

'What is it? Don't worry about me, Josh. I am much better today.'

Shaking his head, 'Ignore me, I must make a call.'

Why so urgent as he had only arrived home a few minutes ago? Josh wandered down the garden with his phone glued to his ear. Then with purpose he came back while still talking, 'Have you your mobile?' His smile had gone. 'Can I see the pictures from the shopping centre of Maddie?'

Stepping away from me, he checked both his phone and mine. 'What's all this about, Josh?'

Holding up his hand to me, I waited as he made another phone call. 'Tom, you'd better come over here.' Josh crossed to me. 'Let's sit in the shed. You will find out, so I'll tell you now.'

'Tell me what?'

He guided me into the shed and pointed to an upturned large pot with a piece of sacking on top. 'Sit. It might be a shock.'

'Josh, what is it?' My stomach twisted and turned. The shaking returned to my hands.

'The murdered woman was Maddie.'

'Oh, my God!' I stared at the picture on my phone. My shaking became worse, I lowered my head into my hands and sobbed. I wanted to leave Blackford. I wanted to go home to my flat in Manchester and be with Scott.

18

Josh found it hard not to think back to school when he'd done something wrong. The sunlight from the window streamed in as he stood in front of the Chief Inspector's desk. Tom shuffled uncomfortably next to him. The glaring sun warmed the room. The Chief, in shirtsleeves, mopped his brow and picked up his fountain pen to make notes. His spicy aftershave filled the room. Josh straightened his shoulders and waited. Tom shuffled again and gave the slightest of groans.

'It's poor policing, you're the most experienced officer in the station, Constable.' The Chief Inspector laid down his pen. He rested his elbows on the table and steepled his fingers together, his expression grim. The steely eyes rested on Josh, 'You are supposed to be a detective.' He wanted to speak but had learned lessons the hard way and stayed quiet. Tom was of the same persuasion, so neither responded. 'Speak up.'

Josh grimaced, 'I should have recognised her, sir. Tom had briefly glanced at the photos, but they were of no interest to the shopping centre case. I'd met Maddie.'

'It's your first case since you've arrived in Blackford and it's not an impressive start.' His voice matched the sharpness of his gaze, 'What progress has been made?'

'It took time to identify her as she wasn't carrying ID.'

'If two officers have either met or seen a picture of the woman, I expect recognition immediately.' He paused while his eyes raked over them. There was no smile and he tapped his fingers on the desk with impatience. 'It's twenty-four hours and we haven't even started on known associates.'

'We're bringing in her boyfriend. A car has been dispatched to fetch him.'

The Chief Inspector huffed, 'I'm must remind you of the basics as I see from the early reports, he has a history of violence.'

Tom gave a small cough, 'Experienced officers with body armour and backup nearby have gone for the arrest.'

'Okay, that's promising at least. What's the Professor given us?'

'Only the preliminary report.'

'What's he been doing?' With an exaggerated sigh, he rearranged the papers on his desk. 'Why can't he position it at the top of his list. This is a murder enquiry.'

Tom checked his watch. Josh resisted a smile. A subtle hint to end the meeting. Josh liked a man who wouldn't be intimidated.

The Chief Inspector picked up his pen, 'You'd better visit pathology and find out why the Professor has not produced a full report. Tighten up both of you.' Then his eyes narrowed. 'I told you to smarten up. You're a disgrace, I expect better and want results!'

With a sense of relief, Josh clicked the door shut. 'Sorry to land you in trouble with the boss, Tom. The fault lay with me, I should have recognised her. You'd only seen a quick picture, but I'd chatted with her.'

Tom gave him a reassuring pat on the shoulder and shrugged. Leaving the police station, they headed on foot towards the forensic department on the other side of the town centre. Tom plodded alongside Josh as the diesel fumes blew across them and car horns blared from irritated drivers in the slow moving traffic. The high street was busy with shoppers and they found it a relief to leave the hustle and bustle to pass between the small warehouses and car showrooms.

'One aspect I don't like about Chief Inspector Haskins is that he harbours a grudge and never lets the matter rest.' Tom clenched his jaw and his eyes narrowed, betraying his irritation. 'If he brings it up again, blame me, that's the easiest way.'

Josh laughed as they stomped down an alleyway between two charity shops. 'Why should I blame you?' They crossed the road and went towards the market.

'You're a young man who wants promotion and will want to avoid black marks. Haskins is renowned for writing his comments, which he will place on your file.'

'Thanks for the warning, but you cannot take the blame.'

Tom gave a growl of a laugh, 'They've run out of paper for the number on my file. The management do not know what job to give me next. They sometimes decide I'm better off in the car but then moan when I do policing my way.'

'What happens then?'

'They give me station duties. If you ever want the police computer system broken, assign me to the case. Chaos reigns when I use computers as I always press the wrong buttons.' He gave another growl of laughter. 'The seniors keep suggesting retirement.'

Tom suddenly changed direction and headed off on a detour through the busy market and homed in on a stall. 'It's legal stuff, Constable. I've learned my lesson.'

Tom nodded to him, then with a slow back bend stooped down and dragged two cardboard boxes from under the trestle table. He sorted through them, then stood up to his full height, which with his helmet topped two metres. 'I'll be back to keep checking on you.'

The stall owner snarled but Tom ignored him and they set off again. Tom's knowledge of the area will be useful on cases as he understands what happens in Blackford. The smell of the onions on the burger bar didn't whet Josh's appetite, though many people nearby were tucking into them with enthusiasm.

'I'd been thinking of retirement,' Tom's smile disappeared, 'but Sandra has had a new lease of life in her fifties. She's into Pilates and Yoga, which always seem to coincide with my mealtimes. Now she has decided the house, which we've lived in for years, needs renovating like they do on the television programmes. I'd have no peace, so it's easier to stay at work and if she's out, I can eat in the police canteen.'

Arriving at their destination, Tom typed in a code to the keypad and pushed open the wobbly steel framed glass door of a 1960s concrete building. The smell of disinfectant greeted them. The clean plastic floor tiles of the small entrance hall had been scuffed and worn over the years. After puffing up the narrow stairs, they entered an office with a thin and cheap carpet. A woman in her late twenties with black hair, a white blouse and a gorgeous smile glanced up from the computer keyboard, 'Hello, Tom. Thanks for the phone call making the appointment.'

Her brown eyes flicked Josh up and down, so he snatched off his beanie and stuffed it in his pocket. The woman smiled, 'You're the new Sergeant. I believe you've met the Professor at the crime scene. He must have liked you, as he rearranged his appointments to see you.'

Tom raised his eyebrows. 'How is he?'

She gave a laugh, 'Same as usual!'

The inner office door opened, 'Ah, you're here. Come in. I haven't long. There's a long line of bodies waiting for me downstairs.'

A gruesome image popped into Josh's mind. He shivered. The Professor took the desk chair in his broom cupboard sized office. Tom stood by the door with his helmet under his arm. Josh sat in the only seat in front of the desk. 'I believe you have identified the victim, Sergeant.'

'Yes, sir. By coincidence, I met her a few days earlier.'

He raised his eyebrows but made no comment. As he moved his mouse, light from the screen flicked over his solemn face. 'The blow with the metal bar didn't kill her. The impact on the rocks as she fell in an unconscious state caused her death. She has been unlawfully killed.'

Josh was keen to ask questions but held back after Tom's warning. 'Have you any other information that might help, sir?'

A fleeting smile crossed his face, 'I found no relevant footprints. Only yours and the Constable's but in areas that I would expect from your initial assessment.' Josh waited as he was more interested in the body. 'No assault. No sexual interference. A little overweight, drank too much alcohol and had salad for her last meal.'

He paused, 'Questions?'

'Sir, any evidence that she was a regular runner on that track?'

'Good question, Constable. From the stones embedded in the soles of her trainers, it would have been her regular route, although the evidence would not stand up in court.'

Josh wanted his opinion but doubted he would receive it. 'She must have known her assailant to allow them to approach close enough to inflict the injuries without assault marks.'

"That's for you to investigate, Sergeant.

There's no forensic evidence to contradict your supposition, but there again there's none to support it either.' He smiled, 'Perhaps someone laid in wait and approached her on the rocks. It would be silent to cross them. A stranger hit her on the head.'

Josh smiled as he considered it was the closest the Professor would come to a sense of humour.

19

I anticipated returning to work with relief as my mind would focus on flying. Resuming my normal routines would help to push the recent bout of terrifying experience to the back of my mind. Josh wanted to meet, which gave me an opportunity to leave the tension of mum and dad, who continued to fuss and had become overprotective. They worried about me, which was only natural but wasn't helping me to return to normality. Rather than staying with them, I should have returned to my flat and Scott.

Thinking about him generated a warm glow. Such a wonderful boyfriend. Would he propose soon? Spending the rest of my life with him would be perfect. The fresh chill air blew across my face as I set off. The old mill town had a dusting of snow. The ravine was picturesque under an icy blanket with crisp whiteness transforming the bare branches into magical shapes. I strolled under the double old railway bridges, which towered high above me. No trains rumbled along its tracks, as many years ago it had been transformed into a cycle path. Following the wide footpath, I headed towards the central park. Josh had arrived before me and waved to attract my attention, 'Hi, sis. I guess you fancied some fresh air?'

I dropped onto a chair at a window table in the large pavilion. 'Yes, mum and dad are driving me mad, they dislike what has happened and have become overprotective. They are treating me like a little girl.'

Josh patted the back of my hand, 'They like to fuss over us. They don't like my job and keep nagging me to change careers. At least they approve of your job as a pilot.'

My fingers twirled the strap of my bag, and a loud sigh escaped from my lips, 'I can't get Maddie out of my mind. Is that normal?'

'Yes. Time will lessen the impact, but I need to ask you questions about her.'

'Talking might help. Apart from the chance meeting in the shopping centre, I hadn't met her for a long time, not since she left the airline.' We settled with a large pot of tea and two delicious looking scones accompanied by blackcurrant jam and thick clotted cream. Tendrils of steam rose from the tea and I lifted it to my lips, blowing across the surface before taking a sip. In such a convivial setting, it was hard to contemplate a discussion about murder. My thoughts raced and a sense of unease gripped me, sending an icy shiver through my body.

Josh reached out and patted my hand in a reassuring gesture. 'Did you find Maddie a trusting person?'

I had to think for a while. 'Yes, she saw the best in people so presumably she trusted them. Why do you ask?'

'We found her in a remote spot, so a pre-arranged meeting is the most likely conclusion.'

'Oh!' Panic raced through me. I hadn't anticipated that scenario. To calm myself I gulped down a sip of hot tea, while Josh's face assumed a concerned expression.

'What's the matter, sis?'

'I assumed she had been killed by a fellow runner. Some unknown person.'

'It would never be that easy, she ran alone. We've picked up two witnesses who noticed her. But we are working along the lines that she knew her killer. Whether the meeting had been pre-arranged or whether someone else knew of her usual route, we are still investigating. Both ways the killer would have known her.'

I shuffled in my seat as the closeness to the crimes made me shiver, but I had an admiration and fascination to see how Josh did his job.

'We find friends, acquaintances and anyone who knew her then we'll try to find a line of animosity towards her. A person kills for a reason. Maddie and the killer had something between them that resulted in the desperate measure.'

His explanation made sense, although it sent shivers through me that an acquaintance had been murdered. Although I hadn't been a close friend with Maddie at school, we were in the same class. Learning had been important to me and I had been a model pupil, but Maddie hadn't fitted that image. Often in trouble, she had been boisterous and outspoken. Josh went to refill our teapot. A group of musicians set up their instruments for an afternoon concert at the far end of the pavilion. Josh returned and poured the tea.

During his brief absence, reflections and memories of Maddie had filled my mind. 'When she worked for the airline, she had an adventurous streak and took any available trip.'

'What about men?'

I raised my eyebrows, 'Perhaps I shouldn't speak ill of

her, but anything in trousers would be appropriate.'

'Have you ever met Jason, her boyfriend?'

'No, I can't tell you anything about him. She had no regular boyfriend when she worked on the airline.

'Had she stayed in touch with any old friends from school?' We were interrupted by the brass band beginning their repertoire. The Floral Dance resonated from the distant stage. We could have talked above the music, but we listened for a while enjoying the repertoire of their chosen tunes.

In a brief lull we resumed our conversation. 'At school she had two friends and must have remained close to them.' Josh's eyes sparkled and his face had a quizzical expression. 'They tried to join the airline but when they didn't succeed, she resigned.'

'Can you remember their names?'

'Danny Mercer and Sean Prendergast.'

'I'm surprised that it's two men.'

'Maddie had no girlfriends that I can remember.'

'One of them is a surname I need to check out.'

Josh spoke in a low voice into his mobile, 'Tom, are you still in work, can you check on Danny Mercer?' He ambled away with his phone pressed to his ear and I relaxed, listening to the music. Josh returned, 'Tom will be here in a few minutes, but I'll try to ensure he's not too intense.'

'Don't worry. The robbery has made me tearful, but you know it's not like me. I'm more concerned about mum and dad rather than myself. Tom's a good guy and I will always be grateful for his bravery.'

Josh smiled, 'Yes, I agree he's a great person.' We settled to drinking our tea as we once again listened to the music.

'Nothing like brass band music at the end of a shift.' Tom slumped into a chair and bit into his scone.

I studied Josh, 'I can see your mind working. What's the question? Is it about Sean and Danny? I can't think they would be involved.'

Tom applied a large dollop of cream to his scone, 'You're jumping to conclusions, Eleanor. If they were close to Maddie, they would know her circle of friends.'

'Yes, I see. Maddie led the group of three. Rumours circulated through the school at one time that the three ran their own protection racket for fag money and they set up a betting ring.'

Josh raised his eyebrows. 'Were they top of the class?' Tom grinned as his head bobbed to the rhythm of the music.

'No. At the opposite end. They wouldn't have qualifications. After Danny and Sean failed to secure a job with the airline, Maddie told me before she left that they had been employed by an international hotel chain. She intended applying to the chain to join them.' The music finished and we applauded. 'Why the interest in them? There's something otherwise Tom wouldn't be here.'

Tom put down his scone. 'The Mercer family has convictions for grievous bodily harm and armed robbery. Two teenage Mercers were at the shopping centre during the raid. I interviewed the grandfather, Arthur, hoping to find information. Danny Mercer is related to a family of criminals. Arthur Mercer is his uncle. It's time we had a chat with Danny Mercer.'

20

The interview would be difficult, but Josh had no option. He left the police station and headed towards the branch line railway station, which appeared tired and tatty. Taking the steep steps down past the station to the ravine, he walked along the suspension bridge that lined the cliff wall. The river rushed twenty metres below him. Stopping midway along the bridge to enjoy the view, the sunlight sparkled on the fast flowing water. The evening with Lynette had been superb, as she was lively and great fun. Although they'd arranged another evening out, he didn't expect it to take place. Now that she knew he was a copper, she wouldn't want to associate with him.

With the sun out, the snow flurries had melted and he enjoyed the pleasant riverside walk to the old mill that dominated the skyline. Many of the Blackford mills were derelict or in states of decay and while Canal Wharf Mill seemed its tired self from the outside, he believed it housed a thriving business. The four storey red brick building with a dirty, blackened exterior and grimy windows, that let no light through, was uninviting from the canal side.

The double front door, old and painted black, appeared heavy but opened with ease. Inside, the lights glared.

The entrance hall had bare, pristine cream walls with no furniture to break the monotony of the colour. Three stout wooden doors led from the entrance hall, which resembled the prison cell of a nightmare, doors with no handles.

A large camera high up faced him. The intense, overpowering smell of food hit him as he stood in the middle of the large empty space. The door in front of him opened without warning. Josh jumped.

A tall, well-built man stepped into the entrance hall and the heavy door slammed shut behind him. The rush of smells were a mix of cooked food and the stench of raw meat. Dressed in white baggy trousers and a white tunic, he had blood smeared down his front. His long hair, held by a fine mesh, sat under a white trilby hat. With no smile or greeting, 'You're not allowed in here, mate. The office block is along the road.' Standing square, he faced him with his hands on his hips.

Josh snatched the beanie from his head and stuffed it in his jacket pocket and held up his warrant card. 'Detective Sergeant Anderson to see Lynette Fredericks.'

'Wait here.' The man disappeared back through the door. Within a few minutes, a smiling Lynette struggling with the heavy door appeared then let it slam behind her.

'Hi, Josh. Sorry, I'm not at my best!' Giggling, she peered down at her front. She wore the same white uniform as the man, but hers had brown splodges. 'The gravy machine exploded.' She laughed again. 'The message indicated that you wanted to talk to me. I assume it's about Maddie, I couldn't believe it when I heard the news.' Lynette never stopped talking.

Josh didn't mind, but he needed to ask her questions. 'Can we sit somewhere quiet as the questions might be difficult for you?'

'Why don't we sit in the sun at the canal marina opposite. I'll clock off and I'll see you in five minutes.'

There had been no animosity towards him for doing his job, which he had anticipated. On their evening out, she had every attribute, chatty, lively and full of fun. Having not mentioned his job during the evening, he had expected histrionics from her when they met, but they had not come as she had accepted the meeting without recrimination. He breathed a sigh of relief. Choosing a small stone wall some distance away from the canal side store, he settled to wait. Lynette's bright yellow anorak and short white skirt caught his eye. With a broad smile and holding two cups of tea, she strode towards him. Mildness had returned and the sun shone over the canal basin filled with brightly painted long boats. The odd plume of smoke came from a diesel engine starting up.

A chandler's store had people coming and going. The boat owners bought goods and carried them back to their boats using the tow path. The movement of the long boats in front of him had kept him occupied while he waited. Happiness radiated from her face, which seemed strange following the death of her friend.

As soon as she settled on the wall, he plunged straight in to an explanation, 'The other night when we met I didn't…'

She held up her hand and laughed. 'Once I found out, I thought it was wonderful!'

'What was wonderful?' He had lost the drift of the conversation.

'I didn't ask what job you did and you never brought up about my family.'

'But now you know?'

'Yes, you're a copper and my brother is a violent criminal.' She smiled. 'That makes no difference to us, I enjoyed the evening.'

Josh grinned, 'So did I.'

Giggling, she looked him up and down. 'I would never have guessed you were the Old Bill. Oh, Josh! Stop looking so serious. He's my brother, I've been interviewed by the police many times about him. What do you want to know?'

He considered his relationship with Lynette was not a matter for the police, although the Chief Inspector would be likely to hold a different view.

'It was a shock when I heard about Maddie. Have you caught anyone, Josh?' With wide-open eyes, 'I know you're at work, but can I still call you by your first name?' Smiling, she had run out of words.

'Yes, Josh is fine. Tell me about Maddie. Were you friends at school?'

'No, we met after my brother, Jason, started dating her.'

'When?'

'About a year ago. I share a flat with him and it wasn't long before she moved in, but it would drive Jason barmy because we were always talking.'

'Do you know where Jason is?'

'No.'

'If you did, would you tell me?' Josh's eyes fixed on her face, searching for a flicker of uncertainty.

'Yes, but not normally.'

'What's different about this time?'

Sipping her tea, 'I'm guessing you want to talk to him

about Maddie.' Josh nodded. 'He won't like it if you pick him up but I can say hand on heart he wouldn't have murdered her.' A canal boat chugged past, the man at the tiller waved and she flapped her hand in response.

Josh studied her. Was she hiding information? 'How can you be so sure he didn't kill her?'

'He adored the ground she walked on.' Lynette gave a slight shake of her head. 'I'd never seen him like that before. He's a rough man and is often crude, but never with Maddie. I know what you're thinking.' She paused, but Josh didn't speak. 'Perhaps if she wound him up when he was drunk, he'd lose his temper.' Josh nodded. 'Over the years I've seen him lose it many times. If you check your records, you'll find it's never against females. Maddie was no saint herself and she would go for him. No reaction from him, nothing. Although he might shout and swear a bit, he'd walk away.'

It hadn't been the reaction from Lynette he'd been expecting. Her smile dropped away and she lowered her head, 'He probably doesn't know yet.'

'Why haven't you told him?'

'He hasn't a mobile phone and as he is on the dole, he's gone to London to catch up with mates. He'll be dossing down wherever he can and he'll sleep on the streets if he can't find anywhere. But I'm worried about him.'

Josh finished his tea, 'If you're convinced that he didn't do it, why the worry?'

'As much as I hate to admit it, my brother is a violent man. You know that from his record.' Taking a deep breath, 'Many of his friends have records. Jason won't trust the police to catch the murderer and he will want revenge.'

'You'll try to deflect him from doing anything daft,

won't you?'

'Yes, Josh. But if he finds out who killed Maddie, then neither you nor I will stop him.'

'What will he think of you talking to me?'

She laughed, 'He doesn't like coppers, I would have thought that was obvious and he won't like me seeing you, but he'll get over it. I don't stand any nonsense from him and he knows it. I'll talk to who I like. He doesn't choose my boyfriends for me and I enjoy talking to you. Pity you're a copper, but at least you're honest.'

A smile came to Josh's lips. 'Who would want to harm Maddie?'

Lynette shook her head, 'She was popular with everyone.'

'What about former boyfriends?'

'Although she's had many, none of her former ones caused her any hassle.'

They dropped into silence, lost in their thoughts as a pair of moorhens scuttled on the far side of the canal. With a brisk movement, Josh rose to his feet. 'Thanks Lynette. I shall need to talk to you again.'

Her eyes focused on Josh, 'I hope so, and perhaps in a pub next time.'

'You'll have second thoughts about meeting now you know I'm a policeman, but I'll text you.'

Jumping up, 'I've clocked off early so will visit the stables. I'm assuming you are still on duty.'

'Yes.'

Leaning forward, she kissed him on the cheek. Turning, she strolled away along the canal path singing.

Josh remained on the wall to enter the details of the conversation into his notebook, but his gaze focused on a boat chugging past. His mind drifted. Two potential girl-friends in a busy week. Both had qualities that he liked; a good figure, a pretty face and a sense of humour. So far, he hadn't asked Gemma out because she was in the police, but she was lively and friendly. He'd like to get to know her better. The evening with Lynette had been brill. Why did she have to become involved in a case that he was investigating? If he continued to date her, he would be in front of the Chief. Should he take the risk? Shaking his head, she would ignore him. It was inevitable. Once she'd thought it through, she would refuse to associate with a policeman.

21

Walking through the huge terminal building with its wavy roof at Bangalore airport, after a straightforward flight from Manchester, I headed towards the temporary offices of the airline. The shell had a mismatched desks and other office furniture. The office logos hadn't been fitted to the walls. Scott jumped up from his desk the moment he saw me. He enveloped me in an enthusiastic hug and his lips brushed against mine as he spoke, 'Hello darling. Do you have the documents?'

Handing him a suitcase, I smiled, 'I hope you brought the clothes.'

'Yes, it's easier for you to bring paperwork for this new office.'

'Why have you asked me to bring so many documents from Manchester?'

'The new office will be large as it will run Asia, so it's a feather in my cap being asked to organise it.' Reaching across, his handsome features appeared anxious as he took the suitcase from me, tucked it inside a stout cupboard which he locked and slipped the key into his pocket.

As we made our way to the hotel, 'I'm worried about you Scott.'

‘Why? What’s the matter?’ He rubbed his hands together despite the hot temperature.

‘You are so jittery.’

He smiled, but it appeared false. ‘Too much work, that’s all.’

‘Is establishing the new office overpowering?’

‘No, it’s the constant changing of time zones that affects me. You have become accustomed to global travel and are relaxed despite a long flight.’ His face brightened, but his eyes were dull and shadowy.

‘Now I’m away from Blackford I’m relaxed and I’m expecting a great evening with my lover.’ I kissed him lightly on the lips but didn’t receive enthusiasm in return and the nervousness didn’t leave his face.

As I showered, Josh’s face kept coming back to me. I worried about him as he didn’t seem so enthusiastic about his job, which seemed strange as he’d received promotion. In our thirties, we had decisions to make.

Josh had to choose whether to spend the rest of his career in the police. I wanted a family and a settled life, not the international continent hopping that I’d done for the past twelve years. With Scott’s promotion, perhaps he will propose. That might be the cause of his nervousness. Shall I ask him? What’s stopping me? It’s not a man’s world anymore. Women are equal. Yes, I’ll ask him this evening. A fluttery sensation swept over me as I imagined the romantic scenario.

Strolling across the busy casino I adjusted the strap on my low cut evening dress. So far, the evening hadn’t lived up to my expectations as I’d had a terrible session on the card tables. Good luck seemed to be in short supply. The first game had been my usual. Blackjack. With no success, I hastened to a poker table and reined back my enthusiasm and took a more measured approach. It hadn't worked.

Nothing seemed to work in my favour with every decision going against me. I'd persevered with low stakes, but three hundred pounds had gone in the first hour. Scott would want to stay the whole evening. As usual, I'd left him to his choices and concentrated on mine. I bought another fifty pounds and went for roulette; I didn't know why because I'd never won at the game. My mouth had become dry despite plenty of water to drink. With growing dissatisfaction, I placed my last chips on Red. I stared at the wheel as the ball popped into black twenty-two. Three hundred and fifty in an hour. It's too much to lose, so I talked myself out of buying more chips to reverse the trend.

I relaxed my shoulders and smiled as Scott drifted towards me. The smart tuxedo suited him and accentuated his slim build. Before he reached me, he slipped a pile of chips into his pocket. I did not know his stakes, but he'd had a successful night.

'You look pleased.' Kissing him on the cheek, I caught his arm. The grin had not left his face. The underlying tension was still palpable, and he hadn't been his normal self for the past few months. The increasing pressure of work seemed to be taking its toll making him sensitive and often irritable.

'Let's go to the restaurant,' A triumphant smirk stretched across his face, 'it's a night for champagne.' Reaching forward he kissed me softly on the cheek.

'That sounds exciting. What are we celebrating?'

'Wait and see.'

My mind bubbled with excitement. Would he ask me? Happiness overflowed and a warm glow crept across my cheeks. Could tonight be the start of a new future?

Scott had been on edge during the meal and only talked about his liking for India, so we never broached personal matters. As we relaxed on the hotel verandah in the warm evening, I gave a sigh of pleasant anticipation as I gazed across the exquisite landscaped gardens of the hotel. Would he pop the question? If the opportunity seemed right, I would ask him. My stomach somersaulted with a mixture of apprehension and excitement.

After he had gone to the bar to fetch the after-dinner liqueurs, his jacket fell from his chair and the casino chips spilled onto the floor. He'd had a good win tonight. As I scooped them up, their worth astounded me. Black chips and a lot of them. How had he won over three thousand pounds? Too much doubt and unanswered questions entered my mind. My stomach knotted. Proposing to him tonight was out of the question.

22

After showing the receptionist his warrant card at the Promenade Hotel on Blackpool's seafront, Josh stood with Tom to one side. The long dark highly polished wooden desk dominated the reception area, which swarmed with Japanese tourists checking out before making their way to the coach parked outside. The worn red carpet was littered with suitcases and trollies awaiting collection by the coach driver.

A young woman without a smile approached them, nodded at Josh's warrant card and led them along a short corridor and down the service stairs. As they descended their footsteps echoed on the wooden treads in the cream-coloured stairwell with its peeling paint. The smell of washing and laundry rose to greet them.

In the basement they entered a small low ceilinged room where the hum of machines was evident. Two young men worked in the warm humid atmosphere. The smell of detergent and wet laundry prevailed, causing Josh to wrinkle his nose. A lithe man eased himself into an upright position and paused from the task of removing laundry from a large drier and flashed a quick grin of welcome, 'Hi, I'm Danny Mercer.' His face was flushed and beads of sweat clung to his forehead. His clothing was not appropriate to his job as he wore suit trousers and a white shirt; his jacket and tie were hung on a chair near the door.

He pointed towards the other occupant of the room, 'That's Sean Prendergast.' Sean, average height with short blonde hair, had a lean, tanned face and wore a suit as he folded the laundry with a bored expression. Josh acknowledged the introductions before showing them his warrant card. His mind whirled. Would it be a productive meeting? Background information about a victim was vital. He needed one small clue to push the investigation forward.

Sean smiled, 'We can stay here or I'll find us a room upstairs if you prefer.' The hot room had a large table piled high with neatly folded towels and tablecloths. A multitude of pipes ran across the low ceiling made strange gurgling sounds as though conversing with each other in their own language.

Although there wasn't much space, Josh didn't want the upheaval of finding and moving to another room, 'Here will be fine.'

Sean dragged four chairs across from the next room and they sat in a makeshift circle and eyed each other warily. Tom took out his notebook and scribbled his first entry.

To break the ice Josh started with a mundane question, 'Is this your normal job?'

Danny laughed as he pulled his suit jacket from the chair and pointed to his hotel badge. 'Trainee management, which means we have to fill in the jobs that need doing. What it should say is, general dogsbody, as we get assigned to the boring menial jobs that no one else wants to do. The staff from this laundry room rang in sick this morning.'

Danny had been holding various papers which he placed on a nearby side table and then returned to the makeshift circle of chairs.

Sean waited until he was settled, 'It's terrible news about Maddie.'

Tom acknowledged his comment with a brief nod, 'How did you find out?'

'We used to live a few doors from Maddie's family so her mum told my family who passed the news on to me.'

Their mannerisms suggested that they hadn't relaxed as they kept glancing at each other, although Josh and Tom had received a friendly welcome.

'When did you last see Maddie?'

'Last week, she visited us here.'

'Did she indicate any plans?'

'She only mentioned a shopping trip with Lynette.'

'Do you know Lynette and Jason?' Tom's brow furrowed with concentration as he wrote copious notes.

'Yes, we've been out with them several times. When we visit Blackford, the five of us often have an evening out.'

Josh allowed the silence to stretch. The two men were ill at ease. They avoided eye contact and their gaze bounced around the room as though they didn't know where to look. Why were they so agitated? 'How long were you friends with Maddie?'

Danny frowned and rubbed the back of his neck, 'We hung around together at school and it continued from there.' His response didn't give Josh a great deal of information. Why was he so reticent to talk about Maddie? Was it shock at her murder? Such a tragic event affected people in different ways.

Desperate for information he ploughed on with the questioning, 'You work in this hotel but Maddie stayed in Blackford?'

'She had a plan,' Danny's face brightened.

Josh stared across at him with renewed interest, 'Tell us.'

'We hoped to find employment in the airline, but it didn't work out, so we joined this hotel chain. Recently, Maddie had also applied to work here.'

'That's a long gap in time since she left the airline?' Tom quirked his eyebrow questioningly.

'She enjoyed working in the Bondi Club and earning money but wanted to travel.'

They would make no progress here, but a breakthrough was required as the investigation appeared to be making little progress. The Chief wouldn't be happy.

Josh and Tom waited until they were clear of the building and strolling along the promenade towards the car park before discussing their thoughts about the interview. Tom paused and leaned on the railings, staring out across the flat expanse of beach towards the grey uninviting water. He'd had a quick word with the manager as they left. 'Their story checks out. The manager planned to interview Maddie soon. He hinted the two lads weren't hard working but improved when international opportunities were mentioned. He confirmed they worked on the day of the raid.' Tom climbed into the driving seat of the Range Rover and settled himself, 'Did you see anything to arouse your suspicions?'

'No, not at all, they are keen on international travel and seem confident it will soon be forthcoming. There were horse racing newspapers and betting slips on the side table for reasonable amounts, but nothing excessive if that's their hobby.'

23

During the return flight from Bangalore, as my co-pilot took over flying duties, my mind had drifted to the reason for not proposing to Scott after dinner at the casino. He enjoyed gambling, but three thousand pounds left casually in his pocket had become a worry. As I strode across the terminal building to meet him after he had cleared customs, I expected a welcoming smile. Instead, I was greeted with a curt nod. Picking up his suitcase, he marched towards the exit expecting me to follow.

Tension radiated from him.

In silence he manoeuvered the car from an awkward parking spot yanking on the steering wheel and muttering to himself. So far, he hadn't spoken to me since we'd arrived back in Manchester. What was the matter? A phone call as we'd left the airport darkened his mood even further. He flicked on loud jazz music making conversation impossible so we continued the rest of the journey without speaking.

As we entered the flat, I tried to lighten the mood, 'Shall we dine out this evening?'

'No! I must find a folder which contains crucial information. There is a crisis at work. I must visit the office.'

My eyes widened, 'It's six o'clock in the evening.' I assumed as he didn't travel often, he had become confused with the time zones.

'I know,' his eyes blazed, 'Have you moved my folder?'

'What does it look like?'

He glared in exasperation, 'Green with black swirls.'

'I've one like that.'

His face paled, but I couldn't work out why?

'Show me yours,' he snapped.

'For goodness' sake, Scott, calm down, it's only a folder.' What was the matter with him? Why was he so agitated over a trivial item?

'It contains the bank details that I need. Have you taken it by mistake?'

I'd had enough of the interrogation. Storming to the back room, I snatched my folder from the top drawer. I stared with a frown for a few seconds.

Scott snatched it from me as I entered the lounge and wrenched it open.

'What's wrong with you tonight,' I squirmed with frustration, 'this is my damned folder, not yours, so get your hands off.' Anger overwhelmed me and I grabbed it back again. Why be so childish?

'I must find it!' he hissed and pulled out the contents of a drawer.

'Where did you leave it?'

'In the wardrobe but I've checked there.'

'Why had you stored it there?'

Ignoring my question, he carried on his search.

'Scott, I remember,' I took a deep shuddering breath unsure of how he would react, 'I picked it up, assuming it was mine as I pop items that I want to take with me on a trip in the wardrobe as it makes packing easier.'

'What the hell did you do with it?' Fury burned in his eyes, he stepped towards me with his fists clenched by his side.

'Don't bloody shout at me.' I stamped my foot and glared. 'I stuffed it in my case, which I've left at my parents.'

'Well, bloody fetch it,' he yelled, jabbing a finger towards my face.

'Piss off, go to work, you're unbearable this evening.' Grabbing his phone and jacket, he stormed out of the flat. Stumbling, I slumped into a chair; I'd never questioned Scott's motives before. Why had that folder become so precious? I needed him to calm down so we could return to our old ways. The large quantity of black chips and now the folder nagged at me. Despite him being unreasonable, I'd taken it by mistake, so I could use this evening to fetch it. On a visit to Blackford, I could assure mum and dad that I had recovered and pick up his damned folder. Anything to keep the peace.

24

My visit pleased Mum and Dad, but I hadn't found the folder. Scott will be unreasonable, but I can't remember where I left it. A bland text informed me he would be late, so I'd take the opportunity to wash and clean the car. It seemed a more profitable approach than sitting in my empty flat waiting for Scott to return home.

'Hello, luv.' A young man in the garage greeted me with a smile.

'Can I have a car wash and vacuum?' Flicking my credit card at the machine, he gave me two tokens. I stared down at them. What were they for? Scott would usually clean the car. I raised my eyebrows enquiringly at him and gave him my best smile, 'I'm not sure how to operate it.'

'That's no problem, luv, I'm not busy.' Calling to a woman in the office, we passed through the shop. 'Bring your car around, I'll start the wash for you.' As I drove the car towards the wash, he signalled to straighten up. 'Close the windows, put the handbrake on and sit there.'

I worried as foam and water sloshed across the car, blurring the windscreen. What would Scott's reaction be when I returned home without the folder? I'd never seen him so angry. What was the matter with him? At one time our relationship had been perfect and I wanted him to return to the affectionate boyfriend he'd once been. I loved him, we belonged together.

Emerging from the wash a few minutes later, the young guy directed me to the vacuum cleaner. 'Thanks a lot.' He returned to the building as I prepared to vacuum the boot. As I cleared an old jacket and a pair of wellingtons, the green and black folder lay in the boot. That's why I couldn't find it in my case. It must have fallen out. At least Scott would be pleased.

A standard folder. So why be uptight? It had been my fault, I'd better apologise tonight and make it up to him. Although he had been over the top about it, so I expect an apology from him. Curiosity overcame me and I picked up the folder. What's in it that's so important?

I gasped as the black leather glove closed over my mouth. Before I could react, I shot forward into the open hatchback. A blow came to my head and a hand yanked at my hair. The black leather fingers filled my mouth. I retched as my legs gave way. Struggling for all my worth I tried to turn but a strong hand jammed my face into the corner of the boot. I couldn't breathe. Panic gripped me. The blood drained from my head and a strange roaring noise filled my ears. The world swirled. Blackness overwhelmed me.

25

'Control to Sergeant Anderson. Urgent message.' Josh and Tom had left the witness who had found Maddie's body but with no fresh information. Josh leaned forward and pressed the response button, 'Sergeant Anderson here.'

'We have an urgent personal message.' His stomach twisted. 'Eleanor has been attacked and has been taken by ambulance to hospital.' Josh glanced at Tom but he was already sitting up straight in the driver's seat and with one fluid movement the car lurched away with a squeal of tyres. The blue flashing lights reflected from the other cars in the street.

'Why would anyone want to hurt Eleanor?'

Tom shook his head and barked into the radio, 'Status update, if you haven't received one, patch me through to the hospital.'

The radio caller came back within a minute, 'Not badly hurt, but suffering from shock.'

'Give me the exact location in the hospital and inform them we will arrive.'

Josh hadn't been able to look, as Tom drove at high speed the entire route to the hospital. As the Range Rover screeched to a halt, Josh jumped from the car and headed through the endless corridors. Concern for Eleanor filled his thoughts as he rushed along and worse case scenarios swarmed through his mind. Why had she been attacked? He disliked coincidences. What had he missed? Had some vital snippet of information been pushed aside? They'd informed Chief Inspector Haskins on the way and he wanted a report when Josh had spoken to Eleanor.

His mind raced. The attack, it must be connected to the death of Maddie or the shopping centre raid. As he rounded the corner of the corridor, the hunched figure of his father, slumped on a hard plastic chair in the brightly lit corridor, filled him with anguish. His dad raised his head as he heard the rapid footsteps on the tiled floor and with a pale face his sorrowful eyes followed his approach.

Josh slumped onto the chair next to him and held his breath as he waited for his father to divulge the news. 'They are still waiting for the specialist and are monitoring the machines. The X-ray has given the all-clear, at least her skull hasn't been fractured.' Visibly shuddering, his eyes watered as he stared questioningly at Josh, 'An attack on a defenceless woman. What's happening?'

It appeared his father had reached the same conclusion. Was there a connection with Maddie's death? The young constable, Gemma, who'd given Josh a tour of the police station, strode towards them along the corridor. 'I'm sorry about your sister, sir. Wrong place at the wrong time.'

Josh nodded, 'Have you been sent?' But he didn't finish the sentence as he worried about the effect on his father.

'Yes, by the Duty Inspector. I've been told to stop all admittance apart from family and hospital staff.'

Dad jerked his head up from staring at the floor, 'Are

you taking the attack seriously?'

'Yes, dad. The police dislike coincidences.'

'I am worried about the significance, which is why I've sat outside as I wanted to monitor any unusual activity. Your mother is with Eleanor.'

'Don't worry, you may be assured that Gemma will stand guard.'

Acknowledging with a brief nod, 'I'll take your mother for a break if you'll stay with Eleanor.' His father's worried face sent a wave of resentment sweeping through him. Had his job with the police brought this attack on Eleanor? If his family were in danger because of him, he'd quit the job immediately.

'Go in, dad, I want a word with Gemma.' With a grim expression, he closed the door behind him as he entered Eleanor's room.

She screwed up her face. It would not be good news. 'The Chief told me to leave the Incident Room and sent me here. He stated that you were to check out your sister, but as the reports have indicated she's not badly hurt, he wants you back on Maddie's case.' Josh's brow creased and he scowled and his whole demeanour grew in severity. Gemma gave him a cheeky smile and raised her hands, palms forward, 'Hey, don't shoot the messenger.'

Josh tried to remain calm despite the twisting in his stomach, but it was difficult. It would be imperative that he discovered who was behind the attack on Eleanor. A mixture of worry and uncertainty coursed through him. The Chief had followed standard police procedure as he couldn't be involved as a member of his family was the victim. Sighing with exasperation, 'What else did he say?'

'His initial reaction is a mugging and an unfortunate

coincidence.'

Josh shook his head. What a naïve conclusion. 'There must be a link.' Gemma's eyes never left Josh's face. She went to speak but stopped. 'What is it?'

Stretching out her hand, she caught Josh's arm, 'Stop thinking about your poor sister and start sifting through the evidence. You're a copper. Use your skills. Even if it's not your case, you can determine if it's a mugging.'

Josh managed a weak smile. 'Thanks, Gemma. Do you know who's leading. Is it Claire?' Josh didn't want her assigned to the case but wasn't sure why.

'She's been directed by the boss to take a quick overview. If it's a mugging, then to hand it over to me.' Josh tried to stop raising his eyebrows, but the surprise registered on his face. 'He wants senior constables like Tom to work on the two crucial cases. I'm inexperienced, but I'll do my best for you.'

Josh's shoulders relaxed. 'Thanks, Gemma, you'll do a good job.'

'I cannot give you the progress on the case, but if we met for a drink then I could relay the chatter in the station.'

'What a star, Gemma.' Chuckling at her deviousness, 'Text me.'

'Will do. Now check on your sister.'

Josh rested his hand on the door handle to Eleanor's room. The sound of a woman's heels echoing in the corridor made him hesitate. Claire approached without a smile. Although he tried hard to like her as he had to work with her, he could find no endearing features. Career orientated, nothing else mattered to her. With her blinkered and self-centered approach, other people's feelings were irrelevant. Did she ever let her hair down and have fun?

Claire scrutinised him and with an expression full of disapproval, 'How's your sister, Josh?' He bristled as even her voice seemed to have a disinterested and formal edge to it.

'I've not visited yet, but dad informed me they are monitoring her.'

Squaring her shoulders, her piercing brown eyes glared. 'You know it's my case.' Josh nodded, as he attempted to keep his expression bland and composed. He didn't want her to sense his disapproval. 'I must interview Eleanor as soon as possible.'

Josh tensed his shoulders. He doubted that her interview technique would be compassionate. He wouldn't allow it to take place if Eleanor weren't strong enough. Keeping his voice steady with a great deal of effort, 'I'll have ten minutes first and then check with the doctor. It will be his decision whether you will be able to have an interview.'

Claire scowled at Gemma, 'It's a waste of time you staying here. A community support officer can do this job so contact the Control Centre and request one be sent to the hospital. As soon as they arrive, you need to return to the garage where she was attacked and finish the interviews.' Josh took a deep breath, controlled his frustration with Claire, and opened the door to Eleanor's room.

26

Mum's pale face with tears and tension glanced towards Josh as he crept into my room and then she re-focused her attention back on me. The hospital room door gently closed behind him. The small beeps from a monitoring machine broke the drone of the outside traffic. Several cables led from me to the machines, which were set in layers on trolleys either side of the bed. I had one pillow and my arms rested on the sheets. Moving my head allowed me to smile at Josh. It would be an unspoken communication, but he would understand.

Dad frowned and his shoulders tensed as he placed his arm around mum, whispered to her and led her away with tears in her eyes. Mum wrapped her shaking arms around herself as though cold. I concentrated on Josh even though my eyelids were heavy. Approaching the bed, he stooped over and kissed me gently on the cheek. Worry was etched across the lines of his face. What could I do to support him?

'This is terrible! Josh,' I stuttered with a weak voice.

'Are you in pain?'

'No, I'm bruised but nothing more.'

Pressing my lips together, I tried to quell the panic

inside of me. 'I'm fuzzy, but the doctor expects that will clear.'

'Tell me what happened? When you're feeling up to it, my colleague will want to talk with you.'

I wanted to concentrate because it could help Josh. 'He hit me on the head and shoved me into the boot so hard my head became trapped in the corner.' Gulping, I closed my eyes and searched my memory. Josh caught my hand and gave it an encouraging squeeze. 'The worse part came when he stuck his fingers in my mouth.' I shuddered with fear, 'I couldn't breathe and passed out.'

'You're doing well, Ellie. When you arrived at the petrol station did you see anybody suspicious?'

'No one else apart from the young man who showed me how to operate the car wash.'

'Someone will take his statement.'

'Is it something to do with Maddie?' I whispered and clutched his hand.

'I don't know but you will be protected. Leave the worrying about catching people to us. There's an officer outside the door.'

'Why?' Panic gripped me.

'To ensure you can rest and recover.'

'I've thought of something.'

'What?' he whispered.

'I haven't taken you shopping and you still have that terrible beanie. When I'm better, we will shop together in Manchester. That beanie is being discarded into the waste bin. It's not fit to donate to a charity shop.'

He kissed me gently on the nose, 'No chance.' A doctor entered the room. Josh showed his warrant card, 'This is my sister.'

'I'm Thomas Marchant, the Registrar treating Eleanor. What do you want to know?'

They whispered, but I could hear. I struggled with my heavy eyelids as I didn't want to fall asleep. I might miss something important.

'How is she?'

'Nasty bruises around her neck and two twisted fingers, my guess would be when she tried to protect herself. Our primary concern is the time she lost consciousness, so we're monitoring her.' The doctor must have seen a reaction in Josh's face. 'Relax, she's not badly hurt and there are no unusual readings, but we'll keep her under precautionary observation.'

27

Tom's large imposing figure, wearing a yellow, fluorescent jacket and traditional police helmet, lumbered along the hospital corridor after parking the patrol car and checking in with Central Control about further developments. Patients and staff studied him as he made his way through the building. He'd been a frequent visitor to the hospital with witnesses, suspects and his back pain.

'Ay up, Gemma.' He strode towards his patrol partner sitting outside the door of a private room, 'Have they sent you as the guard.'

'Hi Tom, yes. Not the most exciting job, but necessary. Claire told me to find a community support officer to cover, so I'm waiting for Control to find someone.'

Tom frowned and dropped on to the chair next to his colleague with a noticeable groan. 'Us coppers have many boring jobs. While the risk is low, it's your job to make sure nothing happens. I don't like community officers covering for a police officer's job.'

'Are you expecting trouble?'

'There are too many connections between the cases and that makes me concerned.'

'I'll stick with it,' she swivelled to face him, 'and keep

my eyes open until I'm replaced.'

Tom rubbed his chin, 'There are two aspects of policing and one of them the force is in danger of losing. Preventing another attack is one, but the other is reassurance. It comforts Eleanor's parents, it's like in the days of the copper on the beat.'

'I've only ever done foot patrols at major events.'

'On a regular route through a neighbourhood the public notice you and that reassures them.' Tom gave a loud sigh and shook his head regretfully. 'However, times change.'

A man strode towards them, checking room numbers. 'You need to do your job.'

Tom ambled away along the corridor and chatted in a low voice into his radio.

Gemma stood in front of the door. 'Is this Eleanor Anderson's room, officer?'

'Why do you want to know, sir?'

'I'm her fiancé.'

He attempted to step past, but she blocked his way. 'I'm afraid it's family only, sir.'

'Don't be so ridiculous, I'm practically family, I've heard the news from her father and I've hurried over from work in Manchester.'

Tom squared his shoulders; his call had finished and he listened. The man exaggerated his travel time from Manchester, but he would let his junior colleague handle the situation. 'The family is not here, but on their return, you may speak with them.'

'Listen to me,' his lip curled, and he peered down his nose in an arrogant manner, 'I'm not sitting here waiting because you're being awkward.'

'Just doing my job, sir.'

'Well, it's not damned good enough,' he snarled. 'Even though her brother is a copper, you lot couldn't protect her. His face reddened and his voice rose. 'Now out of my way.'

'No sir, you may not enter the room. The restriction will remain until you are escorted by a member of the family. If you know them well, perhaps you might like to ring them.' Gemma's voice remained calm despite his belligerence.

'You're a damned impertinent young woman and who the hell do you think you're staring at?'

Tom's face remained impassive, 'If you persist in being aggressive and rude, then I shall require your name and address.'

'I can refuse.'

'You have admitted that you know the victim of an assault, therefore it is within our rights as police officers to ask you questions. If you refuse to answer, then I shall arrest you.'

He gave a loud huff and stormed away along the corridor. Both officers waited until he was out of sight. Tom hadn't been impressed by his overconfident attitude.

'Would you have arrested him, Tom?'

'Yes, I might have more information than you, but he mentioned fiancé, however when I've spoken to Eleanor, she only referred to him as a boyfriend. Perhaps he likes to exaggerate, but I would have arrested him. Confined in a police station affects people's attitude.' He chuckled, which made Gemma smile.

28

Josh hadn't expected a call so late, but as Gemma's voice came on the line he smiled. A chance to meet and discover the details of the investigation concerning Eleanor. When he'd rung Claire earlier, she hadn't been forthcoming and gave him a standard answer about matters progressing.

Josh pushed open the heavy door of the Grapes pub in Market Square. The music and heavy atmosphere of the crowded pub hit him. Stopping near the door, he couldn't see her, so he eased his way past a noisy group of men chatting loudly about cars. At the end of the bar, Josh spotted her tucked into a corner table. The bar was too noisy to call out, so he made a drink gesture and she mouthed white wine.

Carrying the drinks with difficulty across the crowded space, he reached the corner without spilling them. 'Hi, Gemma, thanks for the call, I didn't expect one so late.' He placed the drinks on the table, stuffed his beanie in a pocket and unzipped his leather jacket.

'My shift didn't finish until ten and a quiet meeting here in my uniform would be difficult.' She had changed into jeans and a loose jumper. Her eyes, accentuated by make-up, lit up her face as she smiled. 'You will be worried about the attack and Miss Superstar would ignore you.'

Josh laughed at her description and took a swig of beer, 'I presume you mean Claire.'

Gemma sipped her wine, 'That woman is a pain in the arse. Nothing I ever do is right.'

He nodded in agreement, 'She is hard work. Every discussion is an uphill battle.'

The smile slipped from Gemma's face, 'Why I'm assigned to her I do not understand, but I'll keep you informed.'

As she picked up her bag, it gave him a chance to study her. When in uniform she arranged her hair in a bun, but now it hung loosely on her shoulders. The delicate makeup transformed her face. She wore many rings on her fingers that were not permitted on duty, and a large silver necklace hung down the front of her jumper. Stunning was the only word that crossed Josh's mind. Having found what she wanted, she pushed her bag to one side and placed her notebook on the table between them.

'It appears to be a mugging in a quiet area behind the garage. The bushes would give an easy place to hide.'

The choice of words caught Josh's attention, 'You said appears to be a mugging, what makes you doubt it?'

'Credit cards were stolen, but the cash was left behind.'

'Perhaps he took the credit cards and was disturbed, so he did a runner.'

She replaced her notebook in her bag, 'It must have been opportunistic and my guess would be the attacker chickened out, but it would have been a nasty experience for your sister. That's twice within a week.'

Josh tried to link the two incidents together but

couldn't think of a plausible connection. 'It's been a busy few days.' His shoulders slumped and he pushed his hand through his hair, 'I'm exhausted.' Her glass was empty. 'Would you like another drink?'

'Yes, please. That would be lovely. Shall we meet later in the week, so I can update you with more news. I finish at eight on Friday.'

'Let's catch a meal, shall I book the new Italian across the square.'

A broad smile lit her face, 'Good choice.'

As Josh returned to the bar for another round, his resolve not to date in the police force had evaporated. With Lynette never likely to wish to meet again, should he ask Gemma out? Friday could easily be interpreted by her as an informal meeting with a colleague. He would leave the thoughts until Friday and discover how the evening progressed.

29

As I entered the room, the man rose to his feet and greeted me with a broad smile, 'I'm Chief Inspector Jeremy Haskins and I'm please to meet you Eleanor, but I would have preferred it to be in less stressful circumstances.'

The smart blue suit, matching tie and white shirt contrasted with Josh's scruffy appearance as we congregated in a tatty television room the hospital had arranged for the meeting. He waved a hand towards a young woman who had remained seated, 'You have already met Sergeant Claire Harris.' I did my best to smile, but she remained nonplussed. 'Claire is dealing with your case. Josh will talk to you while Claire and I listen. One of our principal lines of investigation is potential links between the various incidents and you are a key witness for us, otherwise we would leave you to recover.'

My hands shook, so I forced them still in my lap as I tried to relax my shoulders, 'Chief Inspector, I appreciate you need to go over the old ground and I'm prepared to help if I can.' I trembled but hoped they didn't notice. The Inspector returned to his seat, settled himself and fixed his eyes on my face.

Josh moved next to me, 'Eleanor. We don't meet frequently as we lead separate lives. You fly all over the world and I've been in Manchester.'

A strange way to ask questions, but I was content to settle to the direction that Josh wished to follow. The approach had no doubt been agreed with his boss. Claire stared with cold eyes; she hadn't smiled once since I'd entered the room.

'Before you answer my questions, please think carefully about the past weeks and months.' I'd expected direct questions about the attacks. 'Have you had serious arguments either in your job or private life?'

My mind circled back over the recent months, 'I can't think of any arguments I've had.' I didn't want to mention Scott, although our argument about his behaviour at the hospital still hung in the air between us, as did his ridiculous posturing about the missing folder. Did Josh mean to include him or not? I didn't want Josh to know about the rows with Scott. They were just a small blip in our relationship which would be back to normal before long. Pushing all thoughts about his unacceptable behaviour aside, I took a deep calming breath and forced my voice to sound calm, 'No, I've had no arguments.'

'What about threats? Have you upset someone at work or at the airport? Any road rage or angry passengers because a flight has been delayed?'

'No, I can't remember any disagreements. At work, I rarely meet the passengers, the cabin crew take the brunt of the delays.' My stomach somersaulted as an image of Maddie in her air hostess uniform swept into my mind. She'd mentioned that passengers could be aggressive. How had she handled awkward situations? Smiling and using her undoubted charm.

Josh focused on me with an intensity I'd rarely seen in his face, 'Scott made a scene at the hospital yesterday. Tom thinks he could become nasty.'

Oh, I hadn't expected questions about Scott, but I must remain calm and in control. There is no need for them to know that the relationship hasn't been plain sailing recently. I'd been looking down at my hands, but I resumed my gaze into Josh's face. 'Scott is stressed out. There are changes and redundancies in the admin office where he works, and he's struggling to cope, but they don't affect me apart from being given daft flying schedules.'

Josh, the Chief Inspector, and Claire considered my every movement and facial expression. I let out a deep breath, 'Scott is overprotective of me. I've known him a long time before we went out together, he's an intense character. Yesterday, I'm sure he would want to protect me from matters he can't control. Normally he's sweet, but he made a fool of himself and I told him so in no uncertain terms.'

Josh shuffled on his chair, 'The attack at the petrol station.' I shivered. 'Any thoughts about smell, voice, body odour?'

I shook my head, 'It happened so quickly. The attacker didn't speak. A grunt came as he shoved me into the corner of the boot. Then his gloved hands covered my face and my mouth.' I closed my eyes as images of the frightening experience swirled through me.

'From your description you have assumed the attacker was a man. Were there any similarities between the attacks?' Josh's voice had a calmness I didn't possess.

'Such as?' My voice wavered despite my attempt to keep it on an even keel. 'How you were grabbed.'

I could see how they hoped for a clue. The tension of the questions overwhelmed me and I gulped but shook my head.

'Tell us about Maddie?'

Whether he was aware of the intensity or wanted a fresh approach, I couldn't be sure, but he leaned back in his seat. Once again, the image of Maddie wearing her air hostess uniform sprang into my mind. In my images of her, she always smiled. 'I don't talk a great deal to the cabin crew as we arrive at hotels at unpredictable times and after long flights I go straight to my room.'

'Can you think of one unusual aspect of Maddie?'

What a question! 'Maddie had crushes on much older men.'

'A teacher?'

'Yes.' I nodded and thought back to my school days. 'The rumours were about a young teacher.' The Chief Inspector wasn't concentrating, I could tell, 'Will this help?'

He frowned, 'We're making no progress with Maddie's connections apart from her current boyfriend, but she's been with him a long time so we're searching for a trigger. If something in their lives changed, for example, her becoming involved with someone else, it could provoke a violent reaction.'

Claire tapped an impatient finger on her notebook and frowned, 'Can you tell me where your boyfriend Scott is? I want to interview him.'

Why does she want to do that? It's bad enough between us without her interfering. Neither Josh nor the Chief Inspector will stop her. Why interview him as he wasn't in Blackford when the attacks took place? He won't enjoy being questioned by the police so will blame me and it could cause another argument. I will marry him if he ever asks me. It's imperative to be patient, but it will happen soon, I'm sure. Opening my bag, I passed her Scott's business card. 'Today, he's at work in the Manchester Airport office.'

30

'We haven't chatted about working together since I started my new job.' Josh held the door open for Claire after finishing the meeting with Eleanor. The Chief had taken a phone call and stayed behind. Claire's top lip curled, but she didn't break her rapid stride down the corridor.

'Do you want to do it now?' Her voice was low pitched and edged with impatience.

Josh shrugged, 'Yes, unless we meet for a drink after work.'

She didn't immediately reply as they strode through the crowded reception foyer of the hospital. As they cleared the main doors she stopped, 'Let's do it now, I'm busy after work.'

Josh hadn't suggested a specific day, so she had given him a brush off. The rain wasn't heavy, but he pulled his beanie from his jacket and tugged it on to his head. Claire pulled up the hood of her blue summer anorak and pointed to an empty smoker's shelter about twenty metres from the entrance. It was a poor location for an important conversation. Discarded cigarette butts were strewn across the floor and the litterbin in the corner overflowed with cardboard sandwich wrappings and plastic bottles. Although open on two sides to the elements, the stale smell of cigarette smoke lingered.

Claire perched on the hard plastic seat with shoulders hunched, narrowed eyes and a pinched expression. 'What did you want to talk about?' Her tone was abrupt, making it clear that she did not want this conversation.

With that attitude, they would not hit it off. Josh wouldn't be deterred. His stubbornness rose to the surface. Pushing the negative thoughts aside, he opted for a professional approach rather than the friendly manner he usually preferred. 'The cases are linked.' Perhaps the statement would make a good starting point for a discussion. He'd taken off his beanie as they were away from the rain, but she left her hood up.

'But they might not be. I would want firm evidence of any link before suggesting to the boss a joint approach. My intensity of effort is on the shopping centre raid. It's coincidence Maddie shopped at the time of the robbery.'

Josh raised his eyebrows questioningly, 'Shall we arrange some short regular meetings in the diary to exchange views on the cases? Don't forget I'm new.'

'I'm too busy for speculative meetings, I'm sorry about your sister but I see that as a mugging, so Gemma can manage the incident.' She huffed a sigh of exasperation, 'I'll interview Scott, but I'm sure it will be a formality.'

The tension in his stomach tightened as he couldn't believe a fellow Sergeant would be so unhelpful. But she'd made her point. 'Okay, it was only a suggestion.'

A fleeting smile crossed her face, but the sternness returned. 'I appreciate it's hard to start a new job when all hell has broken loose. We'll sort these crimes, then see how we can work together.' She glanced at her watch. 'I'd better go as I've arranged a meeting at the police station and I need to interview Scott, so I'll see you back at base.'

Josh's eyes followed her retreating form as she moved between the parked cars. He pressed his lips into a straight line and battled with the annoyance that surged through him. She had dismissed him; her attitude would make his life difficult. Full of her own importance, she wanted the accolades for solving the cases. He'd been landed with an awkward situation. A meticulous Chief and a dismissive fellow Sergeant. She will keep information to herself, so she can take the glory.

His enthusiasm for the role of a police officer had faded. When he'd first started in the force, he'd viewed his job through rose-tinted glasses. Solving crimes with ease. Keeping law and order. But the reality was much harder. Masses of paperwork, which he hated. Unravelling criminal activities often eluded him and the irregular hours played havoc with his social life.

Shaking aside his melancholy and negative thoughts, Josh stared across to the hospital entrance, where to his surprise, Tom emerged wearing civilian clothes. How strange, he's not in uniform.

Josh waved, Tom spotted him and lurched his way to the shelter where with a loud groan he eased himself onto a narrow seat. 'Is it your rest day, Tom?'

'No, I'm on late shift, but it's police business that brings me here.' Josh raised his eyebrows, curious to know the reason. 'The Superintendent has insisted I have a full medical check.'

'Not good news?'

Tom wriggled around on the hard bench with a groan and rubbed at his lower back. 'It's my opinion the management have decided that they want me out,' he gave a worried shake of his head, 'and will use my back as an excuse to pension me off on grounds of ill health.'

'What did the doctor say?'

Tom rubbed a hand across his lower back, 'She's done a detailed report for the police. For the last hour I've had to perform a load of exercises, lots of bending, stretching and twisting my body around in impossible angles. Sheer torture and that's made my back ache.'

'Did she give you any conclusion?'

'As usual with medical staff she was non-committal but will send the full report to the police well-being team.'

'Let's hope it's okay.'

'Yes, otherwise I've had a taste of the future today.'

'Why what are you doing?'

His shoulders slumped and he let out a long groan. 'Sandra has decided we haven't decorated the downstairs rooms in the house for ages.'

'Are you employing someone to do it?'

'I wish. Sandra is particular. So despite my bad back, I must stop at the builder's merchants to buy decorating materials. I don't expect an enjoyable day off tomorrow. DIY all day and no fishing.' He shook his head in dismay. 'I'd prefer to be at work.'

31

The breathing of his colleagues in the lorry focused Josh's attention, although he couldn't see their faces. The first light of dawn crept across the sky. Heavy clouds emerged from the blackness and burst forth with a deluge of rain which drummed on the roof of the lorry. He'd been on dawn raids before and they always gave him a nervous concern about what would happen. The driver whispered, 'Tango Two and Tango Three ready to go.' Josh sat behind the driver.

Next to him sat a uniformed Sergeant responsible for the smooth operation of the raid. Josh placed his hand on the Sergeant's shoulder, 'Let's go.'

The Sergeant used a low voice into the microphone. 'Tango One. Go. Go. Go!'

A low reply, 'Tango One Operational.'

Josh waited as the Sergeant stared at his watch. He counted down the seconds. 'Tango Two. Go. Go. Go!'

Josh braced himself back in the seat. Another ten seconds count and they would move. The Sergeant touched the driver's arm. The lorry tyres skidded as they slipped on the gravel of the derelict site where they'd been waiting. Finally, they gripped and the lorry shot forward. It skidded to a halt at the back gates of Mercer Demolition.

Spotlights from the lorry lit the gates as the police officers swarmed towards them. Distant cries of police resonated through the air, but the early morning raid didn't expect anyone to be present on the site. Josh ran with several of the officers, dressed in black and heavily protected with riot helmets and stab proof vests, to the house owned by Arthur Mercer, which backed onto the industrial complex.

Three officers nipped through a gate into the back garden. Josh banged hard on the front door. An accompanying officer shouted, 'Police! Open up!' No sound or movement emanated from inside the house. Again, the shout, accompanied by hammering on the door, 'Police! Open up!'

Josh shouted, 'Ten seconds and we're coming in!' The door received another pounding. Nobody could remain asleep through the noise. Too dark to see his watch, he counted down, knowing that the rest of the team at the back of the house would hear him via their radios.

He'd reached nine when a loud voice from inside yelled, 'Piss off!'

'Open the door or we'll break it down!'

The door opened to reveal a bleary-eyed Arthur Mercer in baggy tee shirt and boxer shorts, 'What the hell do you think you're doing!'

'Further to information we have received we have a warrant to search this house and the adjoining works.'

He snarled, 'Have you broken down the bloody gates?'

'Cut through the padlocks.'

'I'll sue you again,' he hissed, 'you've no right.'

'Get on with it, lads.' Josh's team pushed past Arthur Mercer.

His wife came down the stairs wrapped in a thick shocking pink dressing gown, 'Bloody filth!' Then she had to step smartly to one side to avoid a large pair of boots as they thumped up the stairs.

An officer muttered, 'Come on, luv. Off the stairs or you'll get trampled.'

'Don't you bloody 'luv' me. I'm not a friend of the filth.' But she stomped down the stairs to join her husband near the front door.

'Anyone else in the house?' Arthur Mercer shook his head and picked up the phone from the hall table. 'You can't use that.'

'I've a right to a solicitor!' Snarling, he dropped the phone back on the table.

Josh snapped, 'Give us his number, we'll check it out and then ring him.'

'I want to speak with him.'

'You can do it on my phone but I'm listening. You can have a private conversation when he arrives or at the police station.'

Arthur reduced the level of his voice, 'What information have you received?'

'I'm not telling.' Josh gave a tight smile and switched his attention back to the raid as an officer descended the stairs and shook his head. Other officers leaving the house also shook their heads. 'Get dressed, we're off to the works.'

Josh waited outside, leaving the front door open to listen in case he attempted to make a phone call. Arthur reappeared fully dressed in jeans and a thick jumper. He strode into the back garden. The styled borders and the grass merged into a small wood. A winding path of flagstones through the trees led them to a steel fence and gate.

Police officers waited on the other side. The site lights gave clear visibility across the compound.

'Take us to the offices.' Arthur grunted and passed the silhouetted silent machinery to the bright lights of the portakabins.

'You won't find anything here.'

'It's strange, Arthur, but I'm not taking your word for it.' The police officers were carrying out a detailed search of the large site.

Tom sat at a desk in the main office of the cabin.

'That's all I bloody need,' muttered Arthur as they went in, 'What's he doing here?'

Tom almost seemed pleased, 'Some containers are locked. I'm searching for the keys, but if you prefer, we can force them open.'

'Bloody coppers. No common sense.' He yanked open a desk drawer and snatched a bunch of keys. 'If anything is damaged, you'll be paying for it.'

'Sit down, Arthur. It's time for a few questions.' Josh wiped his forehead. The dark suit and personal protection equipment made him hot.

Arthur slumped into the desk chair, 'I will not speak until my solicitor arrives.' Tom stared down on him. His face, a composed mask, gave nothing away. 'Who stitched me up?' He slapped the flat of his hand down onto the wooden surface of the desk. A pen, balanced on a pile of folders, shot to the floor and rolled out of sight.

Tom flicked his eyes in an exasperated gesture, 'You know we won't tell you where our information came from.'

A police officer entered. 'Sir, there's a small concrete building hidden in the bushes.'

'What do you mean hidden?'

'It backs on to the wood but is surrounded by bushes and trees. The tarmac goes past it with no sign of an entrance.'

Arthur's expression darkened and his eyes stared unwaveringly at Tom. His face gave nothing away.

'Is it derelict?'

'No, sir. It's new and well maintained.'

'Can you see in?'

'No, the steel door is locked.'

'You've no right.' Arthur banged his fist down on the desk. His eyes widened and he glared in blatant fury.

Would this be a breakthrough? 'It's on your property so the search warrant applies to any building. Let's go.' Josh beckoned and moved towards the door. 'I'm sure you've a key.'

Arthur snatched a key from the drawer and slouched out of the office muttering, 'Filth!'

Josh stepped between the maze of bushes to a well-hidden concrete building with no windows and a steel door adorned with a large lock. An air conditioning unit attached high on the wall gave an intriguing perspective as to its use. Arthur glanced at Josh, but the serious frown remained on his face.

'This is cosy.' The diffused automatic lighting came on as they entered and gave a bright space with no shadows. The garage-sized room had several filing cabinets and a large desk. The plastered walls, painted cream, contrasted to the thick wooden heavily varnished floor. The air conditioning had been set to automatic so gave no musty smells. At the far end a large shelf stretched the width of the room with cupboards underneath.

A constable entered and gave a small discreet cough,

'Sir, there's a solicitor outside demanding to see his client.'

'Show him in.'

A small rotund man, already sweating, but dressed in a dark blue suit with matching tie appeared in the doorway and snapped, 'Who's the senior officer?'

Josh showed his warrant card, 'Detective Sergeant Anderson.'

He didn't introduce himself but snarled, 'What is the meaning of this intrusion on my client?'

Josh held up his hand. 'And your name is?'

He thrust a card at Josh, 'Thomas Cruickshank.' He went to carry on speaking, but again Josh raised his hand. He tutted in irritation and his face reddened, 'I need to ask Mr Mercer whether he wishes you to represent him.'

'This is preposterous, Sergeant,' his voice rose and he huffed an exaggerated sigh.

Arthur Mercer moved next to his solicitor, 'This will cost you your job. He's my bloody solicitor, you rang him. Are you stupid?'

Mr Cruickshank's well-modulated voice interrupted, 'I remind you Sergeant that the police authority has been successfully prosecuted for harassment of my client and the next time we will expect far more than a token payout.'

Tom drew himself to his full height, 'We are aware of the previous settlement but will never shirk our duty when seeking criminal activity.'

The solicitor snarled, 'Oh, it's you. You should have been pensioned off.'

'They've insisted I stayed on because they knew you would miss me, Mr Cruickshank.'

'I wish to speak to my client in private so you will leave us.'

'No.' Josh gave a mirthless laugh, 'I wouldn't trust you in this room on your own. You may go outside but an officer will watch you and you may not leave the premises.'

'That is unacceptable, Sergeant.' His face reddened again and his lips tightened.

'Very well. A car will take you to a police station interview room.'

'If you have not arrested my client, he is free to go wherever he chooses.'

'If your client fails to follow police instructions or attempts to leave the premises, I shall arrest him.'

'For Christ's sake, let's go outside and talk.' Arthur stood with his hands on his hips in the middle of the room watching the police movement through narrow veiled eyes.

Tom had lost interest in the conversation. He opened a cupboard under a large shelf and found a concrete case which surrounded a grey heavy steel safe, with a combination dial and a large brass handle. 'Open the safe, please.'

'I'm sure that is unnecessary. I doubt you have served the warrant correctly and are exceeding your search area.' The solicitor flicked through the warrant.

'Open the safe.'

Arthur Mercer stood and scowled. His new bravado had arisen from the presence of his solicitor. 'No way.'

'Very well,' Josh spoke with confidence, 'I will arrest you and charge you with failing to comply with the warrant. The safe will remain under police guard until the manufacturers open it.'

Arthur and his solicitor stared long and hard at each other. Arthur bent down and entered the combination.

'Stand back,' instructed Tom as Arthur went to reach his hand inside. Tom groaned as he bent down. Another officer filmed the removal of the contents. He took out two cardboard boxes and ceremoniously placed them on the table. Arthur closed his eyes. Tom removed the box lids.

Both were full of used bank notes arranged into packs with rubber bands. He took them out and examined them. 'I would estimate about £20,000.'

32

Josh stood near the gate as the police car containing Arthur Mercer and his solicitor pulled out of the demolition works. Arthur's sons had arrived and had taken over the watching brief on the police who were still searching the large site. Tom and Josh plodded back to the main offices.

The purpose of the concrete building remained a mystery. Why build a secretive office? The main offices were secure and surrounded by a well-protected site. The police had taken a substantial amount of paperwork from the filing cabinets in the office, but at first glance it held no interest. 'Do you think the money is from the raid, Tom?'

'How much was stolen?'

'About a quarter of a million. They expected a busy weekend. The few teller machines in the shopping centre frequently run out of money. People rely on the building society for cash. The raid had been timed as the cashiers loaded the tills for opening.'

'Have we checked whether there was inside knowledge.' Tom tilted his head to one side in a questioning gesture.

'Don't know. Claire's not communicative. The Chief told me to check, but then he transferred me to Maddie's murder, although it seems worthwhile to follow it up. Unless they guessed and got lucky.'

'Building staff activity is visible as the windows are never covered. With a café opposite, it makes an ideal place to survey the sequences and procedures in the building society.'

'Have you checked the cameras for that idea?'

He laughed, 'It's only just occurred to me, but I'm sure I'll be examining them again, so I'll check.'

'You know Arthur Mercer well. Why is he likely to have a large stash of used notes?' They trudged past a large caterpillar demolition machine, its enormous jaws hanging close to the ground. 'This appears a successful business.'

'When young, Arthur drifted to the wrong side of the law. After spending time in prison for a bank raid, he turned to business. I'm guessing the hideaway is a cover for his other activities, but the main business has become successful, which has surprised him. He's not a man who will pay taxes unless forced into it.'

Josh entered the office and stood at the window. The large yellow demolition machine reminded him of a Tyrannosaurus Rex. He smiled at his fanciful imagination. Tom grimaced, 'His accountant of many years is serving time for fraud.'

'Arthur appears intelligent as he knows when to speak and when to stay quiet.'

'I've known Arthur for years, he's a wily old bugger. The only time we've nicked him was when someone grassed on him.' Tom stopped to examine a wallchart about safety procedures. 'I've given up counting how many times we've had search warrants and found nothing.'

'Did you know about that building?'

'No. It's a long time ago since we last raided these premises. I'm sure it wasn't there then. The last time the police paid him damages for harassment, he could afford a clever Queen's Counsel from London.'

Alone in the main office, 'Do you reckon twenty grand is Arthur's cut?'

'What for?'

'Masterminding the raid.'

'There's been no suggestion he's tried anything like a robbery for nearly twenty years. It would be extraordinary for him to return to his old ways. We have visited the site on many occasions often to support local government officers as he terrifies the life out of them. He employs old lags which we have picked up here. There have been minor motor bike offences but nothing serious for years.'

A car pulling up in front of the cabins caught Josh's attention, 'Come on, Tom.' He made a despairing grimace and nodded towards the entrance. 'The Chief's here with Claire.'

Tom growled, 'That's all we need.'

They descended the steps from the main office to the Chief Inspector who stood glaring around the site, 'What's the update.'

'We're on our way to the police station to interview Arthur Mercer.' Josh forced his voice to sound confident and enthusiastic. 'About twenty grand, in used notes, has been found.'

The Chief scrunched up his face into a disbelieving scowl. 'Show me.'

Josh led the way in silence towards the far side of the site. The Chief Inspector stood in the middle of the concrete building while his sharp eyes scanned the room. Josh pointed towards the open safe, 'He tried every trick to stop us opening that.'

'Did he explain the source of the money?'

'He refused to answer.'

The Inspector nodded his head solemnly and squared his shoulders, 'I've been thinking about our cases. The links between the death of Maddie and the raid seem tenuous and that's not the line I want to pursue. The attack on Eleanor was a mystery.' He paused as his narrowed eyes studied Josh's face, 'While we'll keep an open mind, we need some detailed police work on each of the separate cases. Tom, you stay here and double check everything.' Claire crossed the room to stand beside the Chief. A thin hard smile stretched briefly across her lips, 'Hand over anything relevant to me, Josh.' Her voice had an arrogant edge, 'This is my case now.'

'Get back on the Maddie case. Claire and I will interview Arthur Mercer. We won't be able to hold him unless we have more information.'

Josh stood in silence. The Chief and Claire would be a tough pair to deal with. Would he always be second best? His promotion and the return to Blackford hadn't been plain sailing. The attacks on Eleanor worried him. As they trudged in silence back across the site, he struggled to quell the rising frustration towards Claire. Her smugness and her uncommunicativeness were difficult to fathom. What made her tick? Why come to a town like Blackford?

The Chief Inspector climbed into his car and wound down the window. 'What leads do we have on Maddie's killing? Have we found the boyfriend yet?'

'No, sir. According to neighbours and his sister he travelled to London last week.'

'He could have returned to kill his girl as she wouldn't have worried about meeting him in a remote location.'

Josh wasn't convinced but had no evidence to argue against his boss.

'Tom, we're treating the attack on Eleanor as a separate case, but I want you to make sure all cases have a full exchange of information between them. It's your job.'

Tom nodded. He knew when to stay quiet. The Chief Inspector wound up his window and pulled away. Tom muttered, 'Thanks.'

33

'This visit concerns me, Eleanor, can I ask you to think again.'

Sitting in dad's BMW outside a hairdressing salon, I had used the excuse to leave the house. Mum and dad continued to be overprotective. Resuming a normal life was imperative otherwise the trauma of the attacks would never go away. I'd relived those terrible moments repeatedly. Not only did they nag at me during the day but haunted me during my restless nights.

'Dad, I'll be fine, I'm better today. Apart from the fright and a few bruises, I've not been badly hurt. The hospital wanted to keep me in purely for observation. There is nothing wrong with my results.'

'You were in a wheelchair at the hospital yesterday.'

'A precautionary choice as Josh and his boss wanted to ask questions and we agreed the wheelchair in case weakness overwhelmed me.'

'I didn't like how that constable interviewed you at home.'

'Dad, he did his job, Tom's a brave man.'

'I don't want to leave you at the hairdressers, but I'll return in an hour if you are adamant.'

'Stop fussing dad, my hair's a mess and I yearn to be pampered. Nothing can happen as I'm in a busy salon.'

'I'm worried they haven't caught anyone. Perhaps they are following you.'

'In a few days, I'll return to flying, so I won't be in Blackford.'

'I'm not sure that's a good idea.'

'The airline won't let me fly unless they have fully checked me out. An appointment with the doctor is a prerequisite and when I pass then you'll know I'm okay.'

Nodding, he lowered his eyes. 'What is it, dad?'

'There's something I want to ask while your mother's not here.'

Normally, he wouldn't worry about mentioning matters in front of mum, 'What is it?'

'How's your relationship with Scott?'

'Why do you ask?'

'I wasn't eavesdropping, but I'd gone out to the garden and could hear you raise your voice to him.'

'Scott is under pressure at work and it keeps bubbling over, I've told him unless he can sort himself out then he'll be off with stress. It's nothing more and we need a relaxing holiday which will solve his problems.'

'Yes, good idea. Are you sure you are okay with him?'

'Perfectly fine dad, he embarrassed me at the hospital by being rude to the police and I told him so. He had no right to criticise them. As he plans to stay for a few days you can chat with him.' Dad didn't look convinced which isn't surprising as something is amiss with Scott. Has he overstretched his gambling money? Also, he has asked mum for a separate room. Why? It wasn't like him to pass up an opportunity for sex. Glancing at dad, his face was solemn and lines of worry creased his forehead.

'I'll return in an hour.'

I jumped out and he pulled away. Stepping into the salon I was greeted by a smiling face, 'Hi, I'm Kirsty. This is your first appointment with us, isn't it?'

'Yes, I work in Manchester but I'm visiting my parents locally.' The familiar smell of the hair products pervaded the salon. The stylist's mirrors reflected the light from the myriad of spotlights sunk into the ceiling. Slightly overweight, Kirsty wore a black blouse and black trousers which seemed to be the expected uniform for the staff which milled around. The brown hair had been cut to her collar with a hint of blonde highlights and suited her petite face.

With a pleasant expression, 'Come and sit over here and we can discuss your style preferences.'

'Can you keep the same style and tidy it?'

'Yes, it's been well cut before so I'll keep the shape, but would you like it shorter?'

'Yes, please.' I relaxed back in the chair to enjoy being pampered. After having it washed, I returned to the cutting chair and made myself comfortable.

A man entered reception, 'I need a trim but don't have an appointment.'

Glancing in the mirror, a tall, good looking man flashed me a small smile, so I gave him a fleeting grin and returned my attention to the magazine on my lap.

'Ellie, is that you?'

No one ever called me Ellie. When my parents did the other day, it didn't sound like me. It took a few moments to recollect the face, as it had been many years since we'd met, but he hadn't changed. An icy shiver passed through me and my hands shook as I didn't want to be recognised and in my current anxious state wished to remain anonymous.

Kirsty noticed. 'Are you okay?' A query formed in her eyes.

I smiled reassurance and focused on the man who had spoken my name. 'Hello, Brendon.' I'd met him once at a social gathering since I'd left school and he insisted I called him Brendon although it seemed strange as he had been my teacher. Tallish and slim with brown hair, he had no sign of grey. He wore jeans and had a thick fleece over a polo shirt. Bright trainers told me he wouldn't be at work today.

Meeting Brendon unnerved me. Josh didn't like coincidences and I agreed. With an effort I attempted to control the trembling which had spread from my hands to my body and behave normally. I attempted to breathe deeply, to calm myself.

Having taken the chair next to me, he twisted towards me in a conspiratorial manner, 'Did you see the news about Maddie?'

Nodding, my heart hammered, I gripped the magazine as though trying to flatten the pages into thin air, as I didn't need reminding. 'Such a tragedy.' I muttered the words through clenched teeth as I didn't want to talk about her.

'I didn't know you were friends.'

His words confused me. It seemed a strange statement. Why did he assume we were friends? Brushing off my questioning thoughts, I had doubted everyone and everything since the attacks. Didn't he remember that we were at school together? I'd better elaborate, so I paused for a few moments, collecting my thoughts and breathing deeply. 'We worked together for a short while, but we met at the shopping centre before the raid took place, you must've heard about it.'

'Yes, I did, I shopped early, but I didn't see you or Maddie. As soon as I heard the sirens and the public announcements I left. Did you become caught up in the commotion?' His eyes studied my face.

'Yes.' Anxiety swirled through me as the memories came flooding back. The knot in my stomach twisted. I gripped the edge of the chair and tried to make my voice sound normal. 'Unfortunately, wrong place at the wrong time. Terrifying, but it's over.'

'Could you help the police? Did you see them?'

Oh, why did he want to talk about it? I'll try to be brief. 'No, I couldn't help.' I wouldn't tell him about being held at knifepoint. If he had been at the shopping centre and he knew Maddie, could he help Josh? No, I'm becoming too involved. The conversation ceased while he went to the basins to have his hair washed. I didn't want to dwell on the meeting, so I started on my magazine but couldn't concentrate. I hate Josh being in the police, but I would not interfere with his investigation and if Brendon left the shopping mall as soon as he heard the sirens, then he won't have seen anything.

When he returned to his seat for his trim, he resumed his conversation, 'I was mortified hearing Maddie had been murdered.'

'Yes, it came as a shock, especially after meeting her.' My voice sounded normal and controlled, but inside my head I was screaming at him to stop talking about her. 'Before that I hadn't seen her for about a year.

What about you?'

‘I stayed in touch with several from your class for many years, including Maddie. Sometimes we would meet for a drink and enjoy parties but as time passed people drift away. Maddie hadn’t gone far, but she had a new boyfriend who didn’t like her old connections.’

This conversation was upsetting. To divert the conversation away from Maddie, I blurted out, ‘Who else do you know from school?’

‘Her good friends Sean and Danny were often there, but they moved away with their jobs. If they come back to Blackford, we meet for a beer.’

‘Are you still teaching?’ Once again, I attempted to shift the conversation onto more mundane matters.

‘No, I gave up. No real reason but I decided on a change and I’m in the personnel department of the local government.’

I’d finished, so I stood up, ready to leave, ‘It’s been good to see you again, Brendon.’ The words tumbled from my mouth, although they held little real meaning as I hadn’t enjoyed talking to him. It had stirred up too many unpleasant memories.

Surprising me, he caught my hand and kissed it. ‘It’s great to see you again, Ellie.’ I couldn’t be bothered to tell him about my name. ‘Today we’ve talked about unpleasant matters that have happened and we haven’t caught up on the good times and I’m planning a world trip.’

‘That’s exciting.’

‘When we last met, you were training to be a pilot.’

‘Yes, I qualified many years ago.’ I gave a satisfied smile and pulled myself up to my full height as I was proud of my achievements.

‘On a commercial airline?’

'Yes, I fly Boeing 777s.'

Would you like lunch one day, as you're an international traveller you could give me some advice about suitable locations to visit.' Tilting his head to one side, his penetrating gaze probed my face.

I would have refused but didn't relish inactivity for several days. Whilst his conversation had upset me, I couldn't blame him as he didn't know of my harrowing ordeal. 'Yes, lunch would be good. Here's my number.' Giving him a business card, 'Ring me.'

34

Josh stared at the screen but couldn't summon the enthusiasm to search the Police National Computer for tenuous links. The room buzzed with conversation. Sitting in the admin area at the end of the Murder Incident Room he heaved out a long hard sigh. He'd had a poor start to his new job in Blackford. His boss, a meticulous man, had told him he'd missed two reports. Despite interviewing many of the leads and witnesses across the cases, he'd made no progress. A breakthrough seemed a dim and distant dream. Maddie for reasons unknown had exercised in a remote location and been murdered. Had she met someone she knew there?

With no sexual assault or robbery, it appeared an attack without a motive. A brief argument following an accidental meeting and a quick shove which sent Maddie hurtling down from the raised area to the rocks below. But before she was pushed someone hit her over the head. The person must have been carrying a suitable weapon. So, it must have been premeditated. Josh's brain twirled in circles.

Different scenarios presented themselves but no plausible solution arrived. Cases with no motive, but an easy opportunity, were the most difficult to solve. What to do next? Restlessness gripped him. He was making no progress. Josh let his pen doodle in the corner of the empty paper.

'Sarge, someone is asking for you at the front desk.' Any help or information would be useful. Josh strode to reception. A man in his thirties, scruffy, thickset and heavily tattooed, scowled at a nearby police officer. The Constable opened his hand, 'This is Sergeant Anderson.'

Josh raised his eyebrows to the Constable in a questioning manner. 'This gentleman wouldn't give his name but informed me he wanted to speak with Sergeant Anderson.'

The man didn't offer his hand. The body odour suggested he had been sleeping rough.

'I'm Jason Archer.' He had an aggressive tone of voice. 'What are you doing about catching Maddie's murderer or must I do it for you?' Standing in the middle of reception, he glowered at Josh. His hands, clenched into fists, were ready for a fight.

Despite his hostile attitude Josh smiled and keeping his voice calm, 'Come through to an interview room and let's talk.'

As they entered the room, he sneered, 'I suppose you've been looking for me. Bloody police couldn't find their way out of a paper bag.' His voice held a hint of menace as he slumped his large frame on a chair on one side of the plastic-topped table. The chair groaned under his weight and he grunted his disapproval as he attempted to become comfortable. Shifting his bulk, he leaned back and observed Josh through narrowed eyes.

The harsh fluorescent lights enabled Josh to see his

face. Round and tanned, he hadn't shaved for several days. The dark shadows accentuated the aggression in his grim features. The large hands clenched into fists resting on the table, adding a further dimension to his tough and hostile personality. Not the person Josh wanted to meet in a dark alley late at night.

Josh waited in silence while attempting to keep his facial expressions neutral. He didn't want to question him as he hoped that Jason might be talkative. Jason's expression darkened and his unblinking eyes bored into Josh as though he could see his innermost thoughts. 'My mate told me last night that she'd been killed.' He huffed out a long and audible sigh. 'So, I travelled this morning, by train to Blackford and I walked from the station.' He grimaced and gave a dismissive wave of his hand. 'Despite the cameras and walking past coppers no one even spoke to me. You lot are a joke.' He laughed, but there was no amusement attached to the noise and his whole demeanour had an air of hostility and suspicion.

Their eyes locked across the table. Eventually, Josh broke the heavy silence, 'I intend to caution you and record the conversation.' He switched on the recorder at the end of the table as he issued the standard caution.

'Yeah, I know all about that. I want him caught soon or there will be trouble from me.' He slammed his fist on the table, then with slow precision, he drew his forefinger across his throat. 'If I catch him, he'll be dead meat.' His muscular body shifted uncomfortably on the insubstantial plastic chair.

Josh didn't doubt his intentions, but he blocked such thoughts from his mind and forced his attention back to the present. Aggression oozed from every pore of Jason's body. 'Do you want a solicitor?' Josh's eyebrows lifted fractionally as he posed the question.

Jason slapped the flat of his hand on the table. 'Don't be so bloody daft, they're even worse than you lot. I have done nothing wrong, so why would I want one of those money grabbing scum.'

'Explain to me where you've been for the past week.'

'In London, but I'm not telling the fuzz where I stayed or who I met. You'd only hassle them when they've done nowt wrong.' Crossing his arms, he scowled.

'That approach won't help you. You've a history of violence and your girlfriend has been killed.' His voice was clipped and sharp. Pausing for effect. 'You need to provide information or I will arrest you.'

He eyed Josh with contempt. 'Yeah, I know how the police think but there are two crucial bits of information. He waved two fingers across the table at Josh in a provocative manner and smirked while he waited for a reaction to the obvious insult. With a smug expression on his heavy grim face, he announced, 'I was at the Spurs match on the evening she died. This is the ticket, check the cameras.'

Josh's interest was grabbed but with a dismissive shake of his head, 'No, it's not a foolproof alibi, you could have travelled when the match finished.'

Jason huffed in annoyance, 'I had a drink in the Kings Head after the Spurs match. And before you ask, I wasn't involved in the punch-up. The pub had cameras, so did the filth when they arrived.' Anger burned across his face. 'Scum!'

Josh nodded blandly, ignoring the aggression, 'We could hold you while we check it out.'

Jason jerked himself straight and thumped the table

with his fist. He snarled, 'Bloody useless. And before you get smartarse about me rushing around the country. The following morning, I visited the Tesco supermarket in the same road as the pub.'

'What's the road called?'

'No bloody idea. Even a detective should be able to find a pub called the Kings Head and a Tesco supermarket near White Hart Lane.' He pulled a face and his hawk-like eyes smouldered.

'The Tesco store isn't any proof unless you've a receipt.'

Shaking his head, 'I didn't notice whether they had a camera, but the staff will remember me as we had a good laugh. I think one of them fancied me.' Grinning, he raised his eyebrows in amusement.

Josh turned quizzical eyes towards him, 'Okay, we'll check out what you say.' It could be an elaborate hoax, but he wasn't a man for sophisticated planning and alibi management. He would act on impulse and didn't have a premeditated approach. His life appeared to be ruled by anger and his fists. He guessed he had been told the truth, but he'd have to confirm, as he wanted no further blunders with the boss. That was too depressing to contemplate. If it hadn't been for Tom's camaraderie, he'd be truly fed up.

Jason leaned back in his chair, pleased with himself. He almost managed a smile as the corners of his mouth lifted a fraction. Suddenly, he leaned forward and rested his elbows on the table. 'That puts me in the clear.' His jaw clenched. 'I want to know what you are doing about catching my bird's killer.'

Josh remained calm and kept silent, waiting for the man's tension to ease. Jason's breath stank. 'Did she have an argument with anyone recently? Anyone threaten her?'

Jason's lips curled with contempt, 'You haven't any idea, have you? You must be joking. Anyone going near her would have to answer to me.' Pointing a finger at his own chest, he shook his head in mock horror.

'How long had you been together?'

'Over a year.'

This interview was not producing any relevant information. Time for a change of tactics. Could he provoke him? What would happen if he threw him off track and tried to confuse him? Let's see how he reacts.

Josh raised expectant eyes towards him, 'I liked Maddie when I met her.'

Jason's eyes screwed up. Josh had expected immediate aggression, but he stared. His fingers tightened, but he stretched his hands. 'Where did you meet her?' His tone was low, but he eyed Josh with a mixture of curiosity and contempt.

'I was shopping with a friend who worked with Maddie on the airline.'

'Yeah, that was a good job, but the club paid her more.' The surprise had caused a reaction but didn't upset him.

'Who were her close friends?'

'My sister and two blokes.'

'What did you think of them?'

'Not much. She went to school with them. Don't worry, I monitored them, but they didn't visit her that often.' There was a pause and his haunted eyes focused on Josh. 'Why would someone want to hurt her?'

'You're still on probation for the last assault and affray.'

'For Christ's sake.' Shifting on the small chair, it

creaked alarmingly. 'This won't catch Maddie's killer. I'm innocent.' He waved his arms in a wild gesture. 'Once you lot fasten your claws into someone it's hard to shake loose.'

The interview had been dictated by Jason. He remained confident being near the police, which wasn't the behaviour of a man who killed his girlfriend. Why had he come? He wanted information and intended taking the law into his own hands.

There was one last question that Josh wanted answered before the interview ended. 'Do you know Arthur Mercer?'

'Why's that relevant?' Jason grunted, his voice devoid of any interest. 'Jason, you know that we follow up coincidences. Have you any connections with Arthur or his family?'

A worried expression fleetingly crossed his face but was soon replaced, by a crooked grin. 'You lot and Arthur don't get on, one of Maddie's mates is his nephew, Danny.'

35

Dad's face was anxious, 'We don't like leaving you on your own, but we expected Josh to be here. I've just received a text to say he's been delayed.'

'Josh always works unpredictable hours as being a policeman isn't a nine to five job. Scott will be here soon. Before he arrives, I will shower and then have a relaxing evening with him. Bye, mum, bye dad.' I shooed them out the front door before they could find an excuse not to go as I needed breathing space from their constant worrying. 'Have a good evening out.'

After the traumas of the attacks, a hot shower was a wonderful relaxation. The light grey fully tiled ensuite with fluffy dark maroon towels and accessories made a perfect place to relax and pamper. When I return to flying, the horrific few days will pass into oblivion. I have too much time on my hands, so it's hard to shift the traumatic memories and move forward. My life needs normality, so I want to return to the flat I share with Scott and pick up our loving relationship, but he's been so jittery even before the attack at the car wash.

Hopefully, we'll be able to pinch a week's holiday soon. My mind filled with images of blue skies, white beaches and warm lazy days and I smiled in anticipation. Somewhere hot and relaxing.

As I towel dried my hair, the chance meeting in the hairdressers with my old teacher came to mind. Was it a good idea to agree to meet Brendon? But a quick lunch and chat with my old teacher will let me leave the house. Sitting around moping isn't good.

The crunching of the gravel on the front drive by a car caught my attention. A pang of worry shot through my stomach. This is ridiculous, I'm safe in the house. I tried to convince myself but rushed to the window. As Scott stepped from his smart BMW, I relaxed.

Leaning over the bannister as he entered, 'Hi darling, I'm up here.' Sluggishly he hauled himself up the stairs with a weak, 'Hello.'

'You look shattered.' Leaning to kiss him, he backed away. Then he seemed to realise what he'd done and he gave me a small smile, then a hug. There was no kiss. Not even a peck on the cheek. Scott had changed as he always greeted me with enthusiasm and a kiss. Often a long lingering one on the lips if we were alone. He suffered from more than stress. Did he want to finish with me? No, we are made for each other. The perfect couple.

'Come and talk while I dress.' I made sure my voice sounded bright and enthusiastic, I could lighten his mood as I'd managed it in the past. 'Then I'll fix you a drink and food.'

'I've eaten, I didn't expect you to be here this evening as I guessed you would accompany your mum and dad.' His voice was flat and tension lurked in his eyes.

Continuing to keep lightheartedness in my voice, 'Change of plan.' With an enthusiastic smile and a flourish of my arm for dramatic emphasis. 'I wanted to shower and to wait for you.' He slumped on to the edge of the bed. 'What's the matter, Scott?'

'Nothing. Work is horrendous.' He wrung his hands together and he drew his eyebrows together in an anguished expression. 'I'm okay,' he muttered, 'only exhausted.' I took a tee shirt and leggings from the wardrobe.

Something in his manner and words convinced me he had not told the truth, but I became determined to find out. In an exaggerated flourish I took off my dressing gown and stood naked in front of the full-length mirror brushing my hair. Then with premeditated precision, I passed close to him to fetch lotion from the dressing table and then returned to the mirror. If I'd teased him back at the flat, he would be behind me with his hands on my breasts within a minute. His eyes scanned my naked body, but then he turned away and yawned. The lack of attention convinced me it was over between us and he would dump me.

36

Tom Collins sat in his patrol car mulling over his next fishing trip. The anticipation brought a smile to his lips. A pile of papers littered the passenger seat. During the early morning raid at the Mercers, they'd taken away documents and he had come to return them. The visit was an excuse to have a chat with Arthur. Unlike his colleagues back at the station, who were convinced Arthur was connected to the raid on the building society, Tom was certain he'd had no involvement. Why would he? He had a successful business.

Trying to squeeze information from Arthur was an uphill battle. He hated the police who continued to hold the money pending an explanation as to its origins. Tom picked up the documents from the passenger seat. The papers revealed nothing of relevance to the police, although the tax authorities would be interested. But that wasn't his concern.

Taking his traditional helmet from the back seat, he locked the car and with a resigned expression ambled towards the Mercer's business ready to do battle with Arthur. The gates were wide open. The overcast sky with a brisk wind did nothing to lift the gloom as his eyes swept across the heavy machinery arranged haphazardly on the site. Inside the gate, he waited as a large excavator rumbled past him on its way to the back of a nearby lorry which belched diesel fumes over the entrance. Tom tried not to breathe deeply and sauntered forward, keeping his wits about him.

He spotted Arthur high up in the driver's seat of a huge caterpillar vehicle which had tracks that were only slightly less than Tom's height. Standing to one side and shielding his eyes, he gazed towards the glass cabin at the front of the excavator and guessed that Arthur had seen him.

'What the bloody hell do you want?' Arthur bellowed as he glared from his elevated position.

It was the usual welcome that Tom had expected and he ignored the aggression in his tone. The noise of the excavator being loaded onto the lorry was a noisy operation and Tom had to shout. 'I've brought back the rest of your papers.' Tom pointed to the folders he carried.

'Since when were you a bloody errand boy?'

Tom allowed a moment's pause before replying, 'I wanted a word.'

Arthur waved his arm dismissively, 'What happens if I don't want to speak to you.'

'Are you coming down, I don't want to shout.'

'Tough.'

'Okay. That's no problem, I'll bellow as loud as possible and everyone will discover your secrets.'

A long pause followed this comment. Tom stood and waited, keeping his expression under stern restraint. It was important to show no reaction. 'I ain't bloody coming down, you can climb up here. There's a foothold in front of you.' Arthur, standing up in the bulldozer's cab, pointed.

Tom lumbered his weight up the foothold on to a short ladder, taking him up onto the metal grilled platform outside the cabin. His back griped in protest. Arthur ignored his presence and focused his attention on repairing the door to the cab.

There was no greeting from Arthur who scowled, 'I'm suing you lot for wrongful arrest.'

Tom glared down at the little man and adjusted his helmet with an air of indifference. 'That's of no interest to me.'

'I ain't saying nothing to you. I don't have to. Now bugger off.' Arthur returned his attention to the broken door.

Tom rubbed his chin and peered around at the yard. From this high vantage point, he spotted a gate near to the secret building they'd found. Recently installed, it measured the width of a car. Why install a new side gate? He might have a look another time.

After a long silence, during which he continued to fiddle with the hinges on the door, he finally lifted his head.

Tom snarled, 'You're wasting my time.'

'You've a bloody cheek.' Arthur kicked at the door in frustration, which rattled and shook. 'What about my time and business? I ain't helping you. No way, my solicitor will add it to the list of harassments.' With a look of unmitigated fury, he frowned, 'Now leave me alone, I'm trying to mend this damned door.'

Tom reached out his large hand and gripped the door firmly. Arthur glanced up at him. The steady door allowed him to tighten the screws.

Tom's steely eyes glared, 'If you break the law how can

it be harassment from the police?'

'What do you mean? You talk in riddles, man. Spit it out, let me deal with my business, I still intend to sue you for that raid.'

Tom ignored him and released the door which worked perfectly as Arthur opened and shut it a few times. 'When we served the warrant, I had a look around.' Tom's face became a composed mask giving nothing away.

'Don't I know it, complete disruption.'

Tom pointed. 'That lorry over there.'

'What about it?' His eyes followed the direction indicated.

'It's back trailer tyre is badly worn on the inside, it's not legal.'

'Oh my God,' he slapped his hand to his forehead in an over dramatic gesture, 'are you going down that route?'

Tom ignored him, 'That crane handrail is rickety, its rusty and dangerous.'

Arthur narrowed his eyes and he pulled a face, 'I know all about health and safety, I get the picture. You will hassle me until I answer your questions.'

'We've known each other many years.' A small smile flashed across his face but disappeared.

'Too bloody long.' Arthur slumped down into the single worn seat of the excavator and gave a loud yawn to indicate his boredom.

'If we had information to investigate, it would occupy my time. I'm advancing in age and can only deal with one matter.' He paused, allowing his words time to sink in and then continued his theme. 'If I were fully occupied, I'm sure I wouldn't remember lorries and cranes.'

'Trivial stuff,' snarled Arthur, 'they're no big deal.'

'I could forget about some invoices in these folders,' Tom kept his voice calm but firm, as he handed the folders back to Arthur, 'especially the ones that don't seem to have VAT.' Arthur snatched at the folders, threw them onto the floor of the cabin and glowered. Tom's flat voice continued, 'Personally, although it's not the current line of thinking at the station, I don't think you had anything to do with the raid at the shopping centre.'

'I didn't.'

'As you've a history…'

'That was bloody years ago.'

'As you've a history of bank robberies in the family and a pile of unaccounted money, then the police become interested.'

'Don't forget I'm suing you.'

Tom chuckled, 'The court cases will take years and will cost you a fortune. The police will deny it through to the Supreme Court. So, two years plus a lot of hassle won't be worth it, as you probably won't win, anyway.'

Arthur looked away, 'I'm not a grass.'

'No one said you were.' Tom scanned the area from his high vantage point and pursed his lips. 'Give me a hint about the money.'

'No chance.' Arthur had lost interest in Tom as he surveyed the loading of the lorry near the entrance. He shouted, but because of the general noise he couldn't be heard, so he snatched his mobile from his pocket and pressed the keypad. The man supervising the loading checked his mobile he'd taken from his pocket. He answered it.

Arthur barked into the phone, 'The bloody thing isn't straight on the trailer.' The man gawped up towards the digger where Arthur stood waving his fist at them. 'If I need to climb down and sort it out, I'll sack the lot of you.'

Tom waited for Arthur to return his attention to him. 'There's something that surprises me, perhaps you might solve my curiosity.'

'I don't want to know.'

Tom took no notice as Arthur stared hard at the improvements in loading the lorry, but he was listening as his body remained tense and motionless. Tom spoke as though he was telling a bedtime story to a child. 'A night time demolition.'

The sudden turn and sharp look meant that Tom had hit the mark. He'd caught Arthur out, which pleased him and a small smile appeared on his lips.

'Don't know what you're talking about.'

Tom moved his shoulders to relax and didn't seem interested in looking at Arthur. He'd already seen enough. His eyes scanned the busy site. 'There are many laws to break in the demolition business.'

'Tell me about them,' Arthur grumbled.

'Knocking down a listed building without permission. It's not a job for the police. It's a local authority responsibility. If the law is broken and they don't receive cooperation, then they would contact us.'

Arthur's large calloused hands moved and gripped the railings. His stare at the lorry being loaded had ended. 'Who else knows about your guess?'

'No one.'

'That's good because it ain't true.' Arthur spat out the words through clenched teeth.

'I listen, watch and I read what's happening and then I reach my conclusion.' He shifted his feet and assumed a chatty tone of voice. 'I don't hold with these fancy computers.'

'Go on, amuse me.'

'Well, I asked myself, why would a demolition firm have twenty grand in used notes.'

'What conclusion did you come to? That I'm good at monopoly and always win?'

Tom ignored the jibe. 'The raid,' Arthur appeared edgy but shook his head. 'Or a tax avoidance scam.' Once again, he shook his head. 'Or perhaps secretive night work that wasn't invoiced.' This time Arthur didn't shake his head. Tom continued, 'I searched the local paper and found the information I needed. A man's small house in a large plot had been demolished overnight. Strange, it happened during darkness to a listed building. He runs a series of large scale discount shops so takes a lot of cash.'

'Why are you telling me this?'

'I have two options.' His eyes focused on Arthur's face, watching for a reaction to his words.

'I return to the station and raise the matter in a formal report which we would then investigate. Naturally, that would involve the local authority, inland revenue, vat, etc.'

Arthur slapped his hand down on the railing, 'Okay, I get it, the complaint must be withdrawn.' He sighed with annoyance, 'And I must answer other questions.'

'As they say, we seem to sing from the same hymn sheet, although personally I'm not fussed about whether you withdraw your complaint. That has nothing to do with me.'

His face slumped, 'Try me with a question.'

'What is your nephew Danny like? Do you see much of him?'

He seemed surprised and his eyes widened in unconcealed curiosity, 'Don't see him often, although I spoke to my sister about him recently. She mentioned that the murdered lass and Danny attended school together and had remained friends.'

'What's Danny like?'

'Hang on, I'm wise to you.' His expression darkened. 'It's not about the raid but the death of that lass. You're barmy if you think it was him. He's a likeable lad, wouldn't harm a fly. Forget it, you're barking up the wrong tree.'

'Another name I'm sure you've heard of is Jason Archer.'

'Yes, I know him, he worked for me for a while.'

'After he came out of jail?'

'Yes, I don't hold it against them if they're prepared to work.'

'Is he still here?'

'No, sacked, he's a nasty bit of work.'

'Did you know he was her boyfriend?'

'I wouldn't look for anyone else then, it's obvious who did it. Now, piss off.' He waved his arm in a dismissive gesture, 'I've a business to run.'

37

'It's too soon,' Scott muttered as we pulled into the staff car park at Manchester airport. It had been a tedious journey from Blackford. Scott, still morose, wouldn't chat and had switched on loud jazz music to make talking difficult, so I gave up and pretended to be engrossed in the ever-changing views. We had a problem in our relationship, but I couldn't rectify it until I understood the cause.

Would he dump me?

'I can't sit around doing nothing, I must return to work.'

'No one in the airline will let you fly; it will be weeks or possibly months as you were knocked unconscious in the attack.'

'For Christ's sake. Stop being so negative, you're telling me not to work. How the hell do I spend my time? Shall I become a recluse and spend my life moping in a safe environment? That's not for me.'

As we approached the admin building, I expected him to kiss me on the cheek to say goodbye, but without a word, he marched away. A wave of sadness washed over me. Had our relationship finished? What had happened to the man I loved? I tried to block out the myriad of depressing thoughts and unanswered questions that filled my mind. Brushing away an escaped tear, I strove to calm myself. Underneath my misery, I seethed with anger at Scott's attitude.

I sat alone on a hard plastic chair in a small white painted anteroom with a bare minimum of functional furniture. The water cooler in the corner gave an occasional gurgle. The roar of jets taking off broke the silence, so I amused myself by determining the plane from the engine noise. There were no windows, so I couldn't check whether my guesses were correct. But my self-imposed game helped to pass the time. I needed a distraction, then I could let Scott have the space to solve his problems.

'Eleanor Anderson, come in please, I'm Dr Sutcliffe.' The tall man in a dark grey suit with glasses perched on the end of his nose led me into the consulting room. Sitting behind his desk, he indicated a facing seat. Flicking at the mouse, he studied the screen then gave me a small smile. 'Thank you for completing the tests for your return to work. Unfortunately, I cannot authorise you to fly.'

I'd guessed that would be the result, 'Can you tell me why? I'm over the unfortunate incidents and I'm feeling fine in myself.'

The results show a variance from your previous scores.'

'Which tests?' I tried to contain my irritation.

'Calm down, Eleanor, your reaction shows that you're still anxious. Let me explain.'

'Yes, please do,' I forced myself to relax and focused on taking large slow breaths. I placed my hands in my lap and listened.

'You are a model employee and an able pilot. Your medical readings have been far more consistent than many over the years. The results today aren't disastrous. It's not my job to recommend, but in your case a holiday is needed. Your pulse and blood pressure are up. Nothing that's a medical problem, but you need to return to your usual levels. Performance test and reaction times were poorer than normal.'

'Can I see the results?'

'You can, but you're not listening to me.' That stopped me. 'During the first interview we discussed what had happened to you. It's terrible and you're remarkable in having readings as good as they are, but they are not the results necessary that will allow you to fly a plane in charge of five hundred people.'

This was the conclusion I'd anticipated however I wanted permission to fly. 'How long?'

Glancing across at his computer screen, he shook his head, 'It's difficult to estimate, as you need a break to distance yourself from the unfortunate events in your life.'

After the meeting, I wandered to the admin block to grab a cup of coffee and collect my thoughts.

No matter how much I wanted to return to flying, it wouldn't happen soon. The doctor wouldn't change his mind. Taking up his suggestion of a holiday would be a good start, as it would facilitate my return to normal and it would help my tension if my relationship with Scott improved. Perhaps if I attempt to be more like my old self, Scott will loosen up and meet me half way. I will find him and suggest a holiday.

The neatly organised pods of the admin office emanated a busy buzz of activity as I entered the area. Scott had a large pod with a small table and four chairs. Determination gripped me as I needed to fly and Scott could help me as he organised the rotas. Greeting a few colleagues with a cheery hello and a forced grin, I attempted to bounce out of my depressed mood. Walking through the principal office, the view through the panoramic windows showed an Airbus 370 taking off.

I leaned casually on the partition wall and glanced into his pod as he typed away, choosing to ignore his difficult mood of earlier. 'No go with the quack,' I huffed out a loud audible sigh, 'it won't be long, but he wants another check to guarantee I'm medically fit.'

'It's what I expected.' He had a cool, almost bored edge to his voice.

Isn't he interested to hear the results of my interview with the doctor? Doesn't he want me to resume my job as a pilot? Using a positive voice to gain his attention as he still hadn't stopped typing or faced me, 'I'm almost back to normal. If you remember I'm still officially on holiday so can you slot me into the schedule for my normal return date? I have a week left of my holiday before having another check.'

The typing stopped and he briefly made eye contact but seemed distracted by the pen he twiddled in his hand. The offhand attitude rattled me. With an expression of withering contempt, he shrugged in a half-hearted manner. 'You know the rules. If you're not fit for work, you go on standby.'

Open plan office or not, it was time to sort out Scott. This was not the attitude I expected as we were lovers. Didn't he care about me anymore? Normally he would have slipped me into the schedule unnoticed. My phone rang. Damn! How inconvenient, but I flicked it open, 'Hello.' I didn't intend snapping as it could be someone senior in the airline.

'Eleanor. This is Tom Collins.' My heart sank. I wanted to be dismissive, but I had to support Josh. Swallowing hard, I squared my shoulders and with the phone pressed to my ear I shambled away from Scott. With a heavy heart I slumped down onto a nearby bench close to the large windows facing the runway.

Forcing my voice to be positive, 'Hi Tom. Good to hear from you. What can I do for you?'

'Can I ask some questions about the car wash attack.'

'Okay. I'm available whenever its convenient for you.'

I liked and admired Tom, but how could he spend his whole working life as a policeman? 'Could we do it today?'

'I'm at the airport.' With luck, my location would cause the interview to be delayed.

'I'll come to you.'

Before I responded or could invent an excuse, the connection went dead.

38

Within twenty minutes, Tom and I were settled at a table in an unused meeting room on the ground floor of the admin building. 'What did you want to ask?'

Relaxing his large frame on the hard plastic chairs as best he could, he took out his notebook. 'One of my colleagues is managing your case but as I've interviewed you before, we agreed I would follow up on the previous discussions. First, a snippet of information. Your credit cards were stolen, but no attempt has been made to use them.'

'That's a relief.' Suppressing a shudder, I didn't want to think about the attacks as they would harm my readings at the next medical examination. I needed to relax and leave the incidents behind me.

'Sorry to make you recollect bad times but have you remembered any other detail about the attack.'

'No, nothing beyond the information I gave to the first officer on the scene.' I kept my voice casual, hoping this interview would soon be completed.

'Okay to ask a couple of questions?' His tone, like a benevolent uncle, undermined my confidence, but I didn't know why.

'Yes, Tom.'

'Can you tell me exactly what you were doing when the attack took place?'

Focusing back to the incident, I pictured it in my mind. 'I'd started to vacuum the boot.' Looking quizzical, he shook his head in confusion. He opened his mouth as though intending to speak but promptly closed it again, 'What is it, Tom?'

He studied the paper in front of him. 'The statement says that you received a hard push on your shoulder blades.' I nodded. 'If you were leaning over vacuuming the boot of your car, then it would be difficult to push you hard unless on your bottom.'

I thought through his observation, picturing myself in various positions at the boot of my car. 'Yes, I see what you mean. Let me think.' I reluctantly forced my mind to drag up the sequence of events at the car wash. 'I intended leaning forward to vacuum out the boot, but I hadn't started. First, I moved old coats and boots that I always keep in the car out of the way. Then I discovered a folder which I didn't expect to find. I'd stood up straight and opened it when the man pushed me.'

'That clears that up.'

'Sorry, I wasn't sufficiently precise.'

'Don't concern yourself, you've done nothing wrong. Let's move on. The scene of crime guys are methodical. Was it a green and black folder?'

'Yes, that's the one.' I gulped as my heart pumped uncomfortably. That stupid folder had caused such a row between me and Scott. It was the reason I had returned to Blackford that evening as he was insistent that he wanted it back.

Tom once again checked his papers. 'It still contained

a variety of papers, so I'm guessing nothing was stolen from it. Was there anything valuable in it?'

I shook my head and studied my hands, which were unconsciously twisting nervously in my lap. Getting agitated would not help my next medical checkup. Try deep breathing commanded a small voice in my head. Tom stopped talking and drummed his fingers on his notebook with a confused expression. 'The contents were betting slips and some pieces torn from racing newspapers.'

'Not mine.' I gave a laugh which sounded false. 'The folder belongs to Scott, who you've met.' Tom acknowledged with a brief nod. 'He likes a dabble on the horses.'

'When we returned your car had anything else, apart from your credit cards, been taken?' 'No, I checked. The thief had left the money in the dashboard tray I use for parking coins.' As I thought about what had been stolen, I shivered. Not from the attack itself, but from what it meant.

'Tom, can I ask you a question?'

'Yes.'

'I'd been to the cash machine and had two hundred pounds in my bag. The tray is stacked with pound coins. Why did he steal credit cards, then not use them and leave the cash behind?'

'That's what I've been asking myself. Muggings go for cash. Experienced ones can disable the victim, search and leave with the money in seconds.'

Tom had a wonderful gentle manner, but each time we met I finished more on edge. Would he find the reason for the car wash attack? It made no sense. Remaining calm and relaxed was essential as I wanted to return to my normal work schedule.

Waving goodbye to Tom as he drove away, my mind returned to my major issue of the present and I needed Scott's help to regain my place on the flying rotas. How could I persuade him? Normally, he would cooperate. Would he be different this time? Tom's visit had made me uneasy as he'd dragged back the memories of the attack.

I hadn't opened the folder before being pounced on, but it contained betting information. Scott told me he had an occasional flutter on the horses, but to keep a separate folder with additional data sounded more than an occasional dabble. What has Scott been up to? Am I becoming too suspicious?

Scott wasn't in his pod, but his diary, open on the desk, showed he didn't have a meeting. I'll wait for him. A holiday would return our relationship to normal. That's what we need. Sunshine, pampering and relaxation. While I'm waiting, I'll browse the internet to find a suitable location. I'll use his computer.

He hadn't logged off, so I intended closing his account to open mine, but the details on the screen caught my attention. Guilt surfaced as I shouldn't look, but I couldn't avoid the information. His pay for the recent months was displayed. I gaped at the figures in disbelief; he earned such a low salary. At that point I should have stopped, but I stared mesmerised at the screen. How did he pay for smart clothes and evenings at the casino? Does he have a private income?

We had never discussed money, but his wallet was always stuffed with cash and he rarely used credit cards. Leaving the pod, I wandered away to watch the planes. From an early age, I'd loved the thrill of watching aircraft take off and soar into the air. They would offer a distraction as my mind raced. I thought about Scott's parents, who must help him out with money. Last time we met Scott's dad, he talked about investments. Perhaps that's the source of his money.

39

Josh wandered in as the briefing room filled with officers from the different cases. It was a large room and had a small raised area and rows of moveable seats. The black tiled floor did nothing to help the drab pale grey walls and doors. Josh yawned.

Although he'd been trying hard to find some new facts, he had made no progress. Frustration with the lack of physical evidence gnawed at him making him unsettled and grumpy. Had he missed an important clue? Finding a solution would allow Eleanor some relief. The point that niggled him most was that he didn't believe in coincidences.

As usual, the Chief had identified Josh's lack of detail in his reports and a failure to adhere to strict punctuality. He needed a breakthrough otherwise the Chief would continue to find fault. The only one who offered any encouragement was Tom. At every step of the investigation, he had supported and reassured him. Josh could relax in his company. His dry sense of humour coupled with his laid back approach to modern policing routines came as a breath of fresh air.

Claire continued to be unfriendly and must have been

given permission to miss this briefing as he had seen her leaving the police station. After the last failure he had not attempted any further meetings with her. The buzz in the room quietened as Chief Inspector Haskins strode in, swept through the line of chairs and mounted the raised dais.

Rapping on the table with his knuckles the sharp noise reverberated around the room. The shuffling movement subsided. The door clicked open as another officer arrived. The Chief snapped, 'You're late.'

Josh's body sagged and a small sigh escaped from his lips. This briefing was destined to be heavy.

In a commanding voice, 'This meeting is to review recent serious crimes in Blackford.' Silence except for the outside drone of the traffic.

'Frankly, ladies and gentlemen, your efforts are not good enough.' A twinge of anger laced his voice and the silence in the room suggested that everyone was holding their breath. The Chief Inspector's probing eyes rested on Josh and he stiffened under his withering glare. Determined not to be intimidated, he raised his chin and returned the stare with unblinking concentration.

The Inspector was the first to look away which afforded Josh a moment of smug satisfaction. 'We have a robbery where we have hundreds of witnesses and we've made no progress.' It was Tom's turn for the angry glare. 'Have we any leads from the computer analysis and the review of the witness statements?' Tom kept his expression neutral and shook his head.

The Chief paced in front of the twenty police officers like a caged animal prowling back and forth. 'Well.' No one wanted to speak. The entire room sat in silence like a class of naughty school children.

The tension needed breaking. Josh spread his hands regretfully and shrugged as he addressed his boss, 'No, sir.' His voice, neutral and controlled, echoed across the silent room, 'So far there have been no links worth pursuing.'

The Chief greeted his news with a frown of disapproval, 'Let's move on to the murder of Maddie. Have we completed the house to house and relevant searches in the area?'

'Yes, sir,' called out a detective constable sitting in the back row.

'Have we any useful information worth following up?'

'No, sir.'

The Chief's eyes narrowed to crinkled slits and he slammed his hand down on the table. 'Within the first few hours we had two witnesses who noticed Maddie on her own jogging up the track. From then, we've produced nothing new. It's not good enough. The first few days of an investigation are crucial.' His loud irate voice echoed around the silent room. 'Sergeant Anderson update me on the report about the prime suspect. The boyfriend has a background of drunken violence.'

Some of his colleagues studied him, but most had glazed eyes wishing the meeting to finish. All stayed silent. Josh reluctantly stood up as his mind whirled and reached the conclusion that the best approach was to answer the enquiry. Taking in a deep breath, he raised his eyes and stared fixedly at his boss, 'He was in London but wouldn't name the people he stayed with, however he supplied other evidence which we checked out with the help of the Met police. They verified his movements in London late on the night of the murder and early the next morning.'

'Have you questioned him about hiring a hitman or using one of his friends?'

Josh hated having to stand there and be interrogated by the boss in front of everyone. They would have sympathy for his predicament and would be relieved it wasn't them in the spotlight.

Josh pressed his lips together and inhaled deeply, 'A hit man is unlikely. He hasn't money and draws the dole. A friend is a possibility but doubtful. The principal reason for not considering him as the main suspect is according to statements, he idolised Maddie. There is no history of violence towards her.'

The Chief tensed his jaw and scowled, revealing his deep dissatisfaction and frustration, as Josh sat down, 'Where's Gemma? I wanted a report from her.'

'Sick,' called out Tom.

The Chief Inspector huffed. 'Tom, where are we with the assault on Josh's sister?'

He lumbered to his feet and flicked open his notebook and thumbed through the pages before he spoke, 'No further, sir. Credit cards stolen, but no attempt to use them. Cash left behind and nothing else stolen as far as the victim knows.'

The Chief slammed his fist down on the desk making the papers flutter, 'I repeat, this is not good enough. The only reason I've drawn the three cases together is Josh and several others have suggested there must be links. I'm not convinced, but we have no leads on any of the incidents.'

He lifted the glass of water to his lips and took a large gulp. Silence filled the room. No one moved or shuffled. The Chief drew himself up to his full height and pulled back his shoulders. There was no smile. Drops of sweat beaded his forehead. 'This is the plan. The robbery team, and that includes Tom, are to revisit statements and camera outputs. We have missed a clue.'

Josh dreaded his turn. The tension within him increased and a band of tight pain circled his lower ribs, making deep breathing difficult. His mind circled for excuses to whatever the Chief suggested. More than anything else, he wanted the meeting to finish. 'Josh.' The single word sliced slowly through the pulsing in his head.

'Sir.' This time he didn't stand.

'There was no evidence of sexual assault or a fight, so Maddie knew her murderer. They cannot materialise and disappear. Start again.' He paused. His words hung in the air like a heavy grey blanket. 'Trace her movements, look at anyone she knew, go back through her life. She had friends from school that she kept in touch with. Check out whether we missed someone from the old days. I want a list of people close to her, then find their alibis. We can work out a motive later.'

Josh nodded in acknowledgement as no words formed on his lips. With reluctance, he forced himself to admit that it was a reasonable approach. Perhaps they would get lucky and discover a breakthrough quickly.

'I shall lead the teams and will revisit the Eleanor Anderson case as Blackford does not need attacks on a defenceless woman. It's embarrassing for us, gives no peace for the victims and showers us with negative publicity. Ladies and gentlemen, I want results, especially from you, Josh.'

Why pick on him? His obsessive and fussy attitude was wearing Josh down. Didn't he realise that there were other important traits necessary to make an efficient policeman? Did he offer no encouragement or praise?

40

Tom ran his finger around the tight collar of his new shirt. This was an evening that he had attempted to avoid, but he'd run out of excuses and the Superintendent had insisted. Thankfully, with a small guest list, the event could be finished within half an hour. He hated presentations, particularly if he was in the limelight to receive an award.

Sandra had been full of enthusiasm for the event and had spent many afternoon's shopping for the right outfit. With his hand on Sandra's arm, they crossed the car park, with its rough concrete surface. Wearing new high heels to match the colour of the recently purchased turquoise dress, she tottered, but he had a firm grip to stop her falling. Pausing at the entrance, she surveyed Tom with a critical eye, then brushed a speck of dust from his shoulder and straightened his tie. 'This is an accolade for you, which you can remember into your retirement. What a pity Harry could not be here with his wife.'

Tom mulled over her words. Their son, Harry, was busy in London with his new job and family. To his mind it would have been unrealistic to expect him to travel the length of the country for a short presentation ceremony. He patted Sandra reassuringly on the arm, 'He will be complimentary when we meet. Let's allow him time and space to settle into his new life.'

Sandra leaned against him, 'You are right, Tom, but he would be so proud.'

He nodded his agreement as he opened the large double doors, 'Mind the step.'

Retirement remained at the back of his mind, despite having received many prompts from Sandra. Apprehension gripped him as he didn't want his wife to raise the topic with the Superintendent. Walking across the police station reception area, a constable approaching from the opposite direction grinned, 'Posh suit, Tom. It's a special night for you. Well done.'

Giving a slight nod, 'Thanks.'

On a midweek, early in the evening, the police station was quiet. A short distance along the corridor they reached the Superintendent's office. He waited at the door for them. 'Come in, Tom. The others have already arrived except for Sergeant Anderson.' Tom grinned as Josh would always be late, but he didn't mind. Glancing over his shoulder his lips curled with amusement as Josh marched swiftly along the corridor.

The Superintendent was in a relaxed mood as he enjoyed such social occasions. With a warm smile, 'Welcome, Sandra, it is a long time since we last met. You must be proud of your husband.'

'Yes, I am.' It's such a pleasure to return to the police station as I have so many happy memories of my time working here.'

Tom nodded to the assembled thirty people, who clapped enthusiastically as he entered the room. Most were police service colleagues, some of whom had retired. He appreciated their willingness to attend the presentation.

'Come this way,' he ushered them into the centre of the room making Tom grimace with embarrassment as all eyes would be focused on him. 'I will make the presentation, then it is the buffet. Don't worry Tom my award speech will be short,' his eyes twinkled with amusement. 'You have frequently reminded me that they are embarrassing.'

True to his word the presentation speech was short and Tom breathed a sigh of relief as the buffet started. Josh approached holding a glass of wine and shook hands. 'Congratulations, Tom. You deserve the award as you are a brave man.'

'Thanks, but I hope the evening will end soon.' Josh threw back his head and chuckled. Tom waved as Gemma entered the room. With a quick nudge in Josh's ribs and a mischievous wink, 'Join her and find an excuse to leave.'

Sandra whispered, 'Who is the smart woman in black trousers with a white blouse.'

Tom hid his face and opted against saying Superwoman or Miss Perfection. 'She is a Detective Sergeant who has joined Blackford police from London since you were last here.' Tom helped himself to another sausage roll.

'Will you introduce me? It's so interesting talking to new people. Quick, she's looking at her watch so might leave.'

Tom took a deep breath and stepped towards Sergeant Harris. With a small cough to attract her attention he introduced his wife. A slight smile came to Claire's face. An unusual occurrence as during working hours she was focused and her face rarely showed any emotion. To give

Claire a little background information, he explained, 'Sandra worked as a civilian in the police station and knows many officers and was keen to meet you.'

Sandra shook hands, 'It is good to become acquainted with new staff.' Tom received a fleeting glance, without a smile, from Claire. 'But don't let me delay you if you need to leave.'

Claire's shoulders relaxed, 'No, there is no urgency. I am renovating my cottage and need paint, but I will not manage to buy any tonight, otherwise I shall be late for my Pilates class.'

Tom groaned but changed it quickly to a cough. The single word sent a spasm of pain through his body. Pilates should never have been invented. Why would anyone want to twist and bend their body into positions it was not designed for? It would only result in more pain. He shuddered. His back ached at the mere thought of it.

For the sake of harmony, he would enter the spirit of the evening, but any form of keep fit activity and DIY remained his worst nightmares. But he couldn't bring himself to use Claire's first name as superwoman remained stuck in his mind. With wide eyed amazement he munched through the remains of his sausage roll before speaking. 'I didn't know you were keen on renovation and Pilates.' She gave him a look he didn't understand, but he persisted, as it would not be an evening to be awkward. 'What a coincidence as they are Sandra's greatest interests.'

He had never seen Claire's eyes open so wide as she smiled, an unheard of occurrence in the line of duty. Sandra grinned as she had found a kindred spirit. Claire's eyes moved to him. 'Do you enjoy both?'

Before he could reply, Sandra jumped in, 'No, he

doesn't believe Pilates will help his back.'

Claire grinned, 'But it will, Tom.'

He struggled with the change in her attitude.

Before he had a chance to reply, 'As for DIY, he is capable, but has no interest. He has a list of jobs for when he retires. I enjoy the design, paint and decorating and watch all the programmes on the tele.'

Claire's eyes were as bright as he had ever seen them. 'With my house, I struggle to complete what is required. Let's get another drink and you can tell me the problems you have with your house, Sandra.'

Tom chose a scotch egg in preference to a wine as no beer was available. Forcing a smile, he rejoined the ladies as Sandra explained, 'The lounge door needs rehanging as it is sticky and draughty.'

Claire took the smallest sip of wine, 'Can you wallpaper and paint?'

'Yes, that is easy.'

'Should we share expertise?'

Sandra frowned, 'What do you mean?'

Tom had guessed but didn't want to explain the obvious answer. 'If Tom doesn't like DIY, I could come and rehang your lounge door, then you could help me with the painting. I'd get a better deal as hanging a door is quicker than painting."

'What a great idea. Time isn't an issue to me.' Sandra giggled with enthusiasm.

Tom's mind raced. He needed clear thoughts as days and weeks of DIY loomed. Sandra would scowl at him if he made a negative comment. This evening he wanted to visit the Steak House, have a few beers and relax with his wife. The Black Forest Gateau sitting in the middle of the buffet table would tide him over until the late evening meal. He forced a smile, still eyeing the gateaux, 'It's interesting you both like Pilates.'

With Sandra, she needed no second introduction to talk about her favourite pastime. Claire jumped in first, which surprised him. 'I've not been able to find a good class. The one I attend is okay, but it tends to be rather repetitive and doesn't extend my capabilities.'

Sandra brightened, 'Look no further, my instructor is excellent as she is also a physiotherapist. The sessions are often hard and demanding but great fun.'

'Could you introduce me?'

'Yes, most willingly.'

He grinned and the women gave him a quizzical look. Taking his leave, he headed towards the buffet table. On the positive side if they indulged in their interest, then he could leave them to their enthusiasm and have a quiet time fishing or at the football.

41

Scott hadn't returned to his pod, but after seeing the screen and his low wages, I needed time before speaking with him. Unsure of my best way forward, I wandered through the terminal building, but my mind whirled with thoughts. I'd known him a long time as we had attended the same school although we were never close friends as he was older. In recent times, we'd met occasionally in town when out with friends.

Then about six months ago we had met up again at a party and had started dating. After two months our romance had blossomed and he moved into my flat. Life was perfect. He was so attentive and loving. But his attitude had changed in the last few weeks. Why is his salary so low? What to think? How does it fit together? Low salary, heavy gambling and the development of moods has caused him to distance himself from me. Only a short time ago, I expected him to propose and I would have accepted as I love him. What had changed?

I couldn't avoid him so would return and suggest a holiday when we could have a serious talk about our relationship. The heavy downpour forced me to take the long route to the admin block. Drifting through the ground floor section of the multi-storey car park, I passed Scott's car just as he entered the area. The low ceiling of the concrete structure increased the sense of drabness and cold, as the wind howled through. Pulling my jacket tighter, I hurried towards him with a smile on my face. On seeing me he halted and a grim expression covered his face.

Trying to sound cheery. 'Hi Scott, we need to talk.'

'There's no point, I've left you a message on your phone.'

'What message, it's been switched off.'

'I'm leaving you as I can't cope anymore.'

'Scott, don't speak like that.' I stood in front of him and waved my arms helplessly. 'Let's solve the problems together.'

'It's over.' His expression darkened and anger filled his eyes and edged his voice.

'Tell me why. What have I done wrong?' The shock of his words had swept through me and my breath tightened.

'For some unknown reason you've assumed we were drifting towards marriage and babies, that's not what I want, we had a good time, but it's finished.'

Two women sauntered into the car park, laughing and chatting. One of them called out, 'Bye, Scott.'

Waving his arm to acknowledge, he didn't look at them but remained staring at me through narrowed and hostile eyes. When the door opened again as more people entered the car park, he unceremoniously grabbed my arm, his fingers digging into my flesh and yanked me behind a large van which meant we were out of sight.

'Let go of me!' I tried to shove him away, but his powerful hands pinned my arms to my sides. I couldn't move as his eyes glinted and his grip tightened, 'That damn well hurts.' I shivered as a tremor of fright assailed me. His breath reeked of alcohol. Releasing me with an aggravated push, I staggered backwards. The sharp eyes never left my face and I became uneasy under his intense scrutiny. Spluttering as my throat tightened with tension, 'Has the gambling become out of hand?'

With eyes glaring, his face turned red and his nostrils flared. His hands which he had dropped to his side gradually rose and became fists. My heart thudded and fear clogged my throat as he was acting like a maniac and I was trapped in a concrete corner. His lip curled into a snarl, 'I want a good time and all you want to talk about are babies.' The anger cooled, but his fists remained clenched. 'I'm moving out of the flat.'

I gasped. This couldn't be happening; he didn't mean it. He loves me as I am the girl of his dreams. He's told me that ever since we began dating. 'No! No!' I gave a nervous laugh, 'We can sort this out.'

'No, we bloody can't as you're snooping on me. First the folder and when I returned to my desk, my computer should have shut down, but someone told me you were using it. You've been stealing my folders and now delving into my personal files on the computer. Get out of my life!' He raised his hand as though he intended to slap me so I cowered deeper into the corner. 'You're untrustworthy, you're a thief. I don't want you in my life.'

I slid down the wall and laid my head on my arms as tears flowed.

42

Sitting in the entrance hall of the terminal building, I gazed but nothing registered. Scott's outburst had been uncompromising, he'd acted like an aggressive animal. I'd smelled the alcohol on his breath. Had he been drunk? Where had he obtained alcohol during the day? His grip on my arms had hurt when he shoved me behind the van, but he'd never been violent before. Quite the opposite, he'd always been loving. The words had been hurtful, but were they caused by stress?

Sitting hunched on the bench, the problems between us must be my fault. My chin quivered and tears spilled unchecked down my cheeks. Had I supported him when he was under pressure? No, I hadn't helped. Why did I miss the obvious signs of stress? Would he make my job difficult? Yes. The anger on his face in the car park had been terrifying. He controlled the schedule and staff rota. Would he give me the rubbish work? He's never been vindictive in the past, but he's changed.

The time passed with agonizing slowness. I replayed the confrontation with Scott constantly. It didn't change. The anger and aggression had shocked me.

Lifting my arm, I gave a small wave as Josh strode

towards me. Dropping on to the seat, he wrapped his arm around me. 'What's happening to me, Josh? I've had an almighty argument with Scott and he's leaving me.'

Saying the words out loud became too much and I buried my face in his shoulder and wept. He held me for a long time, gently stroking my hair and didn't speak, but he didn't have to. I gulped, sniffed and then sat up. Clutching my handkerchief, I mopped up my tears. I shook my head in despair. Crying would not bring Scott back. 'I'm grounded which means a load of tests before I can fly again.'

'Bad news as you will want to take me shopping.' Despite the tears, I smiled. Since we'd been youngsters, he knew how to lighten my mood. 'We want the same thing, sis. To settle down.' With his arm still resting around my shoulder, his warm voice comforted and enveloped me.

'Do you have a current girlfriend, Josh?'

'No,' he pursed his lips and gave a slight shake of his head.

'Some don't like me being a policeman but with others, it's my time keeping. It's hopeless to plan arrangements, as I never seem to be able to keep them.' Josh's phone rang.

Giving him time and privacy, I took the gap in our conversation to visit a nearby cash machine. 'Damn.' Even the cash machine wouldn't cooperate. I stuffed my new debit card back in my bag and huffed in exasperation. Perhaps I'll try another teller machine later. By the time I returned, Josh had finished his call and had a mischievous grin plastered across his face. As I settled next to him, he caught hold of my hand and gave it a reassuring squeeze.

'I told you I'm not dating anyone. Lynette just called to ask me why I hadn't been in contact, but then added that I seemed the shy sort and needed prompting into action.'

I laughed as the twinkling eyes and amused expression flooded across his face. 'Will you see her again?' The first signs of lightness in my voice appeared.

'Yes and no.'

'Oh Josh, what's that mean?'

'She's a little flamboyant for my tastes but I like her.'

I laughed, 'She might bring you out of your shell. Go for it with her Josh, you deserve a good time.'

43

Josh shoved open the door to the Murder Incident Room. The few night-shift officers had slumped shoulders and gazed mindlessly at their screens. He crossed to the tables littered with papers and plonked the remains of his cold coffee among the debris. The wastepaper baskets were overflowing and the plastic cups used for teas and coffees were dotted throughout the room. Weariness enveloped him, but his day hadn't even started.

He'd settled Eleanor last night, but it had been a long evening. They had been out for a meal because she couldn't face their parents. When they'd returned home, they had talked into the early hours. Scott had changed recently and his behaviour had become erratic and unpredictable. At one time, Eleanor's relationship with him had seemed perfect. What had happened? Had he found someone else? That seemed the most obvious solution, but why hadn't he admitted it? Poor Eleanor. She will be distraught without him, especially as she'd expected him to propose.

Half of the incident room's lights were off. The blinds remained at a variety of rakish angles. There had been no breakthrough on Maddie's murder. Josh nodded to fellow officers but detected resigned looks. The cases would be escalated with new officers taking control. Josh would soon be sidelined and assigned to a mundane job not connected with the current investigations. His new boss would not be impressed. Even before he started his mind was drained and empty. No fresh ideas had surfaced. With a silent groan he slumped at the computer and stared at the blank screen.

'Wakey, wakey guys. Home time! Give the professionals a chance.' Gemma entered the room with a flourish and wave of her arm. She ignored the comments thrown at her, flicked on the lights and pulled up the blinds. Then armed with a black plastic bag she swept up plastic cups, the contents of wastepaper baskets and anything else in her wake. Her presence gave a breath of fresh air through the room. She smiled and winked, 'Nothing new, Sarge. Do you want to ask the boss about a reconstruction?'

Josh shook his head, 'He'd go berserk about the budget, and apart from the usual nutters, I can't see it would help because of the remote location.'

'We're not on shift for another half an hour, are you coming for breakfast?'

His stomach rumbled and he had a sudden urge to be in Gemma's company. Her smile was infectious and her enthusiasm always cheered him up, but he had little option and had to refuse. 'I'd love to, but I must check with the robbery team otherwise I'll be in trouble with the Chief.'

'Are we still on for our date tonight?'

'Definitely. I've booked the Italian restaurant in Market Square.'

'Perfect.'

Josh was in two minds about starting a relationship with a fellow officer, although he'd had a short romance with a woman from the Manchester crime team. That had caused no problems, even after they split. He would see how tonight's meal panned out. Gemma was pretty and he enjoyed her company. Perhaps dating a policewoman would solve the problems he faced with relationships. She would understand the strains of the job.

Eleanor had made a pertinent comment to him in the dead hours last night. Relationships only work if you try hard. The truth of the comment kept coming back to him. Even in her distressed state she would try again with Scott. Josh stayed quiet as he remained undecided about her decision. Scott's behavior indicated another woman, but he had not voiced his thoughts.

With slumped shoulders, Josh drifted along the empty corridor to the incident room coordinating the robbery at the shopping mall. It had a feeling of deja vu about it. Tom hunched over a computer screen and peered at the flickering images with complete concentration. Josh pulled up a chair next to him, 'How's it going?'

'Not well,' Tom grunted and rolled his shoulders.

'Hey, that's me!' He gestured with a flick of his head towards the video that Tom studied.

'It's endless trawling through the videos, so I have been taking a fresh perspective rather than hours on the same camera.'

'Okay, so what are you doing?'

'This is a map of the camera locations at the shopping centre.' He pointed to a document spread out on the desk next to his keyboard. 'There you are and I'm tracing you through the centre onto this camera.'

Josh acted the fool on the video. 'That's where Eleanor told me the reason for the visit to the shops.' Tom smiled but concentrated on his task. 'We had already met Maddie and Lynette.' Josh studied himself, wandering through the centre with Eleanor.

'Yes,' Tom nodded, 'I've already tracked you after that meeting.'

'We should have recognised her when we found her body.' Josh squirmed with humiliation.

'I don't think we'll ever live that one down.' Tom returned his attention to the screen, 'I've been through this once with you and Eleanor. After the smoke, I lost you until you reappeared outside looking for her.'

'This is a good idea, Tom. Let's trace Lynette.'

'After leaving you she went out the far door to the bus stop and caught a bus headed towards the canal.'

'What about Maddie? It might give us a clue if she met anyone else after leaving Eleanor and me.'

Tom worked the keyboard, 'This picture is when you're chatting to Maddie and Lynette.' He grinned, 'You seemed to like Lynette.'

'How embarrassing, skip that bit.'

'Maddie's looking around,' Tom pointed towards her on the screen. Josh narrowed his eyes as he studied the jerky pictures. 'Did Maddie say she was expecting someone?'

'No, she didn't mention anyone, although she appears jittery.' Maddie moved from one foot to the other, glanced around and checked her watch. Josh hadn't noticed her agitation when they met, as he had been busy chatting to Lynette. He smiled at the memory.

'Perhaps she's meeting her boyfriend?' suggested Tom.

'I thought he'd gone to London, but she doesn't look

settled. Nor does Lynette. When I've met her since, she's calmness personified, but she isn't settled in these pictures.' They turned their attention back to the screen and focused on Maddie.

'There she goes out the door near the loos and the kiddies' area. The camera at the far end of the car park has picked her up.'

'When we were chatting, she told Eleanor she'd travelled on the bus.'

'Interesting,' Tom's expression stalled and grew serious.

'Why?'

'If she's going home, then she's headed for the wrong bus stop.'

'Is she? I never use a bus.'

'It's the wrong direction. The 52, which would take her home, goes from the front of the centre.'

'Move on to the next camera. Is that her, it's hard to tell because of the shadows. I can't decide if it is Maddie. Perhaps she's looking for someone. No, wait. This could be the lead we wanted. Stay on that camera, Tom.'

Tom nodded and moved the video recording forward, 'She's moving past the bikes and heading for the centre again. If it is Maddie, she didn't leave the car park. That's the kiddies' area. She has passed by and entered the loos. When does she come out?'

Tom scrolled through photos from several cameras.

'How long is this before the attack?'

'About ten minutes. We've checked the cameras nearest to the loos, umpteen times. I'll check the log. Someone must have spotted Maddie coming out again.'

'Five minutes later. This is the frame.'

Josh leaned closer to the screen, 'It's blurred but something isn't right.'

'What isn't?'

'Blow up that picture and look at her wrist. The woman is wearing a large bracelet.'

Tom flicked back to previous pictures, 'Maddie isn't wearing a bracelet.' He leaned back in his chair and shook his head. 'We missed it. Maddie moved past the bikes then went into the toilets but never re-appeared.' 'We need to revisit the footage of Maddie again.'

44

Josh rubbed his face to refocus his concentration. A video technical guy who'd been drafted into the team was scrolling through the recorded images. Five studied the relevant footage repeatedly. An officer leaned back, 'That's two hours and there's no more film.'

The technical guy swivelled to face them, his eyes alive with anticipation, 'I've a match!'

The constable on Josh's left punched his arm in the air in a gesture of triumph, 'Well done Tom, you old goat. You're a bone idle sod most of the time, but you suddenly find inspiration. It's the breakthrough.'

Maddie had been a robber at the shopping centre. Josh texted the Chief who stormed into the room, 'What breakthrough?'

'Maddie checked on the bikes, then changed for the raid. Jack, our technical star, has matched the shape of Maddie to one of the raiders dressed in black. It had been the only clear picture because they continually dropped smoke capsules to obscure the view of the cameras.'

The Chief frowned, 'Trace the remainder of the gang on the same cameras?'

'There's a corridor entrance out of the range of the

cameras. Maddie had been the lookout, so she checked nothing had occurred to prevent the raid starting.'

The Chief nodded, 'Combine the two incident rooms. We've a motive. I want checks on who she spoke to. Do we have pictures of who delivered the escape motorbikes?'

'No, sir.'

'Why hasn't it been checked. You're experienced policemen, do I have to keep reminding you what to do.'

Tom sighed, 'The entrances have been checked so the four bikes must have entered the car park the wrong way past the exit gate. When we received the call, I knew I could drive in the exit. That's what the bikes did.'

The Chief frowned, 'Any info on the bike that wouldn't start?'

Tom shook his head, 'False plates. The bike was built from standard parts, easily available and untraceable. There were odd fingerprints, but nothing the police computer recognised. It had been wiped down. It had traces of straw, so we've guessed it had been hidden in a barn.'

The Chief straightened up and rubbed his back from bending over watching the video footage, 'Josh bring in Maddie's boyfriend and his sister. Claire can interview Jason. Josh, you start with Lynette.'

The Chief Inspector leant close to Josh and Tom, 'I can't believe you didn't find this earlier. You fouled up on the recognition of her body. Now this. You've let me and the station down.' The hostile tone was clear, Josh bit his lip to stop the words which bubbled up. It was so unfair as he wanted to highlight Tom's inspiration. 'Your only hope is that it doesn't go any higher in the management. Now get on with the investigation.'

Josh struggled to remain silent. What an arrogant

man. Pressing his lips firmly together he looked away as he wanted to argue their case, but it would only make matters worse. As the Chief left Josh issued a huge groan and banged his fist on the table in frustration. It didn't help, but it relieved some of his aggression.

Tom grinned at him.

45

This is my first time in the shopping centre since the raid. My stomach is churning, but I'm prepared to face the past. Should I have agreed to meet Brendon? Hopefully, it will be a quick chat over a sandwich and then I can leave him to his world travels. We're meeting under the main clock, I shivered, it's close to the place where I bumped into Maddie.

There he is. Brendon became popular with the girls at school and I can see why. He's in smarter clothes today, grey trousers with a light blue shirt and black shoes, all of which suited his slim figure. As I approached him, he smiled and gave me a hug and kissed me on the cheek. 'Are you sure you're happy to be here after your experience? All that smoke must have been terrifying. Silly of me but I didn't think when I texted the location.'

'Yes, no problem, I've settled, although I had been a little concerned when I arrived.'

'Where would you like to eat? The centre has a charming Sushi bar.'

'That would be good, I often have sushi for lunch.'

Strolling through the mall, my nervousness lifted as I sauntered among other shoppers pursuing their normal tasks. 'I'm lucky to have bumped into you as I can obtain inside information for my holiday and have lunch with a beautiful woman.'

The charming man trying to put me at ease, but I'd prefer him to do the talking until I've settled. The knot of anxiety in my stomach is easing. Smiling, I tried to relax. 'Why the change from teaching? As far as I remember you were popular and successful.'

'Flattery will get you everywhere,' he chuckled as his hand brushed over the back of mine. 'The first year out of college became a disaster as I couldn't control my classes. That's when I taught your class. Don't you remember the chaos of the lessons.'

I laughed, 'They were noisy.'

'It was lucky that many like you wanted to learn, I'm eternally grateful to you as you were a star pupil.'

Flushing with embarrassment, 'Don't be silly.'

'But it's true, you don't realise what it's like to face a mass of pupils each day, some of whom are willing you to fail.'

'Some of my classmates enjoyed upsetting teachers.'

We strolled past several shoppers carrying heavy bags. Rays of sunshine came through the glass roof and lit the mall as we strolled to the far end.

'Only a few wanted me to succeed. That's why you were so good as you never stopped doing your best.'

Because of my tension I'd resolved not to mention Maddie as we'd talked about her at the hairdressers. If possible, I wanted the lunch to stay away from difficult topics. Why my resolution evaporated, I couldn't be sure. 'How did Maddie perform in class?'

A dour flicker crossed his expression, but he quickly

smiled again. 'Maddie and her friends Sean and Danny were the in-between types.'

'What's that mean?'

'Picture the scene from my perspective. The renegades in class, including Patrick, wanted to wind up the teachers. In contrast, you worked hard regardless of the surrounding chaos. Maddie and her friends would try when under scrutiny, but once I was distracted, they would chat and forget all about the work they were supposed to be completing.'

It hadn't been a good idea to bring Maddie into the conversation. My shoulders were tense and the knot in my stomach had returned. In silence, we sat at the sushi bar watching the food pass on the conveyor belt. With extreme concentration I focused my attention on choosing as the dishes went past. Brendon picked up the hint and focused on selecting his food. It allowed the silence to linger without embarrassment.

I chose Tempura, as the fried vegetables in crunchy batter were my favourite, plus some Tiger rolls and shellfish. The fresh pickled ginger was also a must as it helped to clear the palate between the different tastes. Having made our decisions, we settled with our choice of food.

Changing the topic became a necessity. I pushed the attacks to the back of my mind and nibbled a tempura, savouring the spicy flavor. 'Where are you travelling to on your trips abroad?'

'I thought about South-East Asia, have you been there?'

'Yes, I'm trained for several Indian airports and I'm on the Bangalore route. It's where the airline is opening another office, I love the city.'

Nodding in approval, 'India will be my first choice.'

'You won't be disappointed.' I'd had memorable nights with Scott in Bangalore. Sadness engulfed me and I blocked out the thoughts and focused on the present.

'Perhaps if we kept in contact, we could meet if you are there when I start my travels.' I couldn't think of a reason to refuse and it might be fun as I'd enjoyed his company, so I nodded in approval. As we left the sushi bar, 'Have the police updated you on the raid?'

The question surprised me. 'It's of no interest to me as it's over. The smoke was terrible and it took me days to remove the taste and smell.'

'Someone told me that your brother is a policeman.'

'Yes, but he doesn't talk about his work.'

'What about dinner next week?'

Apart from the mention of the raid, he'd been good company. He kissed me on the cheek and we hugged. Close up, he's a handsome man. So, I nodded my agreement.

46

Tom took a deep breath and brushed the crumbs from the morning toast off his uniform and knocked on the Superintendent's door. 'Come in,' called the distant voice. The Superintendent sat behind his mahogany desk which was meticulously organised as usual. The soft carpet under Tom's boots was a noticeable contrast to the rest of the police station where plastic tiles prevailed. Tom moved smartly and stood to attention in front of the desk. The Superintendent stood up, opening his hand, 'Let's sit in the comfortable chairs by the coffee table. It will be good to relax as I want a chat with you.'

Tom hadn't been pleased to receive the request for the meeting, and a shiver ran through him. The invite indicated the meeting would review the hospital report. A catering assistant knocked and entered with a tray of coffee and biscuits.

'Sit yourself down, Tom. It's time we had a long chat.'

Tom took a biscuit and placed the coffee which had been poured within easy reach. He would avoid groaning as he stretched for the cup. 'Sir, may I presume you have received the report from the hospital.'

'Yes. That's one matter I wanted to talk to you about.'

He took a sip of his coffee. 'Don't look so worried. It's only a chat about the future.'

'So, it's not only the medical report?' Tom feared the worse and the conclusion would be a forced retirement.

'Rumours drift up through the ranks, but I prefer to understand myself. I'll be direct. Are you thinking of retiring?'

'No, sir.' Tom blurted it out.

'You're adamant.'

'I enjoy the work and see no reason to pack up unless I'm forced to.'

'It is a long time since I worked on the front line. It means that I'm away from direct action, whereas you are not. I examined the report of your actions at the shopping centre and assisting the young woman away from the armed attacker.'

Tom managed a wry smile, 'Reports exaggerate and blow incidents out of proportion. You would have taken the same approach.'

'Please don't think I'm criticising. You're a brave man but it's my job as the senior officer to have a duty of care to my staff, which is why I sent you for a full medical.'

'May I know the contents of the medical report?'

The Superintendent laughed. Tom wasn't sure why he was amused, but he waited, 'It's virtually the same as mine. We suffer with bad backs and are overweight, but apart from those minor issues we are good for our ages.'

'I don't want to retire, sir.'

'Then my advice is don't.' The Superintendent nodded with satisfaction.

Tom paused while he digested the information. 'Then I will not retire.'

'Your back does not stop you being a policeman. So, carry on doing what you do best.'

As he closed the door behind him his mind drifted, Sandra wouldn't be pleased. The DIY wouldn't be done. An even bigger grin creased his face. He hated DIY because it made his back ache even more. However, he knew someone who would be pleased. If the opportunity arose, he'd treat Josh to a cup of tea and a bun in the canteen.

47

Josh tensed as he stood outside the interview room, he'd been dreading the encounter but he had no option. The Chief had been clear with his orders. Taking a deep breath, he opened the door. Lynette twisted from her position on the chair by the table. 'What's this about, Josh?'

Holding up his hand, he smiled as best he could, then switched on the recording machine as he sat opposite to her. Lynette shuffled in her seat and pulled her jacket tighter as she stared at the machine and wrung her fingers together. In a neutral and unhurried tone, he completed the formalities. Now the difficult task. How to extract the information he needed from her. She must have known about Maddie's activities as they were close friends. Could Lynette be an accomplice? Did she want a date to discover progress on the investigations? A warning voice in his head told him he shouldn't jump to conclusions.

Her tense face had tears, 'Josh?'

If she had knowledge of the raid or Maddie's activities, then she was a clever actress. 'Thanks for coming in.'

'Oh Josh, what's happening? I had no choice as I've been arrested and cautioned.'

'Standard procedure given the circumstances.'

Fidgeting on the chair, she tucked a lock of hair behind her ear and raised her tear-stained face towards him. 'Is it Jason? Because he's gone again.'

He nodded, 'We're trying to trace him.'

'Is it about Maddie?'

Josh broke the rule of the interview. He nodded and did not voice his answer out loud.

'Where did you go after you left the shopping centre?' Her eyes caught his and he became confused. Excitement and interest shone in her face. The smallest of smiles crossed her lips. 'I must ask you questions, it's what my boss ordered.' The statement seemed lame even to him.

'That's okay with me, I've done nothing wrong. Let me think, I caught a bus to the canal and visited the parade of shops next to the mill. Then I picked up clothes from the dry cleaners.'

'Why didn't you use the one in the shopping centre?'

'Oh God,' she smiled, 'this will be a tedious morning if we continue to discuss my washing and cleaning habits.' Her earlier tension drained away. 'I work in the mill, so I use the local shops at lunchtime, but I wanted to wear the top that evening. After the cleaners, I bought this vest in the shop next door. Do you like it?'

Josh's eyes strayed to the vest and her cleavage, which showed from the low scooping neckline. Forcing himself to concentrate he dragged his eyes away. 'Was anyone with you or did you meet someone you knew?'

'No.' She paused, 'I won't ask what this is about. Can I look in my bag? It's already been searched.'

'As you were arrested, you would be searched for weapons.'

'Are we on television? Is this a joke?' The smile had

gone from her face. Josh nodded to show she could open her bag. 'That's the cleaning bill and the receipt for the vest.'

'Let me check them.' Josh breathed a sigh of relief and left. He entered the Incident Room. 'Tom can you check these receipts. My guess is they will place Lynette in the clear.'

He drifted back to the interview room. The boss expected results. But he struggled to start. Settling opposite her, 'We need your help, Lynette.'

'I said I would help. Nothing's changed. I don't know where my brother's gone, so I can't inform on him.'

'Do you get on well?'

'Yes, fine, but we talk about mundane matters. The news, football and Maddie.'

'Does he like motorbikes?'

She raised her eyebrows at the question, 'Yes, mad about them.'

'Does he have one?'

'Only an old one in the garage gathering dust. If you search his record, you'll find he's banned from driving.'

Tom entered and whispered, 'She bought the vest at the time of the raid.'

Josh gulped, 'What did you do after the shopping?'

'I walked home along the track in the ravine. Do you know it?'

Yes.' Her large eyes focused on Josh. 'When did you last see Maddie?'

'At the shopping centre. I left her there, then caught the bus to the shops near the canal and afterwards returned home. At the shopping centre she mentioned she would be away visiting at the weekend.'

'Where was she headed?'

'She didn't say. Perhaps to see Danny and Sean, but that's only a guess.' Tears welled in her eyes. 'It's only now that you've asked that I've realised it was the last time we met.' She dabbed a tissue to her eyes.

'I'm sorry to tell you but we believe that Maddie was involved in the raid at the shopping centre.'

'Don't be so ridiculous.' She leaned back in her chair and wiped a hand over her face. 'I don't believe it.' Lynette stared at me. 'I understand why you've arrested me if you believe Maddie was involved.'

'With Maddie, there's little doubt, so it changes our approach to catching the killer.'

'I find it so hard to believe Maddie would be a member of the robbery gang so I shall assume that you've made a mistake. Jason hasn't been involved with the recent crimes in Blackford.'

'How do you know?'

'You've a sister, I met her, you understand each other. You could spot a lie from her.'

'Yes, that's true.'

'I asked him straight. Had he been involved in the raid? He said no. He doesn't lie to me. I didn't need to ask him about Maddie as he would never harm her.'

48

I'm dreading this morning, but I checked my appearance in the hall mirror. Yes, I seem okay, but my insides churned. I took a shuddering breath and willed myself to be calm. Forcing a smile on my face, I focused my attention on dad, who hovered at my elbow with concern written across his face.

'Eleanor, do you want me to accompany you this morning, you'll need support.'

'No dad, Josh will be there.'

'But he'll be busy.'

'Can I ring if I need a lift home?' Dad nodded.

Settling ourselves in the car, we'd agreed he would drop me near to the destination. The journey only took five minutes. I gave him a reassuring wave as he drove away, although inside my nervousness increased.

After he'd left me at the top of the road, with slow steady steps I began the descent and concentrated on moving with a confidence I didn't possess. The church stood out from the rows of terraced housing. The grimy, blackened tall steeple dominated the landscape as it rose over the town centre of Blackford which contrasted to the hills in the distance, sharp in the morning sunshine. It would be a difficult occasion. People I hadn't seen for years would drag back memories. Any funeral would be gruelling but knowing the person had been murdered was a step beyond my comprehension.

Trying to settle my nerves, I concentrated on the scene at the bottom of the hill. A crowd milled around the church. The mourners wore black or dark clothing, but they were intermixed with the bright yellow, fluorescent jackets of the police. I smoothed down my black trousers and picked lint from the matching jacket. Maddie had been murdered and was a gang member in a building society raid.

Josh had given me the information as he expected the rumour to be circulating at the funeral. I arrived on the periphery of the crowd. A large arm from a yellow jacket rose into the air and waved. Tom Collins had spotted me and beckoned. 'Mind your backs, lady coming through.'

'Are you related to the deceased?' asked a scruffy middle-aged man clutching a notebook. I didn't reply. Words were beyond me as my throat was tight and my mouth dry. Tom stood behind the lychgate which he guarded with the help of another officer. After speaking briefly into his radio, Josh strode from a group of police cars nearby. The sizeable crowd made my stomach turn.

'I didn't know whether you would come,' Josh caught my hand.

'I wanted to attend but after what you told me last night, I had second thoughts, but I liked Maddie. It's inconceivable to me she was involved in criminal activities.'

Josh guided me through many people in black. Brendon hovered outside the church and gave a small flap of his hand to attract my attention. As I reached him, he stepped forward and gave me a peck on the cheek. Josh caught my eye and I nodded as being with Brendon would be the support I needed as he understood the circumstances of the funeral. Walking side by side we approached the church door. Joining the long line of people waiting to enter, we paused, and he leaned close to me, his breath warm on my neck. With a gentle grip on my arm he whispered, 'The last time I spoke with Maddie she worked at the Bondi Club, I'm afraid her boyfriend led her down the path of crime.'

'Yes, that's what must have happened.' I shook my head, hoping to deter him from continuing this line of conversation.

'Shall we go in?' He nodded and offered his arm. Brendon had appointed himself as my escort. Two men directed those attending the service to the pews. I recognised them even though it had been many years since we'd met.

The sombre organ music resonated through the church reinforcing the gravity of the occasion. A broad shaft of light from the stained glass lit the chancel. Dust floated in the air and a musty smell mixed with the strong fragrance of the lilies that lined the aisle. I gave a gentle smile as I didn't know whether they would recognise me.

Danny dealt with the person in front of me and then turned and opened his arms, 'Darling, Ellie.' Hugging me, he kissed me on both cheeks. A hot flush of embarrassment ran through me. 'It's good to see you again but in such tragic circumstances.'

After the embrace from Danny, I received the same from Sean. After exchanging hugs, 'You're looking well, Ellie.' I didn't have the heart to tell them I preferred Eleanor.

Although my mind went blank, I had to speak, 'Had you seen much of Maddie since school?' Although I knew the answer.

'Yes, we'd kept in touch on a regular basis until recently. At one time we were trying to join your airline, but they rejected us.'

I didn't reply. What could I say?

'When she left, we tried to persuade her to join the hotel chain where we worked, but she took a job in a dodgy club and I'm afraid it led to her downfall.'

'Why did she work there?'

'Don't you remember from school that Maddie could not manage her money. It slipped through her fingers like water.' He emphasised money with a resolution that he expected me to understand, but I couldn't remember Maddie and her wasteful ways. 'We can't talk now Ellie, so why not visit Blackpool then we could take you to lunch and reminisce?'

49

Tom sat in the front passenger seat of the police minibus and adjusted the small camera on his shoulder. The other officers chatted and laughed about the football matches earlier in the day. A riot grill covered the windscreen of the bus. They wore black coverall uniforms. Most had helmets on their laps.

Although the raid should be straightforward, a frisson of tension pervaded the bus. The heavily overcast sky with drizzle made it easier as most revellers would remain inside, so there would be less chance of the club noticing the police presence.

Raids had never been Tom's preferred method. He favoured a quiet, non-threatening approach as it seemed to produce better results. Raids made people less cooperative, but it hadn't been his decision.

The uniformed Sergeant leading the officers sat in the back receiving a ribbing about his team's poor performance in an earlier football match. A silence descended as the Sergeant's radio crackled. Two officers on the street were observing the club and radioing updates. 'We're nearly there. They've closed the doors to the club for the night. Remember the briefing. All names and addresses as we need to check the backgrounds. Backup is on its way if we need multiple arrests. Let's go.'

Silence fell as the officers donned their helmets. The minibus crept along the High Street, then past the shopping centre and along the road towards the nineteenth-century industrial area. The prime of the town's Victorian businesses had long gone. The buildings were derelict or had been disfigured by multiple short-term use. It had become a popular spot for night clubs. With no neighbours, noise didn't become a concern.

The minibus crawled along a narrow cobbled lane at the back of the buildings. As it stopped three officers and the Sergeant slipped out. They would sweep up anyone loitering outside the club, which was sited in a former boiler house of a factory. Surrounded by other buildings, it became easy for the police to approach without being seen. Tom sat in the passenger seat at the front for these raids. The youthful exuberance of his fellow officers would form the initial thrust to gain entry and deal with any resistance.

Tom left the minibus and followed his colleagues into the club. Maddie had been a barmaid here. The deafening music from the dancing area drowned out the shouts of surprise. His value in a raid would be to spot known faces and decide who needed further attention. A sweet smell pervaded the atmosphere along with the cigarette smoke. The fine would be issued as smoking wasn't permitted, but it was a minor misdemeanor compared to the real reason for their visit. The music faded as the first officer reached the dais with the DJ. A megaphone filled the room, 'Police! Stay where you are and keep your hands out of your pockets.'

The drunks would argue. Most would stay quiet, hide

incriminating evidence and give a false name. Tom spotted his prey and raised the visor on his helmet. The majority had become subdued, indicating an increased chance for a smooth operation.

'Good evening, Arthur.'

'Bloody hell. You hassle me at work and now I can't drink in peace.'

'With your sons, Mark and John.' Tom nodded towards the other two men.

'Piss off, copper.'

Tom had never risen to such simple attempts to wind him up. They amused him.

A man on the periphery of the Mercer family, caught his attention trying to slip along the bar away from him. 'Not so fast, laddie. You've forgotten your drink.'

The megaphone had stopped. The atmosphere had become hostile but settled.

Arthur pointed at the police officers, 'One of these scum will recognise you, Jason. Don't get nicked for something daft.'

The man scowled, but after Arthur's words, stood still.

Tom faced him, 'Jason Fredericks, I presume.'

Tom received the usual response, 'Piss off.'

The Sergeant in charge of the raid crossed to check with Tom about information gathered. 'Constable. You seem to know these men.'

'Yes. Let me introduce you.' The men scowled, but by then they were surrounded by Tom's larger colleagues. 'This is Arthur Mercer who has a conviction for armed robbery. He owns the large demolition company on the edge of town.' A small smile creased the lips of the Sergeant. 'These are Mark and John Mercer, sons of Arthur, who also have a conviction for armed robbery.' Tom added in an aside voice, 'Mark acted as the getaway driver on a raid many years ago. Now tell me, Mark, how are your motorbikes these days?'

Tom faced the Sergeant. 'He's good enough on his bike to have won races at Silverstone.'

The Mercer sons glanced at their father, who shook his head. They wouldn't speak until their solicitor had arrived. Tom added, 'Last but not least, this is Jason Fredericks. The Mercers claimed they hadn't seen Jason for ages. Jason has convictions for violence. He and Maddie had been dating for about a year.' The press release linking Maddie to the shopping centre raid had been issued earlier that day.

The Mercers taking their lead from their father stood motionless, but it was too much for Jason as he picked up his pint glass. He lurched forward and his hand containing the pint glass moved towards Tom, who had been expecting a reaction, so he stepped back. Jason finished face down on the beer stained floor. He yelped in pain as his arms were twisted up his back by Tom's colleagues.

Arthur sneered at Jason as he was dragged away. A smile crossed his face, 'I didn't know I would commit an offence by having a drink in a private club with members of my family and a few friends.'

'You haven't. It's been good to meet you again, Arthur. Quite like old times.'

Arthur held up his hand to stop his sons saying anything untoward.

Tom left his fellow officers to deal with Jason and scanned the room. Many members spoken to by officers had now elected to leave. Tom breathed a sigh of relief. At least there had been no trouble and they'd found Jason. Tom went through a door marked Private. A man he recognised sat behind the desk. Tom nodded to another officer, 'I'll deal with him.'

'You're welcome to him. Rude bastard. Do you want me to stay?'

Tom shook his head, 'Trevor and I know each other well, don't we?'

Sweat beaded on Trevor's forehead. His mouth was set in a hard line. He sneered. 'I guessed you'd be here. What's all this about? There's nothing wrong with this club.'

'Smoking is not allowed.'

'You lot don't arrive mob handed to deal with a smoking problem.'

Tom glanced at the desk, 'You've been given the search warrant.'

'Yes, not that it makes any difference. There's nothing to interest you in this club.'

'I want to ask you a few questions.'

He leaned back in his chair, gave a condescending smile and a dismissive wave of his hand. 'I wouldn't bother, we've been here before. You know I won't say a word about the members.'

'Frightened of them, are you?'

'Huh, bloody common sense. They cause me no problem so why frighten them away by being known as a grass.'

Tom had interviewed Trevor many times before. He wouldn't reveal the time from his watch, let alone any information. 'It not about your customers, it's one of your staff.'

'I suppose you mean Maddie.' His voice was brusque.

'How long had she worked here? What was she like?'

His eyes glazed as though searching for any answer. He stared at Tom, then screwed up his face, giving the impression he was thinking through a difficult decision. 'She'd worked behind the bar for about a year.'

'That's a long time, your staff usually have a quick turnover.'

He ignored the barb, 'Regulars liked her.'

'Rumour is she earned plenty of money here.'

'I know how your mind works, copper. She worked a lot of hours. Her boyfriend is a regular.'

'Did she visit when she wasn't working.' Trevor picked up the search warrant and read it. 'Her boyfriend was a regular and she liked the slot machine room.'

'Does Lynette Fredericks work for you?'

'Sometimes.'

'Not permanent?'

'No, part time. Always wanted a shift with Maddie.'

'Didn't they chat all the time?'

'No, both were good workers.'

'Did Lynette work part time because of her other job?'

'No idea. Ask her, not me. You've used up all your questions.' He slapped his hand down on the desk. 'That's it. Now get lost.'

50

I waited to hear from Scott and checked my phone at every available opportunity. Would he change his mind about leaving me? Sitting at the dressing table in my bedroom, I brushed my hair while listening to mum and dad chatting downstairs in the kitchen. Scott will make contact when he's ready and although he's let me down, I still want to hear from him.

Staring at my reflection in the mirror, my skin was pale and there were dark shadows surrounding my eyes, I gave up on my hair. Tapping an irritable rhythm on the wooden surface, I needed to apply make-up. Staring at my phone, I willed it to ring or indicate an incoming message but it remained silent. I grabbed it to check I had no missed messages, but he hadn't contacted me. A text had arrived from Jackie, my next door neighbour, asking me to ring.

'Hi Jackie, it's Eleanor, it's unusual to receive a text from you.'

'I wasn't sure what to do.'

'Why? What's happened.'

'Last evening, I noticed the front door of your flat was open, I checked, but Scott wasn't there?'

'Oh, I'm staying at my parents for a few days.'

'I knocked assuming one of you had left it ajar but I received no answer, so I went in.'

'Is the flat okay?' I became worried we'd had a break-in.

'Yes, I think so.'

'Jackie, what's that mean?' I'd snapped but regretted it. 'Sorry didn't mean to snap, but I'm worried.'

'I kept calling out but found the lounge in a mess. Darren helped me check it out. It was untidy, but we couldn't see any damage.'

'So, had there been a break-in?'

'I didn't want to snoop, but your flat is always tidy. Both wardrobe doors were wide open and one was empty so I assumed Scott had removed his clothes.'

'What had happened in the lounge?' There was a faint tremor in my voice and my hands shook.

'Papers were everywhere as though someone had searched the room.'

'Had anything been taken?'

'I wouldn't say much had gone. Has Scott left you?'

'Yes, he told me yesterday that he intended moving out.'

'Well, he didn't do it carefully. Anyway, we locked the door as we left, so it is secure.'

Closing the call, tears coursed down my cheeks as I didn't think Scott would follow through with his threat to leave the flat. He loves me, so why is he behaving so uncharacteristically? No doubt he will contact me soon but must have had a breakdown. One day we'll look back on these events and laugh about it together. I love him, he's the right man for me, we have a future together. Anyway, it will soon blow over as it's a lovers' tiff. The time for action had arrived. Scott had left, hopefully only temporarily, but I needed to return to work.

If he wouldn't schedule me for good jobs, then I'd go to his boss. I'll pop into the airport first and explain to mum and dad later. As I reached my car, I remembered the folder I had intended inspecting when the attack came. The police told me they had replaced it in the car boot. The loss had riled Scott and caused an explosive argument. I opened the folder to reveal pages from the newspapers and various betting slips. How could he afford to bet such large amounts? I now knew how much he earned. What had he been up to?

Parking in the staff car park, I marched into the terminal area at Manchester Airport to take out cash. When I'd been with Josh the previous night, the teller machine wouldn't cooperate. I placed my card in the slot and pressed the button for cash. The message responded there was insufficient cash available for my withdrawal.

A wave of panic passed through me and my hands trembled while my heart hammered. Sitting on a bench seat, I logged on using my phone, but there was no money in my account. I stared at the screen in disbelief. My stomach tensed and a chill crept through my body. Yesterday afternoon, the entire contents of my current account had been removed.

The number of the recipient account I recognised as Scott's. Checking the timing, it had been after he'd accused me of looking at his private details when I sat at his desk. I took a deep breath and logged on to the deposit account. It had been emptied of several thousand pounds. He must have searched my bag or computer and found the details. Be calm and don't panic, I whispered to myself.

Should I inform the police and my company as he works for them as well? The company will take a dim view and blame me for being careless. Josh? No, he would be angry and would confront Scott. For a short time, I can live on my credit cards, but I'll ring the bank and open a new account for my salary.

I shoved my phone into my bag. My whole body shook and my legs had transformed into jelly as I scuttled towards the admin office. I steeled myself. If he was there, then I would confront him, but I had to choose the most appropriate method so no one else discovered our problems. No scenes, I kept repeating to myself.

Luck was on my side as I entered the main office area, 'Hi, Sheila, just the person I wanted to see.'

The large round lady with light blonde hair wearing a black flowing dress smiled, 'Hello, Eleanor. I know what this is about. Come through.' I followed her into her office and waited. 'Medical won't pass you but you want to be placed on the schedule expecting a return to work.'

'That's part of it.'

She dropped her weight into her chair behind the desk. 'As you cannot officially go on the schedule, you've come to me because Scott's gone.'

Gone; the single word resonated around my head as my eyes widened, 'What do you mean gone?'

Sheila hesitated and studied my face. Popping on the glasses lying on her desk, she intensified her stare. 'Are you still dating Scott?' I shook my head. 'Eleanor. What's happening? You were chatting to him yesterday in the office.'

I had no alternative, I had to tell her. 'Yesterday, he told me that it was over between us.' Pausing I strove to calm myself but struggled to keep the tears from my eyes.

I wouldn't tell her about the bank accounts.

Sheila's eyes never left me, 'Is it because he's leaving, you've split?'

I had missed something, my brain whirled trying to make the connection but it didn't succeed, 'Sheila, what do you mean? Where's he going?'

'Think back, Eleanor. Perhaps because of your unfortunate experiences, you've forgotten.'

Concentrating as I didn't want Sheila to doubt me. 'Oh, of course, I remember now.' It sounded false. 'He planned to visit Bangalore and open the new office. Is that where he's gone?'

'You're right, that's where he is, on a year's contract.'

My face gave me away. 'You didn't know, did you?'

'Not that he intended moving there. When?'

'Within the next few days.'

I left the office in a daze and plonked myself on a spare bench in the terminal. I remained motionless and stared at nothing. What had happened to me? My chin trembled and tears coursed their way down my cheeks. One minute life seemed perfect and now it was disintegrating. What had I done wrong? I flopped my head into my hands and wept.

51

Josh hadn't been invited to sit, so he guessed the Chief only wanted a quick word. At least it wouldn't be another telling off, although he expected one would come soon. 'Anything useful from the operation at the Bondi Club?' He gave Josh an interrogative look from under his bushy eyebrows. 'Nothing concrete.'

Josh kept his face impassive, 'But too many coincidences, so we're checking on the stories.'

'Tell me.' The Chief Inspector's tone was sharp, as he placed his fountain pen on his desk and raised his head.

Josh had his full attention. 'Arthur Mercer and his two sons were there, all of whom are convicted bank robbers, they appeared to be friends with Jason, Maddie's girlfriend.'

'Did we expect the Mercers to be drinking there?'

'No.' Josh shook his head for emphasis. 'We'd checked membership lists before, when asking questions about Maddie, but their names were not listed. The club will never say whether they know a person. Tom mentioned the club often accepts false names or no names if the bouncers recognise them.'

'What about Jason?' His eyes were cold and appraising and his lips tightened, 'We'd been searching for him.'

'When interviewed, he refused to reveal where he'd been.'

'What about the manager?'

'He's been arrested previously for obstructing police officers, by refusing to give information, but he won't say a word.'

The Chief shook his head, huffed out a long sigh, then picked up his pen and wrote a few notes. The silence stretched, broken by the scratching of the pen across the paper. Josh waited. What was coming next? At long last, the Chief stopped; pen poised.

'So, we have known bank robbers and the barmaid takes part in a raid on a building society.'

'One of Maddie's close friends from school is Danny Mercer, the nephew of Arthur. There are connections, but no evidence.'

'What do we know about Danny Mercer? Does he have a record?'

'No. He hasn't come to our attention before, he works at a hotel in Blackpool as a trainee manager.'

'Have we arrested anyone?' snapped the Chief Inspector.

'No sir. The Mercers gave no trouble at the club. Jason Fredericks lost his cool as usual, but his aggression came to nothing so we didn't charge him. Claire questioned him and then released him this morning. But his alibi for the time of the raid looks truthful. Claire has put a tail on him, but as far as we can tell he's returned home to sleep.'

He drummed his fingers on the desk top in an irritated manner, 'I'm changing the organisation of the investigation as we are not making the progress I would expect.' This didn't sound as it would be good news. 'We are combining the murder and robbery teams.'

'Yes, sir.'

'I'm the Senior Investigating Officer but the Superintendent wishes me to appoint a deputy who can assist with liaison to senior management, so I've already told Claire she will be in that role. Normally I would have expected to appoint you, as the more experienced officer in the police, but I haven't been impressed since you arrived. Let's hope it's because you are settling in.' He stared hard, but Josh didn't respond, 'Let's find evidence to arrest the Mercers, who Claire and I believe are at the heart of the crimes.'

Josh left the office. The role as his deputy should be his, but he couldn't fault the Chief for giving it to Claire. It would be an uphill battle for him in Blackford. Would his career in the police force always be so difficult? Nothing had gone according to plan since his unexpected promotion. Should he hand in his resignation? No, he wouldn't admit defeat. He was far too stubborn. Claire had become the Chief's favourite. Josh hadn't taken to her. Like the Chief, she didn't smile.

On the plus side, he didn't fancy her, otherwise working together would have been difficult and the Chief would never be impressed by a relationship between his officers. Claire didn't fancy him, that had been obvious from their first meeting.

Josh entered the Incident Room to find her. He wouldn't harbour a grudge. As she wasn't there, he plonked himself onto the chair next to Tom.

Glancing at Josh, 'A uniformed Sergeant has announced Claire is leading.'

'Yes, the Chief told me. Where is she?'

'Claire has liaised with the Chief and has started again. There's been a call from the building society, so she's gone there.'

'Do we know what it's about?'

'No, she didn't say. You should have been placed in charge as you've more experience than her.'

'Thanks for your support, but I've performed poorly since I arrived.'

The door burst open and Claire stood in the doorway with her hands on her hips, 'Listen up, full briefing in three minutes we have a breakthrough.'

Tom stood up, 'That gives me time to fetch a cup of tea.' He winked at Josh, 'White, no sugar?'

Josh nodded; Tom, an old stager, would not get excited by dramatic hype. He did nothing in a rush apart from the driving of a police car.

Claire remained near the door, her brown eyes glittering with excitement, but as usual there was no smile. Moving to the front of the room she clapped to gain attention and waited for the chatter, shuffling and scraping of chairs to stop before she spoke, 'After a visit this morning to the building society we have new evidence. A cashier who has been absent from work since the raid returned to her job and remembered a crucial fact.' Her voice sounded pompous. She enjoyed being in control.

'Before the raid, the cashier organised her money drawer and noticed a twenty pound note had the word Vanessa written across the top corner. The cashier placed the note at the bottom of the pile, intending to advise it should be withdrawn from public use.'

Josh guessed what Claire had found out.

He glanced at Tom, who had a quizzical expression on his face.

'We have checked the notes taken from Mercer Demolition and the twenty pound note with Vanessa written on it has been located.' She paused and her eyes scanned the room as she allowed the information to sink in. 'We will break into groups to effect the arrest of the Mercer family and Maddie's boyfriend, Jason Fredericks.' A constable read the team members she wanted involved.

Josh wasn't surprised that his name was not mentioned. As she came past, 'Do you want us, Claire?'

Her sharp eyes studied him and then flicked over to Tom, who was sitting next to him. She shook her head, 'No. There's enough in the team to bring everyone in. You can carry on with the background enquiries.' A small cold smile moved across her lips which served to highlight her disapproval of them. They'd been put in their place.

52

After the room cleared of the personnel included on Claire's list, Josh sipped his tea as he mulled over the proposed arrest of the Mercer family. For a long moment he stared at nothing while his mind raced through the evidence. Was Arthur Mercer the brains behind the building society raid? The thought niggled him, however the boss would be please as he would have an arrest.

'It doesn't seem right to me,' Tom pressed his lips together and gave an impatient huff. 'I returned the documents we confiscated during the last raid on the Mercer's premises. While the tax people would be interested, they also showed a successful business. So why would he risk his business by being involved in a raid? The figures showed him to be worth far more than the amount stolen.'

'Could he have spiralling debts?'

Tom rubbed his chin, 'He could, but I doubt it. This old town has large grants for regeneration. Whenever there is a king-sized contract it is awarded to the Mercers. They are the biggest and their signs are throughout the town on redevelopment sites. Everything points to a successful business.'

'Didn't Arthur give you a hint as to the origins of the

money?'

Tom sighed, 'I guessed that he'd struck a deal to knock down that listed building in the middle of the night. He was happy to go along with my suggestion. Perhaps I led him on and he perceived it as a way out.'

'So, where does that leave us?'

Tom touched his forehead in a mock salute, 'Not sitting in this room. I shall visit the man whose listed building has been knocked down. He's a bit of a dodgy dealer, but I'll try to find out his side. I could be wrong though.' He spread out his hands and shrugged, 'Sorry, if I led you down the wrong line.' Retrieving his jacket from the back of the chair, he whistled softly as he lumbered from the room.

Josh rejected a call from Lynette as his phone rang, but immediately a text arrived, Josh. Urgent. Must speak. About Jason.

If the Chief discovered he had dated a witness, he'd be in trouble again. But curiosity surfaced, and after an exchange of texts he set off to meet her. He strode through the wind and drizzle to Market Square. Why wouldn't she give him the information over the phone? Why be so mysterious? The team had left to arrest Jason. Perhaps she hoped Josh would plead on his behalf. For the first time he was apprehensive about meeting her. As he entered Market Square, she sat huddled in a bus shelter.

As soon as she spotted him, she rushed across and flung her arms around him, 'Jason is in danger. Please help him!' She grabbed hold of Josh's arms. Tears streamed down her face.

He eased her back and held her at arm's length, 'I assume he's been arrested. If he's with the police, he can't be in danger.'

With a confused look, she shook her head.

'Tell me what's happened?' He led her to a nearby bench. Lynette trembled and clutched his arm. Josh expected it would have been a heavy handed arrest. No one in the police would take a chance on him coming quietly. They would take him before he could resist. 'Has he been arrested?'

She struggled to speak. The crying had caused her to lose her breath and she gulped. 'No! no! He'd left about five minutes before the police came to the house.' Josh waited for her to explain. 'He'd had a call on the house phone.' Josh tried to piece together what had happened. She wasn't making sense. Why had she become so distressed?

'What call? Who from?'

'I don't know. As he finished the call he shouted out, I know. He grabbed his jacket and ran out of the house. Although I called after him, he wouldn't stop. It was only when I heard the motorbike start in the garage, I understood. He must have discovered who killed Maddie.'

She tightened the grip on his arm, 'You must stop him. He will kill the murderer.'

'Leave it to me, Lynette. I'll do my best. What's the reg number of his bike?'

'It's a track bike. No number.'

With a quick peck on the cheek and a reassuring smile, he strode away across Market Square. Once out of earshot, he flicked open his phone, 'Is it urgent, Josh?' Claire's high pitched voice resonated down the line as she answered.

He ignored the remark. 'Jason Fredericks believes he knows who killed Maddie and has left home to search for them.

He's riding a track bike.'

'Okay Josh.Leave it to me. I'll deal with it.' The line went dead.

53

Wandering around my bedroom, I couldn't settle. Mum and dad were visiting friends, which came as a relief as it would stop a further interrogation from them. Although I'd left messages for Scott, he hadn't responded, which disappointed me. Will I ever stop missing him?

I wanted to give him another chance especially as he needs help, but I'm certain the split isn't my fault and that he's having a mental breakdown. With a loud groan I slumped on my bed. The gambling must have overtaken him. If only I could speak with him, perhaps he would agree to counselling.

Shall I tell Josh and the police about Scott taking my money? The bank has changed my details, I'll put it down to a bad experience as I can't punish Scott, as I want to resolve the issues between us.

Moping around at home must change, as it wasn't helping my return to normality. Sitting at the dressing table I picked up the notes I'd been making. Tomorrow morning I'll tell mum and dad that I'm returning to my flat as I'm fully recovered.

It's the perfect opportunity to check the flat and to leave the pressures of Blackford behind. Josh will be cool with me returning to Manchester. After the funeral, Danny and Sean had been supportive and charming, but I'll give them a ring to tell them I shall not be able to visit them in Blackpool. I'll do it now. That's strange. Taken aback I rechecked, but the mobile number was unobtainable.

Perhaps I wrote it down incorrectly so I'll ring the hotel. 'Can I speak to Sean Prendergast or Danny Mercer, please?'

'I'll connect you.'

'Minesh, Hotel Manager speaking, I believe you are trying to contact Sean and Danny.'

'Yes.'

'I'm afraid they have left their jobs and I have no forwarding number.'

'Thank you,' I cut the call, surprised at their sudden decision. That's strange as they were so enthusiastic about staying with the hotel chain for the international travel.

Perhaps, I shouldn't have accepted Brendon's dinner invitation, but it will be the last time I see him, unless he comes to India, although the chances of us meeting there are slim. Brendon is a charming man so it will be a pleasant evening. I'm determined to relax and enjoy myself. If we steer clear of unpleasant topics like the raid and Maddie's murder it could be fun with lighthearted conversation. Then it is goodbye to Blackford.

My mind drifted to Scott who I would meet in the Bangalore office as soon as I returned to flying. Why hadn't he told me about the year's contract? Can we sort out our misunderstandings? I remained positive and the idea cheered me up, I smiled.

54

As the Chief and Claire were leading the robbery and murder, Josh expected to be moved to a different investigation. It had been a bad start to his new job in Blackford. For a change, he would ensure he had completed the paperwork. His reports needed to be watertight. At least if the paperwork was correct, the boss will moan less.

Josh checked his notebook. Damn! He'd missed one note. Instruction: Contact Maddie's old school. Josh remembered a comment from the Chief that the Friends of Blackford School were active in the local community and Maddie could have connections with them. He'd checked the name and address of the head teacher who had recently retired, and had written it in his notebook, but had never visited him.

It wasn't an encounter he relished, but he had no option. Josh would check his availability for a meeting. After a brief phone call, he left to meet the man who had caused him hassle in his youth. At school he'd always been in bother. Perhaps he wouldn't remember all his former pupils. Would he recognise Josh?

As Josh pulled up, so the front door opened and a short man with trimmed grey hair wearing black trousers and a white shirt came to meet him. Close to where his parents lived, the large double fronted bungalow in immaculate condition had an in and out gravel drive. Within minutes, he sat in a luxurious lounge with a cup of tea supplied by his wife.

'Thanks for agreeing to meet, Mr Johnson.' He showed no obvious signs of recognition. While he was relaxed in his armchair, his sharp eyes focused on Josh. The last time he'd seen him, he had been taking assembly at the school.

'How can I help you, Sergeant, your request to meet sounded urgent? I've returned from my round of golf, so you were lucky to contact me.'

'We are investigating the murder of Madeleine Taggert and we are tracing her contacts, friends and people she knew well.'

His brow furrowed. 'Your presence suggests that you have not yet made an arrest.'

'That's correct, sir, we are looking for background information that may yield clues or evidence of an opportunity or motive.'

'I understand.' His fingers drummed a staccato rhythm on the arm of the chair, 'What do you want from me?'

'Has she been part of the old pupils' network?'

'Not unless she'd joined since I retired about a year ago.'

'Perhaps you could suggest anyone who might know her well. For example, one of her former teachers.' He didn't look impressed and Josh couldn't blame him as he had asked about events fifteen years ago.

Mr Johnson's face implied Josh would be on the carpet for wasting his time. He didn't reply, so Josh added, 'Did you recognise Maddie's name from her school days?'

He regarded Josh in silence and his distinguished face had become brooding. 'You were a troublemaker at school.' The piercing eyes never left Josh's face, who shifted uncomfortably in his chair.

Josh gave a half smile, 'Not my best days.'

'You even became involved with the police, didn't you?' Josh nodded but made no comment while he waited. He didn't want to talk about when he'd been wild. 'Many who caused trouble in their youth turn out to be fine citizens,' but no smile followed this pronouncement. 'Is your sister, Eleanor, enjoying a successful career?'

'Yes sir, she's a pilot on long haul commercial airliners.'

'Yes. That would be right for her.' He took another sip of his tea. Had his former head teacher lost his concentration?

'Madeline, she brings back memories.' He suddenly sat up straight, 'You haven't time for my reminiscences as you need to crack on with your job and I'm in leisure mode, it's not good enough. I'll be succinct.

During Madeleine's time, she had connections with every dubious happening in the school and she caused me to sack a member of staff and to investigate with the Social Services, including the police, serious gambling and sexual related activities. Refer to her sixteenth year and you will find details in the police records.' He took a bite of cake and a sip of his tea. 'It will be more straightforward if you ask the questions.'

Josh nodded, 'Let's start with the gambling and sex, I want the names of people involved with her.'

'The two boys were Sean Prendergast and Danny Mercer. The three tried to set up a gambling ring using lunch money.'

Josh raised his eyebrows, 'What would they bet on?'

'Believe it or not, it started on school sports matches, but moved on to any activity or event.'

'May I assume you stamped it out?'

'It was far from easy, Sergeant. The pupils revelled in the gambling, which spread like an infection throughout the school. Madeline and her friends showed a great deal of ingenuity in avoiding sanctions.'

'Did Maddie lead the group and activities?'

'Yes, undoubtedly, at the beginning.' He paused and the corner of his mouth twisted in exasperation. 'Don't misunderstand me. A charming girl on the outside, but underneath a different character. It was essential to ensure those involved received counselling for gambling, but they either never attended, or it didn't break the habit.'

Josh jotted down a few notes. He summoned a smile. Tension gripped him as he once again faced his former Headmaster, 'You mentioned earlier that there were sexual activities.'

'Yes, although they were more difficult to prove, but it was my firm belief that the gambling led to low level prostitution which involved Maddie and others.'

'Could you elaborate?'

'The local college is located close to the school. Boys from the college were caught in the grounds of the school with Maddie.'

'How did you resolve the matter if you couldn't prove your suspicions?'

'Fortunately, it came at a time of increased break-ins

to schools so the local authority and the governors agreed to install security cameras.'

For the first time and to his surprise, Josh warmed to his old headmaster. 'You mentioned that you sacked a member of your staff.'

He laughed, 'I have probably over stressed my role, because in education and the local authority you couldn't dismiss anyone. I persuaded him in no uncertain fashion that he should leave the teaching profession.'

'Is this related to Maddie?'

'Sergeant, I will no doubt reminisce and wander off the point in my dotage, but fortunately that hasn't happened yet.'

Josh grinned, he wouldn't get the better of his old headmaster. The information so far had been interesting, but it wouldn't help the case.

'Brendon Simons joined the school as a probationary teacher from college, he came with good references and taught Madeline's class who were sixteen. Not long after he started work, I advised him to be less familiar with the pupils, especially the girls.'

'What happened?'

'To be honest, I was never sure of exactly what occurred, but one evening I had a minor social function in town. It involved another junior member of staff who had spoken to me previously concerning Brendon's inappropriate activities. She arrived at the function and asked me to accompany her. Madeline sat on Brendon's lap in a pub. I knew he had exceeded all reasonable actions of a teacher.'

'After that incident did you ask him to leave?'

'No, I reported the matter to the governors and local authority. Brendon apologised and convinced them of his innocence so he continued as a teacher but never changed. About a year later, I forced him to resign by listing the number of times he'd been undesirably associated with the girls in the school.' He paused, and his faint smile held a touch of sadness. 'He became a blot on the teaching profession. Rumours came to me that he continued to see Maddie.'

'How do you discover what happened to former pupils?'

'You rightly mentioned the Friends of the school and there are several reunions held. At those events, I'm told about the activities of friends and former classmates. Brendon, Madeline and Danny along with Sean stayed close.'

'Are there other associated names of former pupils?'

'Sergeant, you must appreciate matters became complicated. The school had an agreement with the local college. The group moved to the college but frequently came back into school, then I noticed one significant addition to their group. any years older, he had been a loner at school but joined their group at college.'

'What happened?'

'Madeline had been the group organiser, but he took over command.'

'Do you have a name for me, sir?'

'Yes, let me think for a moment.' He took a sip of his tea, 'Scott Jennings.'

55

Josh closed the meeting. He had a lead. Scott's name had cone as a complete surprise. Thanking Mr Johnson he returned to his car and made an unsuccessful phone call then dialled Tom's number, 'I've been following up the information about Maddie and have spoken with the former Headteacher of Blackford school and gained a useful lead.

I will return home to talk to Eleanor. I'm sure she'll have information that might help us.' How would she react when she discovered that Scott had close connections with Maddie? Had she heard from Scott and had they resolved their differences? 'Can you join me?'

'I'll be there in ten minutes.'

Josh, with his mind whirling, drove the short distance to his home. Striding across the front gravel as the drizzle fell, he entered the house. 'Ellie are you there?' Silence followed his request. His dad came into the hall from the lounge. 'Where's Eleanor?' He didn't wish to alarm him but needed to find his sister. Josh couldn't keep the relaxed look on his face.

His father opened his eyes wide. 'Are there developments on your cases?'

'Yes, but I must speak with Ellie about fresh information. Where is she?'

Tom's patrol car crunched on the gravel as he pulled into the drive.

'Your mother and I have been out. Ellie is having dinner with someone from her old school. She's met him several times.'

Josh opened the front door. Tom stepped into the hall and nodded. 'Ellie is at dinner with someone from her school.'

Josh returned his attention to his father. 'Do you know his name?'

'Is it important?'

Josh nodded as his father screwed up his eyes, trying to remember. 'His name is Brendon.'

'Brendon Simons?'

'Yes, that sounds right.'

'You mentioned Eleanor has met him several times.'

Dad puffed his cheeks, 'The first time at the nearby hairdressers. I picked her up and she related they had met by accident.' Tom had taken out his notebook. 'She met him for lunch and then at the funeral.' He glanced between me and Tom, 'Is this important. Have you rung her?'

'Yes, her phone is switched off. Do you know where they were going?'

'The new Italian in Market Square.' Tom left Josh talking to his dad. 'I hope she's all right.'

'There have been developments I want her with me until it settles down. Let me know if she rings.'

Tom shook his head as Josh climbed into the passenger seat of the patrol car. 'I've rung the Italian. They are not there. What's happened?' Tom studied his face. 'You are looking worried.'

'After I spoke to the former Headteacher at the school, I tried to contact Danny Mercer and Sean Prendergast but they've left their jobs. Brendon Simons was a teacher at school and was associated with Maddie. Also, the Head gave me the name of Scott Jennings, who became involved with Maddie and her friends in a variety of undesirable activities. He is Eleanor's boyfriend but has been acting in a peculiar manner with her recently. You met him at the hospital. In my opinion their relationship has ended, but she won't admit it.'

Tom closed his notebook, flicked on the police radio, 'High priority, I require an immediate trace on a car owned by Brendon's Simons who lives in Blackford. Please circulate to all patrols and inform Sergeant Harris.'

Josh's phone rang. Unless it was important, he wouldn't take it. Claire's name came on the screen. His finger hesitated, but he pressed answer and switched the phone onto the speaker so Tom could listen. 'Josh, we'll need your help. Is Tom with you?'

'Yes, what's happened? Have you picked up Arthur Mercer and his sons?'

'No, we can't find them. They are after someone. That much we know. It was difficult to get the information, but I gathered that they intend dealing with the person when they encounter him.'

'Any names?'

'No.'

'What about Jason Fredericks?'

The same info as you. He's left to chase down someone, but we don't know who. There have been no sightings of him.'

'What do you want from me?'

'Who might they be chasing?

Have you any idea?'

Josh took a deep breath, 'It's Brendon Simons or Scott Jennings.'

'I don't recognise Brendon Simons but I interviewed Scott Jennings. He was nervous but apologised for his behaviour at the hospital. He mentioned a domestic argument with your sister, nothing more.'

'Brendon and Scott have been involved with Maddie since they were at college together. Eleanor is out to dinner with Brendon. I'm concerned about her safety. We're trying to find them.'

'Okay. I'll message all patrols with their details.'

Josh and Tom listened as the call was transmitted to all units.

Tom radioed control, 'We urgently need to know the location of a phone. Can we get a trace as soon as possible?' I held up my phone with Eleanor's number and he read it to the radio controller.

'Where do we go, Tom?'

He started the patrol car, 'My guess would be the Bondi Club.' Tom swung the car through the streets. He didn't want noise or attention, so there were no sirens or flashing blue lights.

'What did you find out about the demolished house?'

'There was an underhand payment to Arthur Mercer but only ten thousand.'

The control radio blared, 'Any available units near to Canal Street? Badly injured man has been found. Unit Foxtrot-Tango-Three in attendance and an ambulance called.'

Tom in a fluid movement swept on the siren and blue lights. 'That's near to the club. A couple of alleyways connect the canal to the club.' He barked into the radio, 'Any identification.'

'A man, but negative on a name,' came the reply from control.

Josh breathed a sigh of relief as it wouldn't be Eleanor. But where had she gone?

Josh called control, 'Can you check the airlines for Brendon Simons, Scott Jennings, Sean Prendergast and Danny Mercer.'

'Will do, but it might take time.'

'Do it as fast as possible. Summon help from the Incident Room and inform Sergeant Harris.'

A blue light flashed in the distance. A police car and ambulance had arrived near to derelict ground close to the canal. Headlights illuminated the scene so he could see the blood. The police officer who had arrived on the scene approached. 'Young courting couple trying to steal a few minutes of privacy stumbled across him.' He grinned, 'Spoilt their evening.'

Josh plodded over with the officer. Tom joined them and peered over the shoulder of the paramedic. 'It's Sean Prendergast.'

'Will he be able to describe his attackers?'

The paramedic shook his head, 'He's been badly beaten. It looks a malicious attack. Even when he comes around, I would be surprised if he can remember his own name. I would expect no long term damage, but he will need several weeks for recovery.'

They left the paramedics to their job. 'What do you think, Tom?'

'Either he killed Maddie and Jason has caught up with him or he's double crossed Arthur Mercer and his boys have taught him a lesson.'

'If Sean killed Maddie, then he must have been part of the raid. So, it would have been carried out by Maddie, Sean and Danny Mercer.'

'Who's the fourth?' Tom raised his eyebrows questioningly.

'Could it have been Brendon or Scott or possibly someone else from the Mercer family?'

Tom shook his head, 'I'm still struggling that Arthur Mercer would let his family become involved. Sean and Danny were working when the raid took place.'

Josh pursed his lips and tilted his head to one side, 'Hotels are large fluid places. Would they be missed?' He paused and assembled his thoughts, I've thought of the connection. Gambling. Danny and Sean had substantial betting slips. The Headteacher told me they had set up a gambling ring when they were at school. Maddie loved to play the fruit machines, and she'd been part of the ring. Maddie knew the Mercer family. My guess would be a loan from Arthur at a high interest rate.'

Tom gave a bleak nod, 'When he brings pressure to bear for repayment none of them have money so they organise the raid to repay him.'

Josh paused, reassessing the information, 'It's coming together, but we must find Eleanor.'

Tom climbed into the patrol car, 'It fits with why the Mercer's would hunt for someone if they discovered the police had identified money from the raid.'

'Would Arthur deal with them?'

'Not sure. Or would he make sure they confessed?'

'Whatever way it is, we need to find them before someone is killed.'

Tom's eyes were guarded, 'Brendon or Scott.'

'Eleanor has mentioned that she has often spent too much money in the casinos. They visit them because Scott likes to play the tables.'

Josh answered his phone as it rang, 'It's Claire. I'm in the Incident Room. Scott Jennings is on a flight to Bangalore. I'll arrange with the Indian authorities to arrest him when the plane lands.'

'Any other news?'

'Brendon Simons is booked on a flight to Bangalore tomorrow morning. Nothing on the others. I have sent a team to the Bondi Club.'

'Sean Prendergast, the friend of Danny Mercer, is the badly injured man near the canal.'

The radio blared, 'Car registered to Brendon Simons has been spotted without occupants near the ravine.'

'Exact location, please,' shouted Tom as he started the car. Josh didn't recognise it, but Tom nodded. 'It's a makeshift layby near the woods. There are several paths into the ravine. Some are steep and dangerous.'

56

The black void of the ravine stretched below them as Tom halted behind Brendon's empty car which had been squeezed into bushes. Josh and Tom spoke briefly to the officer in the police car who had waited down the road. With a small wave of his hand, he drove away to follow the next set of instructions from Claire.

Claire's voice sounded on the radio. 'Coordinating all units from the Incident Room. We're sealing off the ravine and riverside area as fast as we can.' Josh adjusted the volume of his radio lower and Tom switched off the lights on the patrol car. Easing open the doors they stepped out without a sound. Three paths were easily identifiable leading down from the layby. Tom whispered, 'The paths are treacherous in daytime. They are steep, rocky and slippery.'

'Why go down there?'

'During an incident, a few years ago we discovered a building in the woods. It served a nearby quarry.' Tom pointed, 'It's along the path at the far end, which is the easiest.' Josh crept along the road and peered into the darkness, but no building was visible.

They returned to the car. Claire's voice came through again, 'White van registered to Mercer Demolition has been spotted at a car park near the walkway in the ravine.' With a brief nod to each other they fitted their personal radios with earpieces before they left the car.

It enabled them to hear any further announcements, but it wouldn't make any noise. Tom grabbed Josh's arm and they stopped. Through the still night air, the sound of an engine reached them. Tom leaned in and whispered, 'That's the sound of a track bike, Jason is nearby.'

Standing near to one of the paths darkness surrounded them. Josh's mind raced. Where was Eleanor? The dark would prevent a police search until the morning. The radio crackled in Josh's ear, 'Station Inspector has authorised firearm units, which are being deployed. Several reports of a track bike in the area. All units await further instructions.'

Josh ached for action. Eleanor dominated his thoughts. Could she be down there? Was she safe or under threat? Had she gone willingly? Somehow, he doubted it. He checked his phone. No messages from her. Dad had rung earlier to say she hadn't come home. Nothing must happen to Eleanor, his lovely sis. He'd risk anything to make sure he could take her home safely. A sudden stab of fear hit him in the gut. Time to focus. He needed all his wits about him.

He whispered, 'Tom, how far to the building? I want to have a look.'

'About four hundred metres down this steep path and through the woods. The path joins a disused railway track after the building. The Mercer's van will be about a mile away. Jason's bike could be anywhere in the ravine. My guess is that after finding his target, he will abandon the bike in the undergrowth. Let's take it slow and steady down the path.'

'Good man.' Josh admired Tom, who wouldn't shirk from danger. It would be difficult for him, but he would not make excuses. They edged along the first part of the path which wasn't that steep but was littered with loose stones. It was imperative to remain undetected and any sudden noise would give them away. Twigs broke under Josh's shoes, which weren't suited to rough paths at night. After each hesitant step they stopped to listen. Desperation etched its way through Josh's whole body, and he was sweating despite the cool night air. Progress became painfully slow. Silence pervaded the ravine.

An owl punctuated the distant drone of traffic from the town. As they stepped under a canopy of trees the darkness increased. Picking their way forward without a torch became hazardous. The night became darker as they descended. They methodically made their way metre by metre. Josh's heart hammered and fear for Eleanor gave him a strangling sensation. The grass at the edge of the path had gone. The exposed tree roots were slippery and uneven.

Josh moved quicker than Tom, but he slowed and waited for him every few yards. His hunched shoulders and stooped posture meant he concentrated hard at being silent. Josh gasped as a bat flew past his face, but he hadn't made a noise. The short canopy of trees ended and the sky appeared above them although bushes still afforded them some cover. They continued to follow the path, checking for sounds and movements. Josh had to be careful he didn't fall. His leather shoes slipped on the wet surface, but he could only think of Ellie.

An outline of a building appeared. His legs ached

as he balanced on the wet grass at the side of the track. Tom, a few steps behind him, made silent progress, despite his size. The bushes and trees stopped after the building where the wide gravel track led to the quarry. The rigid shape of the eaves of the single story became clearer as Josh concentrated. Only ten metres away, the weak light from the cloudy moon allowed him to pick out the steel plates over the window apertures. The brickwork building shaped like a garage sat at the side of the track.

Tom joined him. Josh held his breath as he listened, but the noise of the track bike had gone. A crackling in a nearby bush made him jump, but he waited for whatever animal to pass by on its nocturnal journey. Keeping low in case anyone left the building, he crossed the path to the back corner and crept along the wall. A low voice sounded inside. A nod from Tom confirmed he'd also heard it. Josh had become certain that Ellie would be inside. An owl hooted. He willed it to be silent.

A man's voice spoke, but the words were indistinct. Tom caught Josh's arm and pointed back up the path. Josh was reluctant to leave, but Tom pulled his arm more forcefully and he accepted the need to return to the car to call back-up. As silently as they arrived, they moved back along the track. Tom led. He moved slowly while near the building, but then he increased his pace.

He stopped about thirty metres along the track and whispered. 'We'll tell control and then surprise the people in the quarry hut.' Josh nodded his agreement as he didn't want to wait for backup. His worry for Eleanor increased as the minutes ticked past. Nothing must happen to her.

Tom moved faster up the path. Josh stayed with him. When they'd determined they were far enough away from the building he whispered into his radio, 'Voices coming from inside the old quarry building near to the disused railway, directly down the east path from the location of Brendon Simons' car.'

The immediate message came back, 'Await support before continuing.' Tom switched his radio off, winked at Josh, and they began the slow descent once again. It was quicker this time as they knew their target, but his anxiety for Ellie increased with every step and progress still seemed painfully slow. Crouching low they crept towards the building.

It was solid and while it might not be in regular use, it had been made weatherproof. The windows were sealed with steel plates and a sturdy tiled roof showed no sign of deterioration. With slow precision they edged to the front, carefully checking the bushes opposite and the entrance to the quarry to ensure they were alone. A heavy steel door covered the entrance.

Standing motionless, hardly daring to breathe Josh listened again. No sounds or voices reached him from inside the building. They stood in silence on either side of the door which had large solid hinges indicating that it would open outwards. No rust was apparent so the hinges would move with ease. His breathing was slow and shallow as he pulled his stab-proof vest to its correct position, and Tom did the same. His hands sweated, but he gripped the torch which they hadn't used for fear of giving themselves away.

Tom pointed at the door. His sign indicated to pull the door open quickly and to stand to the side in case whoever was inside attacked. Josh's heart pounded, and his stomach churned. Waiting by the wall, his whole body tensed in anticipation.

With a torch in one hand and a pepper spray he readied himself. Tom's hand rested on the handle.

Josh nodded. Tom yanked the handle of the door down and flung it open.

'What the…'

Before any further reaction, Josh bellowed, 'Police! Stay where you are!' Both held their torches wide of their bodies and shone them into the hut. Josh's beam moved rapidly around the space, and then it landed in a corner. A hooded person wrapped in a blanket huddled on the floor with arms and feet bound. Josh gasped, 'Ellie.' She responded by wriggling and groaning. She was alive.

Tom's torch shone on the man standing in the middle of the hut. A gun pointed at them. 'Come in. You can join Ellie.'

'Let her go, Brendon, she's done you no harm.' Josh's eyes were riveted on the barrel of the gun.

Tom growled, 'Leave her to us and make your escape.' Brendon flicked on a light that dazzled after the darkness of their approach. The fluorescent light in the ceiling highlighted the shiny metal of the gun that was aimed at them.

Eleanor wriggled again and moaned, 'It won't be long now, Ellie. Sense will prevail as they will know backup is coming.'

'Bullshit. I don't think so.' Brendon drawled in a confident and arrogant tone. He let out a short, mirthless laugh. 'You'd break orders to come after your sister. I don't believe you've called. Now get in here.' He beckoned them with his other hand, but the gun remained pointed towards them. They hesitated at the door. But they had no other choice. Tom lurched in.

A voice made him jump. 'Do as you're told!' It hissed,

full of menace. Josh twisted and scrutinised another gun. Danny Mercer's hand shook as he waved the gun. There was blood down the front of his jacket. Who's blood?

A tremor ran through Josh's body. Danny jiggled around and scanned the room as though he expected to be attacked. A jittery man with a gun made a dangerous combination. He whispered to Brendon, 'Let's tie them up and leave.'

Josh had his first unobstructed view of Brendon. His eyes were alive with evil. His face was flushed scarlet and sweat beaded his forehead. Josh gradually moved inside, but it was too slow for Danny. With a hard shove in the back, Josh stumbled and sprawled across the concrete floor.

Eleanor groaned again. 'Stay calm, Ellie.' Josh whispered as he rolled towards her.

'My colleagues have not been called, Brendon. You can escape.' Tom spoke calmly, enunciating each word.

'Stop talking. Lie on the floor!' Brendon waved his gun.

Josh had secreted the spray into his pocket, but with two guns pointing in his direction, he had no chance to use it. Josh's concern for Eleanor had eased a fraction as she wriggled and groaned. She was alive and he was nearby. Brendon produced two hoods and pointed at Tom, 'Get down on the floor.'

Tom stood firm, 'The area cannot be surrounded by police in the dark. You can escape.'

He ignored him and focused on Danny, 'Are the bikes ready.'

'Yes.'

Escaping along the paths in the dark would be easy.

The police could block the roads but not the footpaths. If they knew the locality, it would be simple to escape through the cordon. 'Danny, cover them with your gun while I tie them up.'

Brendon put his gun on the ground. He roughly shoved Josh who tried to resist, but Brendon kicked him in the ribs. 'Do what I say. Lie on your front with hands behind your back.'

Tom groaned as he dropped to the floor. Brendon glared and snapped, 'Concentrate, Danny. Keep them covered.'

'There's someone out there.' His voice was hushed and held a note of panic.

Brendon yanked a rope around Josh's arms and pulled it tight, making him wince. 'They won't have called in. No one is outside.'

Josh eased his head to one side so his cheek rested on the concrete. Danny stood in the doorway, facing inwards and flapped his gun around as he hopped from foot to foot. Anything could make him fire. 'Listen! I heard something. There's someone out there.'

Brendon hissed, 'Danny, keep the gun still and pointed at these coppers. I've not tied them yet.' Josh could raise his head enough to see that he followed Brendon's instructions.

A lump of wood crashed on Danny's head and his knees buckled. The impact sent him reeling across the floor headfirst, colliding with Brendon. 'Don't think about reaching for the gun,' yelled Jason as he stormed into the building. He kicked Danny, who was already groaning and bleeding from the head wound. Jason stepped forward and crashed the wood against Brendon's shoulder as he reached for the gun by his side. Jason had been too quick for him. With a swift movement he kicked Brendon viciously in the stomach and crashed the lump of the wood across his back.

'Don't do it, Jason.' Tom shouted.

Danny murmured as he passed into unconsciousness, but Brendon cowered in the corner with his arms around his head as he tried to stop the blows from Jason. Josh struggled to free his hands. Tom attempted to stand but Jason hissed, 'You coppers stay there.'

Tom shouted, 'Do nothing daft, Jason.'

But he was already standing over the whimpering Brendon. 'You killed my girl. Now you will suffer. And believe me, I will make it long and slow. She was the best thing that had happened in my life. Even if I spend the rest of my life in jail, I want revenge for my angel.'

Jason lifted the heavy wood and crashed it down on Brendon's body, who cowered even lower to deflect the blows. 'It wasn't me,' squealed Brendon. Jason bent down and picked up the gun. Unlike Danny, there was no nervousness in him as he pointed it at Brendon.

Another outline appeared in the doorway. A resonant voice echoed around the small room, 'Jason. Stop. They will be sent to jail. Even the bloody coppers know the score.'

Arthur Mercer strode across the floor and grabbed Jason's arm to stop him firing. Jason held on to the gun and attempted to shake off the hold on his arm. Arthur's sons came into the room. One of them picked up the second gun.

Danny Mercer groaned as he came back to consciousness and peered up from the floor, 'Uncle…'

'Don't bloody uncle me. You've tried to stitch me up along with this bastard,' he pointed towards Brendon. 'The filth can lock you up. Don't do it, Jason.' Arthur continued to tug at his arm.

Tom glanced up from the floor, 'The gun, Jason. Put it down.'

Arthur Mercer glared at Tom. 'You're too bloody old for these jobs, why don't you retire?'

Arthur gave Tom a hand to stand up and then pointed at Brendon, 'They raided the building society and tried to pay off their gambling debts to me with the money they'd nicked. The bastards tried to stitch me up.'

Tom moved to Eleanor and whispered to her while Josh struggled to undo the ropes which bound his feet. Jason was still pointing the gun at Brendon. 'Put it down, Jason.' Josh's voice was husky with tension, 'If you go ahead, you'll kill the wrong man.' Jason concentrated his gaze on Josh. 'It wasn't Brendon that killed Maddie. The killer is on a plane flying to India.'

Josh shook the ropes aside and approached Jason. Arthur stood by his side. Brendon whimpered in the corner, hunched in the foetal position. 'Give me the gun, Jason.'

'Please do as he says,' pleaded Arthur.

Josh whispered as he didn't want Ellie to hear, 'It was Scott Jennings who killed Maddie. Brendon did the raid but Scott masterminded the robbery.'

'I hope you're bringing him back to this country,' snapped Arthur through clenched teeth.

Tom had untied Ellie, who he helped to her feet. Jason closed his eyes but handed Josh the gun. 'You'd better be telling the truth or there will be trouble.'

He gave Brendon one last vicious kick and twisted

away. Josh stepped forward and wrapped his arms around Ellie, who sobbed with relief.

Arthur's son handed the other gun to Tom who gave a nod of thanks, 'Shall I call in Arthur?'

'Yes, you'd better before anyone gets hurt.'

57

'What a result!' Josh patted Tom on the back as the pair sat in the Incident Room. The investigation had been scaled down.

Tom stretched his back, 'We were helped by the confession from Sean Prendergast. He's weak and I suspect always has been. The others bossed him around, first Danny at school, then later Maddie. My guess is that when Scott took charge he did as he was told.'

'Yes, you are right he was weak. After they had kidnapped Ellie he bottled out and Brendon beat him up to stop him talking while they made their escape. Scott had the most desperate need. The Post Office raid last year had dealt with some debts, but they were a group of addicted gamblers. When the money ran out, they approached Arthur Mercer for high interest loans.

'A daft thing to do,' scowled Tom.

'You'd think Danny Mercer would know his own family. The pressure came from Arthur's sons to repay the cash so a raid became their only chance for clearing the debt.'

I've been writing up my paperwork, so I don't have the Chief on my back. What's happened to Scott?' Tom's mouth hardened into a thin line. 'I never liked him.'

'The plane carrying him received our call while in international airspace. The Indian authorities didn't want him but held him until he was conveyed back here. He's in jail near Heathrow.'

'Has he confessed to the murder?'

'He's saying nothing but the statement from Sean tells us he and Scott went along the footpath to meet Maddie as they knew it was her favoured running route. She'd been jittery and had suggested they should own up to the crimes. Scott lost it and hit her. Sean denies all knowledge of involvement.'

'But he must have realised that Scott was carrying a metal bar.'

'He denied the intent as Scott had hidden it in his rucksack.'

Tom raised his eyebrows. 'Is the boss happy?'

Josh laughed, 'No, there are unanswered questions and the paperwork isn't complete.'

'I know him of old so I understand the paperwork. But what else isn't finished?'

'The motorbikes used on both raids have disappeared without trace.'

'How's Eleanor taking it?'

'She's returned to her flat and wants to forget the whole affair. I can't blame her. She's not answering her phone apart from to mum. She's texted that she's trying to return to work, but they won't have her.'

'She must be embarrassed as she's chatted up by a man who badly assaulted her at the car wash, although Brendon still hasn't admitted it.'

'But Sean alleged that Brendon mugged Eleanor to

retrieve the papers which had details about the raid. Scott's folder not only had betting slips but a plan of the shopping centre. Under normal circumstances she would have ignored it. It went wrong because by coincidence she was in the shopping centre after telling Scott she would be in Manchester.'

Tom glanced out of the window. 'It's only late afternoon and it's a mild evening for winter, I'll finish the paperwork in the morning, I'm off for a spot of fishing after a bite to eat in the canteen. Sandra's meeting up with Claire for a meal at an Italian restaurant. Since they met at the Superintendent's buffet they have met on several occasions. They seem to be getting on like a house on fire. Life is strange at times isn't it? What are you doing?'

Josh gave a sheepish grin.

Tom chuckled and mouthed, 'Lynette?'

Josh nodded. 'It's over now and Jason wasn't implicated so it can't do any harm. I'll try to tie together as much of the paperwork in the next few hours and deal with outstanding issues before I meet her.'

Josh had not covered himself in glory since his arrival in Blackford, so he needed to ensure a good finish on the case with the boss.

Within the hour he'd completed the mundane reports, but there was still another hour before he met Lynette. The one aspect that nagged the Chief was the getaway on motorbikes. Both the post office and the shopping centre raid used the same means of transport.

Josh wanted to question Sean, but the hospital had refused. Josh hankered for a solution. Both raids had the similarities of motorbikes using footpaths to avoid pursuit by cars. The bikes had not been recovered except the one abandoned in the mall car park. The nearby reservoir had been searched, but no bikes were discovered. While on the escape route along the disused railway track no one had reported anything unusual nearby. Josh re-read the reports. The motorbikes had travelled into the ravine. He loaded a map of the area on his screen and studied it.

58

With the paperwork complete, Josh wandered to the town centre whistling to himself in anticipation of a good evening. 'Josh, darling, I'm so glad it's over and we can meet without a problem.' Flinging her arms around him, she kissed him on the lips.

Smiling, he gave her a warm hug in return. Needing relaxation, she would be perfect company, so full of fun and always laughing. 'Let's go into the restaurant, they've a bar so we can relax with a drink before eating.'

'Great.'

Within minutes they were settled on low slung arm chairs typical of a Bistro-style restaurant. Josh had a Peroni and Lynette her usual drink, a large G&T. 'No talking about the case, Josh as it's been endless.'

Josh relaxed back in the chair as her startlingly dark eyes danced with merriment, 'I wanted to ask you about your brother.'

'The involvement with the police stressed him out, so he's disappeared to London. You're not attempting to arrest him, are you?'

'No, I just wondered how he'd coped.'

'Jason will find his own space. That's what he needs.'

Catching Josh's hand, she winked, 'With Jason in London, there's only me in the flat.' Her eyes twinkled and a mischievous expression lit up her face. 'I'm sure you'll be happy to walk me home.'

'Another drink, your glass is empty?'

Nodding, 'No more about the case.'

'Okay, I give in.' Josh sipped his Peroni and relaxed, 'Tell me about something else.'

'Such as?'

'How's your riding? The first time we met, you told me you were often at the stables. I assume you still ride your horse.'

'You don't understand, do you?' Lynette wriggled around on her seat and adjusted her short skirt.

He eyed the exposed length of lightly tanned thigh with interest. 'Probably not.' With an effort he forced his attention back to her cheerful face, 'What don't I understand?'

'I can't afford a horse.' She clucked with amusement.

'But you said that you ride.' Rubbing a hand across his forehead, he gave a slight shake of his head.

'I help at the stables so I can ride horses there.'

Josh took a swig of his drink from the bottle. The details from the map of the ravine circled in his mind as it had been the last task before leaving the police station. The only unusual aspect of the bike abandoned at the shopping centre car park had been straw. With racing thoughts, he took a deep breath and attempted to keep his voice casual. 'Mucking out doesn't seem an enjoyable task to me.'

Lynette laughed, 'Young girls do that. It's teaching them about horses.'

'So, what role do you perform at the stables?'

'I supervise the youngsters, but I often drive the horsebox to shows or whenever the horses need transporting.'

Josh sat up straighter and placed his Peroni back on the table. His thoughts raced, but he needed to play it cool. Don't rush, a voice in his head cautioned. 'Which farm is it?'

He tried not to allow an edge in his voice, but he didn't manage it. Lynette stared at him. The smile had gone. Slowly, she sipped her new drink without taking her eyes from him. 'Hill Farm.'

He nodded as it had been marked on the map. 'That's the one about a mile along the track from where you live, it's tucked by the woods near a small tunnel which is part of the disused railway track.'

She laughed. 'You seem to know a lot about it?' Her eyes never left Josh as she knocked back the rest of her drink. Plonking her glass down with a bang, she frowned, 'You know, don't you?' Her eyes glistened with tears. 'Oh, Josh, how can you do this to me? We have such fun together.'

'It was both times wasn't it.'

Giving a resigned smile, she studied her hands in her lap, 'Yes.'

'I assume you parked the horse box in the tunnel and left the gate open. No one would take any notice of you driving the horse box to a barn and hiding the bikes.'

Tears escaped and trickled down her cheeks, 'Have you told anyone else?'

He shook his head.

'Can't you just forget about it, Josh. I'll take my chance if another copper finds out, they never did after the post office raid.'

'I can't, Lynette. As much as I would like to.' This was so difficult as even in the short term he'd found her such a perfect girlfriend. Pretty, vivacious and forgiving. He pressed his lips together and took a slow, deep breath. Why did she have to become involved?

'Will you arrest me?' Her voice quivered with emotion.

He shook his head. The Chief would expect him to interview her. 'Go to the police station and offer the information.'

'What now?' Josh gave a small nod.

'We're waiting to interview various people so we can piece together the whole story. Volunteering information will help you in the long term.'

'I'm not prepared to rat on anyone.' She moved away from Josh, her eyes stared with a bleak expression and her hands shook.

Josh couldn't believe that he wanted to advise her what to say, 'Tell them how the bikes entered the horsebox and where you dumped them but answer no further questions until a solicitor is there.' There was nothing else Josh could do, 'Goodbye, Lynette.' He stood up and without glancing back left the restaurant. If she hadn't attended the police station by the morning, he would arrest her.

59

Josh entered the Chief's office, followed by Claire and Tom. Three chairs were arranged facing the desk. This would be no friendly review. As usual, the Chief Inspector sat behind his desk with a notepad and fountain pen in front of him. The desk was never untidy. The polished wooden surface shone in the afternoon sun coming through the large window. Josh had already learned that his new boss never engaged in small talk.

Many senior officers would have a more relaxed manner once major cases had been concluded, but Chief Inspector Haskins came from a different breed. His face, as intense as at the beginning of the case, didn't smile. Opening his hand, he indicated the seats which had been arranged for them. He studied them. 'I've called this review of the case between the four of us.' His eyes focused on Tom. 'Normally I would complete the meeting with my Sergeants, but as Tom has been at the forefront of the cases, I have invited him.'

Claire shuffled in her seat with tense shoulders. 'Sir, I'm not sure of the status of the review you intend holding today, but I would have normally expected only myself and Josh to be present.'

Tom took a deep breath, 'If my presence makes you uncomfortable then I shall be happy to leave.' Josh suppressed the smile that threatened his lips. Tom hated meetings and would find any excuse to depart.

The Chief Inspector's brow furrowed. 'Claire. Tom Collins has more police experience than the rest of us in this room added together. I have given him criticism over the years, but he never gossips and I wish him to hear my review.'

'Very well,' mumbled Claire.

'First, I will update you on my conversation with the Crown Prosecution Service. Sean Prendergast, Brendon Simons and Danny Mercer will be charged with two counts of armed robbery, the post office last year and the building society raid in the shopping centre.'

Tom kept his expression impassive, 'May we presume that Maddie was the fourth person in both robberies.'

'Yes, you're correct. As for Maddie's murder, Scott Jennings and Sean Prendergast will be charged. Sean has already admitted being there. Scott Jennings has denied any involvement.'

'Will the charge against Scott secure a conviction?'

'Yes, Josh, it would be my guess that he will take legal advice which will cause a guilty plea. However, I suspect it will go to trial to determine whether it is murder or manslaughter.'

Tom chuckled, 'What about my old adversary, Arthur Mercer?'

'His case took a long discussion with the Prosecution Service. He took the money in good faith from Danny Mercer and Brendon Simons to repay the loan. Whilst many charges about his operation were considered, it is not in the public interest to pursue them. You're nodding, Tom, I'm surprised that you agree.'

'Despite his previous record which is now a long way in the past I believe he is trying to stay legal. He'll maintain he lent money to his family and friends. The only law breaking is the clandestine demolition of the listed building.'

The Chief Inspector nodded, 'I questioned whether that case would proceed, but it appears neither central government who controls listed buildings, or the local authority, have the heart for a court case, that could easily become intertwined with a murder trial. So, there will be no prosecution.'

'What about Scott Jennings activities?'

'Good question, Josh. The investigations are complex, but he will be charged with embezzlement from the airline. He falsified expense claims to fuel his gambling habit.' He considered Josh and with a resigned smile added, 'I emailed you about one matter, I trust you understand what needs to be done.'

'Yes, sir. Thank you for your consideration.' The man had compassion. 'I will take action this evening.'

'Any charges for Jason?' queried Tom.

The Chief shook his head, wrote some notes, and then regarded Josh.

'Lynette Fredericks has been charged with aiding offenders, although because of her voluntary admission, the prosecution will only press for a suspended sentence and probation.'

Tom shuffled in his seat. 'I've not finished Tom.' He sat still again. 'The cases were not investigated well and that responsibility lies with the two Sergeants within my remit, Josh and Claire.'

Claire went to speak, but the Chief held up his hand. 'Later, Claire. Finally, after pursuing many red herrings, Josh and Tom took the correct approach. While their intervention in approaching the hut without support was contradictory to orders from control, I'm prepared to overlook that indiscretion as Josh's sister was involved. I'm afraid Claire the gung-ho approach to arrest the Mercer's backfired. Perhaps more discretion would have produced the information quicker.'

Claire moved to the edge of her seat, 'Sir, I protest. You're judging with hindsight.'

The Chief Inspector snapped, 'Claire. I'm giving my review analysis and it is not open for debate. You need to learn to accept criticism.'

They were interrupted by a knock on the office door. 'Come!'

The Superintendent's secretary popped her head around the door, 'Chief Inspector, the Superintendent wishes to see you as soon as possible.'

Tom smiled but looked down. The Chief picked up his jacket from his chair as he left. As he reached the door, a resigned smile replaced the usual frown. 'You know what you must do, Josh.'

'Yes, sir.'

The Chief left the room. Tom sitting nearest to the door made his escape, 'I'll see you in a minute, Josh.' He followed the Chief, closing the door quietly behind him.

'I'm sorry Claire, I wasn't much use on the case. My apologies, as you were criticised.' The piercing eyes didn't leave Josh's face and her expression was thunderous.

'I shouldn't have come to a bloody backwater like

Blackford. I'd expected your support as I'm junior to you, but you let me do the hard work then jumped in to pinch the glory.' She stormed out, slamming the door behind her. Working with Claire would not be easy. She was a perfectionist, which didn't suit his style.

Josh wandered through to the canteen as he anticipated Tom would be there. He was ensconced at a table with two cakes and two cups of tea. 'Celebratory meal. For once we weren't reprimanded.'

'Yes, but will it last?' Josh sighed.

'Sorry, I shouldn't be flippant. This case was close to your family.' He paused and took a large bite of his Belgian Bun. 'And Lynette.'

'It's too hard, Tom.' He shook his head in frustration and stared at the tempting bun with its swirl of icing on the top. 'I want a sensible life.'

'Give it six months. I've worked for worse Chiefs. He moans a lot, but he's consistent with his standards. He never falters. Under the paperwork hype, he's a good copper. Besides, I'm happy to be part of your team.'

Josh smiled, 'I want you to be part of it. But I worry you will want to retire.'

'No chance, despite what the rumours say. The Superintendent decreed I can stay, so that's what I will be doing. Sandra has come up with the idea that we could move, buy a derelict house and refurbish it. I envisage being a copper until I'm ninety.' He chuckled. 'We might be a bit of an unlikely pairing, but I can't see the villains in Blackford being too pleased we're together.'

Josh stood to leave. Tom picked up his newspaper and grinned, 'I will have five minutes of peace to finish my crossword then I've a visit to make.'

'Sounds formal.'

Tom finished his cake, 'Once a month I go to a nursing home to see an old copper. He approached the end of his career as I started as a fresh constable, he's nearly ninety but his memory for cases is like an elephant. He remembers the smallest details; I hope I'm like that when I'm ninety. Jack Hardcastle was a great mentor to me.'

Josh shuddered and closed his eyes for a moment trying to disengage from the shame that engulfed him. He dropped back to his seat. The name from the past. One that he could never forget. It had altered the course of his life in a single evening.

'What's the matter, Josh, you've gone white and your hands are shaking. Are you still fretting about Eleanor?'

Josh wrung his hands together. A long silence followed as his mind raced. How could he explain? His stomach rolled and he had a sour taste in his mouth. Stalling for time he grasped the cup and gulped down several mouthfuls of the lukewarm tea he had left. Bracing himself, he controlled his voice with an effort, 'Returning to a role in Blackford was a big step for me.'

Tom shook his head in confusion, 'Why?'

'At school as the Headteacher remembered I had been a renegade always in trouble for fights or disrupting lessons. But one year, when I was fifteen, I became involved with a bad crowd. The fights became more serious and my attitude was hostile and belligerent.'

'Has this something to do with Jack?'

Josh nodded, 'Vandalism,' the single word caught in his throat. 'He caught me.'

'Did Jack tell you off?'

Josh hesitated, 'It was more serious. He'd told me it

would be a caution, at least. Mum and dad would have been livid. He informed me the prosecution would go ahead, but it never did. For months I kept waiting for the letter to arrive.' Josh stared across the room as images of his misdemeanours returned. They'd been caught when attempting to vandalise allotments on the edge of town. The other three lads had vanished, but he was apprehended. Jack Hardcastle had lectured him long and hard and had then suggested he tidy up the havoc he had caused.

For over an hour he toiled, covered in mud, while the policeman watched him in stony faced silence. He broke contact with the other lads but it had been a tense period waiting for the prosecution to materialise. It had been a turning point in his life; a wake-up call. Jack must have contacted his Headmaster, as during the recent interview he'd mentioned a run in with the police. The impact of that night had reshaped his life. It was the reason he became a policeman. He'd never forgotten the policeman who could have given him a record.

When filling in his application forms to join the police, he had excluded the information. Pushing the memories aside he stared across at the calm and impassive face of Tom. 'I'll tell the boss but I'll be in a lot of trouble, as I've always denied I had any involvement with the police.'

Tom stood and rested his hand on Josh's shoulder, 'Do you want me to mention it to Jack?'

Josh nodded, 'It's better to have it in the open. If he remembers me then I would like to visit him and thank him for giving me a second chance.'

60

Tom anticipated a pleasant evening. Sandra would at home and she had promised him Lancashire Hotpot for tea, which was one of his favourites. His mind drifted through the day's activities as he parked the car. Josh's revelation about his run in with Jack Hardcastle had surprised him, but there again nobody was perfect. Jack had remembered the incident and was looking forward to meeting up with Josh again.

It was a relief that the cases had been solved but the continued disharmony between the detectives niggled at him. Somehow, they needed to learn to get along with each other. He pushed the thoughts aside. Work was over for today, so he'd think about that problem another time.

A perfect evening beckoned, starting with a good meal, a couple of cans and then putting his feet up to indulge in the reading his monthly fishing magazine which should have arrived today. Entering the back door, the aroma of the cooking infused the atmosphere. As he closed the door, his brow furrowed and he paused as he could hear voices. Sandra's voice held an excited tone, but the other voice, although female, was more subdued. As Sandra had a Pilates class in the afternoon, perhaps one of her friends had returned with her. He drifted through to the lounge to say hello.

'Hi, Tom.' Sandra's voice reached him as he opened the door.

Stepping into the lounge, he stopped, and his body stiffened.

'Hello, Tom.' Claire looked up at him from the armchair with a hesitant smile.

'Claire came on trial to my Pilates class. She has come to talk about DIY.'

Tom regained his composure after the surprise. He wanted to resist using her name, but he had no option. 'Evening, Claire.' Dropping into an armchair, he was aware of Sandra's watchful gaze. 'Did you enjoy your class?'

'Yes, it was excellent and I've joined. So much better than the class I've been attending. Not only was it fun but it was demanding.'

Sandra stood, 'I've persuaded Claire to stay to tea, so chat to her Tom, while I set the table.'

Before Tom could volunteer to serve the hotpot, his wife had left the room. Tom gave a half smile. No easy conversation starter came to mind, so he would stick with DIY. He went to speak, but Claire held up her hand.

'Tom tell me here and now if you object to me meeting Sandra. We have common interests and might meet frequently.'

Tom relaxed back in his chair. 'Sandra enjoys your company, so you are most welcome to come to this house whenever you wish.' He gave what he hoped a genuine smile.

'Thank you, Tom. Your offer is more than generous as we appear to irritate each other at work. Perhaps if we meet informally under relaxed circumstances, then the interaction between us might improve.'

Sandra appeared with a glass of white wine for Claire and a beer for Tom. 'Don't talk about work. Claire explain how you are renovating your cottage.' She returned to the kitchen.

Tom furrowed his brow, 'Explain to me about your cottage over tea.' Claire's face remained neutral, but her eyes remained riveted on Tom's face. Taking his time, Tom chose his words with care, 'You are correct we do not work well together but for understandable reasons. I'm an old school copper and you are a different generation; a modern police detective so we do not solve problems the same way. I appreciate your comments and informal meetings may ease the tension between us, so please drop into our home at any time.'

'Thanks, Tom I've been lonely since coming to Blackford and meeting Sandra has been exciting as I've someone who is prepared to listen to my thoughts and ideas.'

Lonely would not be an attribute he would ascribe to her, but with regular casual meetings he might discover further information. She smiled then took a sip of her wine as she visibly relaxed back into the armchair.

The sounds of cutlery and crockery came from the kitchen. Sandra's voice came from the kitchen, 'It will be another ten minutes.'

He would be direct. 'Friction between us is understandable, but you and Josh are close in age and the same rank.'

The serious frown returned, 'I appreciate Josh and you are friends. I would like to give you my honest opinion, but you will believe it unjustified and it will ruin the understanding we have agreed.

'Tension is always likely to remain unless we discuss him. Give me your opinion, I will not comment, but it might shed light on the difficulties at the station. Without taking her eyes from his face, she sipped her wine, then licked her lips.

'Very well, I hope I will not regret this conversation. Josh is lazy, his paperwork is terrible. Although yours is too succinct, his is riddled with mistakes and ambiguities. If that were his only fault then I could build a tolerable working relationship with him, but on this last case he withheld crucial information. The headteacher meeting provided the key links, which he didn't share as he wanted all the glory.

Tom pursed his lips, perhaps Claire had a valid point, as she oversaw the investigation. Josh had been annoyed that he hadn't been put in charge, so in retrospect maybe he had been economical with the information he'd discovered. Tom sipped his beer and focused on Claire's face.

Her expression showed that she had not finished. 'Carry on, Claire, I can find validity in your first two statements.'

She took a deep breath, 'As a person, he is unprofessional and deceitful.' Tom's eyes narrowed and he puffed out a long audible breath. Claire gulped her wine.

Tom focused on her eyes, which never broke the stare at his face. 'Please tell me why you think that.' 'It is unprofessional to continue to date a key witness in the case. Even though he met Lynette before the cases unfolded, he should have terminated the relationship.' Tom sipped his beer as he could understand her perspective.

She downed the rest of her wine. 'A man who two-times women is despicable. He dated Gemma and Lynette at the same. She held up her hand. 'Gemma and he did not meet for a quick drink after work. They had dressed for an evening at the Italian in Market Square. I was out on a social evening with friends and we entered The Grapes'.

Putting down her half empty glass she jumped to her feet, 'Your face tells me I have said too much. I'd better leave.' Sandra's voice came from the kitchen, 'Tea is on the table. I will put fresh drinks out.'

Tom stood, 'Although Josh is a friend, I cannot disagree with your interpretation of the events. He opened his hand and smiled almost apologetically, 'Sandra's Lancashire Hotpots are delicious, please stay. Tell me about your cottage.'

61

The Chief laid down his fountain pen. 'Thank you for telling me, Josh. That is a credit to you. When you were recruited to the police force, you denied any run-in with the police. It is essential to discuss the matter with the Superintendent, but I believe it will not affect your service as a police officer as the events took place while you were a teenager.'

'Thank you, sir.'

'I have been trying to write your initial assessment for days but cannot find the right words.' Josh didn't want to hear what would come next. 'On one hand, you reached the solution first in a complex series of cases showing you have excellent attributes as a detective.'

Josh studied the carpet, waiting for the but, as criticism would be forthcoming from the Chief Inspector, 'But your paperwork is sloppy, your dress sense is closer to a tramp and dating a witness is beyond belief.'

'I'll try to do better with the paperwork and my clothes, sir.'

The Chief placed his pen on the desk, 'Despite your assurances me you must now complete what will be the hardest duty of your life.'

'Yes, I will do it.' Without waiting for further comments from the Chief Inspector. 'Thank you, sir.' Slowly, he left the office. Wandering along the corridor, he mulled over his future. Should he resign from the force? Quit before they throw him out? He'd never have solved the crimes if it hadn't been for Tom. Thinking about him brought a smile to his lips. He'd adopt Tom's laid back approach. Perhaps it would help.

With his thoughts swirling, he returned to the canteen to build up his courage for the task that lay ahead and calm the sourness in the pit of his stomach. Hesitating in the doorway, Gemma sat on her own in the corner. She'd been helpful and had given him information that could have earned her a reprimand. He slipped across to Gemma's table. 'How are you?'

'I'm still feeling ill but when I'm better can we try again for a meal. I had a bug starting the night we went out.' She'd been quiet since that evening, but he'd assumed it was cold feet about dating a copper or that she'd found out he had become friendly with Lynette.

'Thanks for your support Gemma, you were great.'

'You didn't answer about going out for another meal? Don't you want a date?'

'I do.' He grimaced, 'But life is tough.'

'Tell me about it.' She raised her hand to her forehead in a theatrical gesture, 'I've been ill, hassled at my flat by the landlord and received a terrible assessment report from Miss Perfection. To cap it all, I've been told I'm in her team. I'm on duty this evening but why don't we drown our sorrows tomorrow, however you'll need your Sergeant's salary to keep me in gin and tonic.'

'Only on one condition.'

‘What’s that?’

‘There is no mention of work.’

‘You better go to the bank,’ she giggled, ‘I will cost you a fortune.’ The exchange lifted Josh’s spirits for the unenviable task which lay ahead.

62

I threw the Airline's letter down in disgust. The only positive part had been my exemplary record and that I would continue on full pay until I could fly again. At least that will allow me to surmount my money issues after Scott cleaned out my bank accounts. Bastard! How could he do that to me? Slumping onto the sofa in my Manchester flat, I had no information about the cases. Mum informed me that Josh worked all hours and was never at home because of his workload, but I was concerned for him after Lynette had been arrested.

I grimaced. No retest for flying for two months. I'd cleaned the flat from top to bottom. All traces of Scott had vanished so I picked up one of the aviation newspapers, but no suitable jobs were listed. Dad had made a helpful suggestion to leave the airline and become a private pilot, but he doesn't realise I have no money to retrain.

The front doorbell echoed through the silent flat. Who's that? I'm not in the mood for visitors. Should I answer the door or not? Forcing myself, I unlocked the door and edged it open, 'Josh! What are you doing here?' I threw my arms around him. I'd missed talking to him, but after the humiliation of Scott, I'd shut myself away in my flat. He gave me a long hug, but he had no joy in his face.

As he had an anguished expression; the cases must have weighed heavily on him. I gabbled, 'You've never been to my flat before. Why the unexpected visit?' Although he still hadn't spoken, I ignored his grimness as I was excited to see him. 'How are you? I'm sorry about Lynette.'

Stepping forward, he hugged me again, 'Hush, sis. Hush.' I didn't want him to stop the embrace as his strong arms wrapped around me was perfect. But my stomach somersaulted, and a shiver fluttered through me. Something was wrong. The tension in his body was palpable. Coldness gripped me.

'Let's sit down.'

'Is there bad news about Scott?'

Guiding me to the settee, we perched on the edge with him holding my hands. The rush of memories flooded back. Josh's face told the full story. Tears streamed down my cheeks, but I wouldn't release his hands.

'There's no easy way, Ellie.' Using my childhood name made me shiver again. Josh sensed it through my hands, but he didn't withdraw and stroked my fingers.

'Tell me, Josh.'

'This morning Scott has pleaded guilty to the murder of Maddie.'

Screwing up my eyes, I stared down at our hands. Never had I been so cold. The warmth of the flat made no difference to the chill that penetrated me. My mind jumped. The smiling face at the casino when he'd won. The passion when he made love to me. I shuddered as it hit me that he could have killed me. A wave of nausea spread through my body. There could be no sympathy for him. I'd been lucky. Deep inside, it registered that my life had been returned to me.

My mind couldn't form words, not even for Josh. I had been determined to marry Scott, but he'd used me. I would always feel tainted. I'd been staring at the carpet, but my eyes returned to his face.

What confronted me wasn't the expression of my brother, but the granite countenance of a policeman. Words wouldn't form. I stuttered. 'Josh.'

Although his face was close to mine, I could barely hear his whisper. I had to strain to hear his words. Hesitant, slow and quivering. 'Scott was the leader of the gang for the raids.' Josh gulped. The coldness deepened.

I shook my head. I'd been so close to him but had never glimpsed his dark side. 'He talked about Bangalore during his confession of embezzlement.'

My eyes opened wide as we had been there together and enjoyed some wonderful evenings together. 'Scott organised the smuggling of the money out of the country from the post office robbery.'

'How did he manage to…' The words died. My stomach sank. I realised how Scott had smuggled the money abroad.

'You have come to fetch me, haven't you?'

'Yes, to take you back to Blackford. Scott has stated that you transported the money in a suitcase for him. Is that true?'

'You know it is Josh.' I sobbed.

Josh waited until I stopped gulping. 'The Indian police found and opened the suitcase you took through customs on the last trip, it contained the money from the building society raid.'

'Scott told me they were admin papers to help him

set up the office in India, but no one will believe that.' The solemn police face revealed the answer. I threw my arms around him and sobbed.

THE END

Enjoy this book?

Thank you for reading my book. If you have time I would appreciate a rating or review. They are a great help to me in developing and writing my books.

You can find more information about my books on my website:

T M Goble's Website

www.tmgoble.com

Action Thrillers
Detective Murder Mysteries
Standalone Murder Mysteries
Historical Fiction
Contemporary Fiction
History of Peak District Literature
Seasonal Recipes

I occasionally send newsletters with details on new releases, special offers and other bits of news relating to my books.